THE
SORTING
ROOM

THE
SORTING
ROOM

———◦•◦———

A Novel

MICHAEL ROSE

PART I

CHAPTER ONE

———·———

Heat drew out the children and the odors on the hottest day along the Eastern Seaboard in the summer of 1928. Blasts from ship horns in New York Harbor rolled over the buildings and dropped into the alley that ten-year-old Eunice Ritter had entered with purpose. She was not an unwitting, innocent little girl who happened upon five older boys playing marbles in the dirt. Curiosity had not tempted her into their keep. Yesterday, when she'd finally gotten her chance, she had won her brother's prized shooter. Today, she was returning to finish what she'd started.

Eunice's brother, Ulrich—Uli, they called him—tried to chase her off, throwing a rock at her feet as she approached. She did not break stride as his missile sailed off target and bounded past her. Dismissing Uli with a smirk, she marched up to the boys who were competing for each other's glass trophies. All of Uli's, she held in her own sack.

Agitated by her presence, the swarm buzzed around the shooting circle they had scratched in the dirt; they had hand-smoothed the pitch's interior to remove pebbles. Two boys knelt in opposition, their bodies tight with concentration. Beads of sweat broke free from rutted foreheads, drew lines down dirty faces, and dropped from noses onto their field of play. With grimy wrists, the contestants wiped their eyes. Eunice waited to take on the winner, her cool calm raising the heat on her adversaries, increasing their perspiration.

Uli's best friend, Gerald, won the round. He stood to unwind his legs and stretch his back. He did not gloat, as was the custom after such victories. Wary of his next opponent, Gerald was silent as he rolled his shooter in his hand. Before Eunice knelt at the edge of the circle and tossed her marbles inside, she first scanned the crowd, freezing the boys one at a time with a personalized scowl.

The high walls of the narrow alley trapped the stifling air like an empty metal boxcar left on hot tracks under a midday sun. Her thin, tattered dress gave Eunice a breezy advantage. She nodded at Gerald, then dug her bare, bony knees into the grit.

Unfazed by their attempts to distract her, in short order Eunice cleared all but one of Gerald's marbles from the circle—a single glass sphere waited in the dirt to be claimed. Anxiety mixed with the thick air as the other four boys leaned over, helpless. No one laughed.

She paused for her final shot. Relaxed and focused, like a sniper timing a kill, Eunice released her thumb at the end of a slow breath and sent on its course her newest weapon, Uli's beloved shooter. After she heard the glass-on-glass *clack*, she lifted her gaze to watch Gerald's last marble roll across the miniature pitch. It hopped on first contact with the gravel waiting beyond the circle's perimeter, then skipped and spun to a stop.

"Your baby sister's a lot better with your shooter than you, Uli."

"Shut up, Gerald!"

Eunice rose into a squat, then rocked back and leaned on her right arm. The heel of her tight fist dug into the dirt. Uli's shooter cupped in her palm, she surveyed the stunned circle before she spoke to Gerald.

"Shoot for shooters?"

Without looking at her, he croaked out his refusal. "Nah, you win. You took Uli's shooter yesterday. You ain't gonna add mine to your collection. You sure you're a girl?"

It was not a novel taunt to Eunice, who was skinny but strong, sinewy, and narrow-hipped, often mistaken for a boy. She scooped up all the marbles she had bet; Gerald had not captured a single one of hers. Eunice then stood, rubbing the skin on her knees as she unfurled. Gerald spread open the mouth of his depleted marble bag and dropped his shooter inside. It made no sound when it landed at the bottom of the empty pouch.

The last of Gerald's glass trophies dropped with a *click* onto the pile in Eunice's bloated leather sack. Uli's shooter followed, and, with the drawstrings twisted around her right index finger, she pulled the bag closed. She flashed a victor's smile, then raised and extended her arms into a V high above her head, squeezing the bulging pouch in her right fist.

"Yeah, she's a girl, all right," Uli yelled, as he lunged at her.

Eunice felt his fist punch her gut. She doubled over and fought for breath, her face close to Uli's belt buckle. He scratched the back of her dress until he had two fistfuls of fabric, then pulled it over her head. He twisted the garment like a turban, trapping her arms at the shoulders. Uli forced her head toward the alley floor. Blinded and suffocating, she pressed her bag into the ground to steady herself. She knelt, grinding her knees into the gravel.

Uli leaned on top of her back, surrounding her like a wrestler. He crushed his elbow into her ribs, and then Eunice felt him paw at the pouch. After she tugged it away from his grip, she reared back to buck him off, then stood, wobbling. She heard Uli snicker as he lost his hold on her headdress. Although he fell silent, she could sense him kneeling in front of her.

Without warning, Uli slipped his index fingers inside the waistline of her exposed panties and pulled down hard. Her underpants crumpled at her ankles like cotton shackles. The boys heckled. She gasped, imagining them all staring at her nakedness.

Eunice squeezed the bag of marbles as she stood gyrating to get her arms free. She kept her feet planted in place, knowing she would trip and fall over if she panicked. The boys spat out invectives that sounded to her like wishful incantations, frantic spells to prevent her escape.

First things first, she thought. *Free the feet, then the arms.* Up and down she marched, alternating her steps upon the hot coals of their taunts, until one foot slipped out.

Panties in a loose bunch around a single ankle, she steadied herself and widened her stance for balance in order to fight her way out of Uli's swaddle. It was hard to breathe. She contorted her arms and shoulders like Harry Houdini. The boys' laughter grew quieter as the material slackened, releasing her arms. She took a hungry breath. Once the dress fell back into place past her hips, she pulled her other foot free from the dusty cotton leg cuffs.

Still kneeling before her, Uli looked up. She fumed, wanting to cow him in front of his friends. Elbows locked, hands clenching his thighs, Uli had left his head unprotected. She held the sack of marbles in a white-knuckled fist and brandished the spoils in his face.

"What're you gonna do? You hit like a girl, Eunice," he said. "Now, give me back my shooter!"

It happened in a flash and felt instinctual, unlike a skill acquired by countless hours of repetitive practice. Not until after she left the boys in the alley would she recall where she'd learned the move, from Pa, who had come home early one night, albeit drunk, as usual. He'd rambled on to his children about fighting, about how to stop an attacker. He had been holding a cold compress to his blackened left eye, the result of an altercation outside a speakeasy, as he said, "When they comes at ya, *box their ears!*"

Pa had dropped his compress and wobbled over to where his son sat, mesmerized. Clapping cupped hands against Uli's head, Pa boxed his ears with intemperate force. Uli absorbed the blows, then dropped off his chair and fell to his knees. He told Eunice later that a white light had blazed in his head when Pa clubbed him.

For years to come, Eunice would marvel at the quickness of her reaction, fueled by fury. Without internal debate, she simply clenched her jaw and struck. An open hand slapped the right side of Uli's head—a sting apropos for the insult. The marble-filled pouch, squeezed in her right hand, cudgeled his left temple. The blow left Uli lying in the dirt, unresponsive and bleeding from his ear, surrounded by his stunned friends. He would never be the same. Nor would he ever torment his younger sister again. As far as Eunice could determine, he never thought to do so.

Out on New York Harbor, a cargo ship blew its horn. The sound sailed past the water through the stale, humid air and drifted down to Eunice's ears. She tugged and twisted her dress at the waistline and then exited the alley, her posture erect. The leather sack, still bulging tight with marbles, relaxed in her hand. The panties she had stomped into the gravel swung from her other hand on a loose hook formed by her pinky.

CHAPTER TWO

—·—

F ew sanatoria did laundry on-site anymore. They simply sent out their dirties to places like Welles Laundry and Dry Cleaning, which offered a proposition hard to turn down: Unpin the diaper, lift the patient, pull the sheet. Wrap it up, diaper and all. Shove the messy wad into a canvas bag and put it outside, and we'll take it away. We'll return every article clean, pressed, folded, and ready to stack on your shelves until needed.

When motor-powered carriages began to chase horses from the streets, David Welles bought a dilapidated vacant stable at a bargain. The building was not ideal, but the lot was massive and the price was right. The new owner ordered the stalls gutted, exposing a long structure with few ventilating windows. The livery's rafters flew high above the hoof-stomped dirt floor, which Welles had covered with concrete. Pads were poured, foundations laid for the heaviest equipment: the ironing mangle and the industrial washers and dryers that fed it a steady diet of clean linens.

Under the old barn's roof, Welles's employees moved filthy loads from the receiving dock through the plant's cleansing processes. He faced no shortage of willing low-wage workers for his labor-intensive business. As Italians and Irish were still flooding the East Coast, unskilled labor was plentiful.

Today was Thursday, the day he went to the bank. The plant had been humming for hours when David exited and confronted, for the second time that day, the scruffy little girl who had met him each morning this week, seeking work. The last thing he needed was a kid inside his plant. David huffed as he brushed away her appeal. She was persistent, difficult to ignore, and he wondered what he might do to get rid of her if she was still there when he returned. Her presence had become tiresome.

Whenever David was away, he left oversight of the operation to his younger brother, Martin, and their cousin Alfred Bittle. David often returned from errands to discover that Martin had slipped off to the racetrack. Alfred might accompany him to play the ponies on days when David would be gone for several hours. This morning he had told them both that he would return before the lunch break. That alone might keep Alfred at the plant. Of late, Martin had grown more petulant, and tiresome, too, testing his brother's patience as if it were a family business, rather than a sole proprietorship.

Alfred Bittle stood staring out into the alley through a window, its panes crusted with a film of grime fused to the glass by the plant's humidity. He watched his cousin David whisk past the street urchin, a young girl who had been standing outside when the plant opened. She had been there each morning this week, pleading for work. Martin Welles sat nearby, poring over the roster for the day's upcoming races at the track.

"That kid's still out there," Alfred said. "She just chased David until he turned the corner. She's a stubborn one. Most whippersnappers get the message after he ignores them for a couple of days."

"Maybe she can't go home till she scrapes up some work," Martin said, without removing the pencil from his mouth or raising his eyes.

"Whatever her reasons, that guttersnipe won't take no for an answer. Tough little kid."

Martin let the racing form drop. "Why not give her a whirl? It'll break up the day. I bet she won't last fifteen minutes with Gussie in the sorting room."

"Aw, come on, Martin. She can't be more than ten years old, for chrissakes!"

"Since when do you care about some snot-nosed kid? Scared to bet? Getting sick of giving me your money?"

"Hey, I win some," Alfred said.

"Put your money where your mouth is, Cousin," Martin challenged. "I bet two bits she pukes and runs out of there in under fifteen minutes."

"I'd take that bet, but you heard what David said: no brats."

"He won't even be back by the time the kid's home, crying in her mama's arms."

"She'll last longer than fifteen, that one," Alfred said. "Any kid that won't take no from a man like David might last longer than you think."

"You're more afraid of David than you are of betting. Fifteen minutes, and she'll be gone."

"You're his brother. You know I can't lose this job, Martin. If she lasts an hour, David could be back before she's out of here."

"If he gets back before she bolts, I'll do the talking."

Martin rolled up his racing form and stuck the chewed pencil behind his ear. Paper tube shoved into his back pants pocket, he slapped his cousin on the shoulder, then shepherded him toward the door to commence the contest. "She'll be out of here in less than fifteen minutes, you wait and see. And she won't be back tomorrow morning, either. David'll be glad we got rid of her."

Three weeks had passed since Eunice had won Uli's shooter. He no longer seemed to miss his glass trophies. When she poured his old marbles back into his empty sack, he looked puzzled as he massaged the leather. Then he giggled and said to the room, "Shoot for shooters, shoot for shooters." His mantra followed her to the door on her way out.

Summer continued to drive her outdoors from their family's tight quarters in the stifling tenement building a few blocks from Welles Laundry and Dry Cleaning. Eunice wanted to work and make her own money. A job at the plant would be simple to conceal from her parents, since they seldom inquired into her whereabouts. Uli had been a tattletale, but now he no longer posed a threat to her exposure, only to her conscience, which made staying home even less attractive.

Two men called to her from the side door in the alley where Welles's employees came and went. The one with a pencil behind his ear asked her if she was still looking for work. She thought that curious. Every morning this week, she had all but accosted them for a job when they arrived at the plant. Still, she nodded and stepped through the doorway.

The pair guided her through various piecework departments. In the first room, skilled workers toiled at removing spots. Next door, several women were busy ironing by hand, leaning downward pressure against waist-high boards. They then entered a room with a row of women sitting before spinning bobbins. Eunice envied the seamstresses, pumping their feet and pushing fabric into the narrow channels of their sewing machines. If she learned to sew, she could mend her rags, maybe even make her own clothes if she could get her hands on some cotton swaths. *First things first*, she thought. She would take any job.

Past the stitching women, they approached the expanse of the plant. Harsh, metallic grinding sounds confronted Eunice as she followed the men into denser air. The deeper into the plant she got, the more she registered the piercing odors. Not the repulsive scents of nature, rot and excrement—these were a result of man-made runoff from unchecked rivers of the industrial revolution. The violent chemical onslaught attacked her nose in a crisp sprint, unlike the trotting stench that greeted her upon entering a barn.

Outdoors, it was a humid New York summer day. Inside, the converted livery became a dank hotbox. Wiping sweat from her forehead, she wondered if the plant's atmosphere was as caustic during winter. Today's stifling mist, laden with processing fluids, burned her sinuses and irritated her eyes. Electric fans delivered a toxic breeze to perspiring workers, who eyed the passing girl as they turned their faces into the blades' currents in hopes of relief.

The high windows above her must have been cut into the sides of the former stables for ventilation. A glass box jutted from an external wall into the plant. It was an office with a tall window that must have also been carved out by the new owner to draw fresh air. Her eyes searched the interior, where she saw what had to be the boss man's vacant desk.

The temperature spiked as they marched into the belly of the plant. The mounting noise matched the heat in the cavern, an area the men told her was called the big room. The high-ceilinged, open space housed gargantuan industrial washers and dryers. The brutish machines were larger than she had imagined as she stood outside each morning.

Along the path through the big room, raised buttocks protruded from carts where women bent to grasp soiled articles hiding on the canvas bottoms. Eunice was startled when one rose to toss the last of her load into a washer. The toothless, sweaty woman glared at Eunice, then rubbed a sleeve across her brow, slammed the door, and locked the handle. After smacking the starter switch, she pushed the dirty cart to the side and spun to grab a clean cart's wooden handle. She rolled the empty cart to a resting dryer, opened the portal, and pulled out a hot load of cotton. As Eunice walked by, she studied the workers and wondered if Uli could manage the simple motions that separated dirty and clean, wet and dry.

The sounds of the plant became sharper as Eunice followed her escorts into the room where the mangle—the largest machine in the plant—yakked, hissing and clanking. At opposite ends of the monster, separate trios of women stood side by side. Three fed a washed, dried, wrinkled bedsheet into the mangle's jaws. Eunice watched as an ironed sheet exited the other end of the contraption. The labor-saving device had pressed the unwieldy fabric in one smooth pass, far faster than if all six workers had glided hot hand irons over the same clean cotton. The awaiting three workers extended their arms over the folding table in the direction of the spinning rollers. In a synchronized reach, they each fingered the advancing edge of the sheet as if they were about to turn the page of a newspaper. As they straightened their postures, they slid the sheet toward themselves, then collected and folded it atop the metal table in a choreographed routine.

The three women feeding sheets into the mangle's mouth had eyes on Eunice from the moment she entered the room. Following her escorts to the exit, she heard the women talking above the noise, guessing whether the young stranger was one of the supervisors' kids or maybe Mr. Welles's own daughter.

"Wearin' rags like us," shouted the oldest-looking worker, as if she wanted Eunice to hear. She was stooped, her chin close to her chest. Hunched over the table, she appeared to Eunice to be even older than the sick, white-haired woman who lived in the apartment next door and would shriek in the middle of the night for no apparent reason.

The snide remarks persisted until Eunice and the men exited the room. Above the racket, Eunice had gathered the workers' sentiments. These women did not want a runt slowing things down, much less working for a lower wage. Eunice had held her gaze straight ahead, refusing to react to the barbs. She would take any wage and suffer their chastisement without shrinking. She wanted to get to work.

The sound of squeaky wheels cut through the hisses, clinks, and clanks. Eunice and her escorts followed a line of women-powered carts along the cement runway that coursed through the back half of the plant. She saw where Welles must have had his builders add an appendage to the old livery. Behind the colossal washers and dryers was a small brick building for the chemical dry-cleaning process. Its windows remained wedged open, no matter the weather, the man with the pencil told her. A coat tree caught Eunice's attention; several tattered sweaters hung on hooks, waiting at the ready for a drop in outside temperature.

The caravan slowed down as it neared the bottom of a ramp that descended from the shipping dock. When the procession halted, the pushers abandoned their carts and turned to walk back toward the big room. Though it was obvious that she was the subject of the group's conversation, Eunice could not hear the words hidden inside their giggles and fading mutterings.

The trio paused at the bottom of the ramp and looked up into outdoor light. The main building terminated at a raised dock where trucks had been backed into loading bays. One driver was exiting the back of his truck, rolling out a dirty cartload. Arms outstretched, head down, with his forward-leaning torso set at a middling angle that split vertical and prone, he strained against what must have been heavy cargo and fought to keep the cart aimed straight as he accelerated. The front wheels cleared the lip of the dock with a *pop*. Eunice understood. If he had taken the wrong angle or gone too slow, the result would have been painful. An abrupt halt would cause the driver to jam his arms at the elbows or smash his chest into the wooden frame that he gripped as a handlebar. The man turned the cart a sharp ninety degrees and pumped his knees to maintain speed until he could reach the ramp and allow the cart to glide down to the floor of the plant.

Bags of dirty laundry were piled high in the cart and bulged out its canvas sides. Eunice lost sight of the driver, except for the hair on the crown of his skull. His head bobbed, alternating between lowered relief and the forward-looking vision required for steerage to the top of the ramp. Once there, the driver raised his head and let gravity take control. His eyes widened when he saw Eunice, and he leaned back to slow the cart. One of her guides grabbed her shoulder, yanking her out of the cart's path. She pressed herself flat against the wall until the driver and his load had passed.

Her destination, Eunice was about to learn, was at the far end of the shipping dock, placed there because of the stench. A wooden chute, next to the last truck bay, fed the room. Brakes squawked and an engine died. A second cart exploded from another panel truck. Once the driver cleared the lip of the dock, he parked the cart and disappeared again inside the back of his truck. Within seconds, he exited dragging a pair of bulky gray canvas bags, each large enough for two children Eunice's size to fit inside. The driver seized one of the bags, apparently unaware of the three witnesses watching him from below. Squeezing his eyes shut, he crinkled his nose and turned his head to one side, as if to avoid a rancid odor. He opened his eyes, took a breath, and held it. Tie-down cord in one fist, he stooped to grab the canvas handle sewn onto the bag's base. With a jerk, the bag cleared the lip of the chute and slid out of sight.

The driver finally spotted Eunice, then turned his gaze on her two escorts as he drew a sleeve across his tight lips. He leaned over to lift the next bag while keeping an eye on the men. The chute swallowed the second bag, and the driver stepped away, exhaling a breath that Eunice was certain he had held through both lifts.

The man with the pencil behind his ear shrugged at the driver and turned to instruct Eunice. Without touching the door-knob, he gestured for the girl to let herself inside. "That's the door to the sorting room. Gussie'll show you the ropes. If you can't take it, just come out here, and we'll pay you a dime for a full hour and show you how to get out of here."

"If you last an hour, I'll give you an extra nickel," the other man added.

"Do I get a nickel extra for every hour?" It was well before noon, and Eunice planned to work until the plant shut down.

"Sure, kid. Sounds like a deal," the pencil man said, as he winked at the other.

After the door closed, Eunice heard the men laughing outside. A Negro woman who appeared to Eunice to be equal in size to the washers in the big room rose up from a stooped position. She had tied her coiled hair into bunches with torn cotton strips. Her eyes were set wide apart on a round face. Blood vessels ran from her brown irises through yellowed sclera. Jelly arms flared out, suspended to prevent soiled fingers from touching the sides of her thin sleeveless smock. Bare feet splayed flat beneath her weight. Eunice spotted the woman's worn sandals resting against the wall.

"Stand there, child. Don't touch anything, ya hear?"

Eunice nodded. The woman kept her hands extended, motioned for Eunice to follow, and then stepped outside. The two men were loitering within ten feet of the doorway; their laughter subsided when they spotted the duo. Both men palmed pocket watches in their open hands. *They're timing me*, Eunice realized, disgusted.

"If this poor child vomits and runs, I'll have to clean it up."

"Don't let her run off before she wipes up her puke, Gussie. Simple—see? Now, go on back in there, and get her working, too. It won't count if she just holds her breath in a corner and doesn't touch a damn thing," the pencil man said, while the other began to pace. "We're beginning over, Alfred. We'll restart our watches when they're both inside."

The sorting room's wooden floor was smooth, worn to a polish from the daily rubbing of canvas laundry bags over many years. Lumbering side to side, Gussie skated on bare feet to a raised washtub. Hulking over the basin, she spoke into running water as she scrubbed an article against a corrugated metal plate. "If ya gotta throw up, get over here to the basin. If ya can't make it, puke on the floor. Out in the open, not on that pile of laundry. Got me?"

Eunice nodded. Gussie fed a stained rectangle of wet cotton the size of a checkerboard through the clothes wringer.

"I ain't gonna puke."

"We'll see about that." Gussie stepped away from the basin

and shuffled back toward the pile in the middle of the floor. "My name's Gussie. What they call ya?"

"They call me Eunice."

"Okay then, Eunice. We got to sort these pieces here and take the dirty-dirties to the tub and run them through that wringer. Go slow, hear?" Gussie frowned at her new apprentice. "Sorry, child. Them men out there playing a trick on ya."

"I got a job as long as I don't puke, right?"

"They just betting on how long ya last."

"I know. I figured that part out when I saw them looking at their watches. But if I don't puke, I get the job, right?"

"Don't know. I don't give nobody no job. Neither do them two."

"Who, then?"

"The big boss man, Mista Welles. But, child, he don't want lil' kids working here."

"I work good, Gussie. Maybe he doesn't know any kids that work good."

"Ya spunky, Eunice." Gussie chuckled. "If ya work good, maybe ya get a job from Mista Welles."

Side by side, the two labored at a metered pace. Gussie talked as they sorted, never breaking her stride. "Use ya head, Eunice. When a bag stinks real bad, drag it to the corner by the basin. After we work the pile down, I'll show ya how to take care of it. Them girls in the big room just grabs 'n shoves into the washers whatever's in the dirty carts. They don't think. They just feed the washers fast as they can. Them girls know that ole Gussie in the sorting room'll take the blame."

"Okay, got it. Bag smells bad, drag it over there."

"Every bag gonna smell some kind of bad. No mistaking the ones that need to visit the basin. Ya smell the dirty-dirties right off."

Eunice did not sprint ahead or fall behind. She asked few questions, her expectations as simple as the task. Gussie showed her how to separate out the colors from the whites, to search for wool and other delicates, then told her to pull out items that might cause damage: big buttons that could get caught, or zippers with gnarling teeth that chewed up other articles. Gussie told her the sorting room was the best chance to prevent damage.

They cleared out what Gussie called clean dirties; a truckload of hotel towels and bed linens that should have gone straight to the big room. Lazy driver, Gussie told Eunice. Lazy or stupid or both.

"Once I found me a fox stole wrapped up in a big ole wad of hotel towels."

"What'd you do with it?"

"I looked out the door. Ain't nobody on the dock or comin' from inside. So I pull it round me head. Rub it back 'n forth over me neck."

"Felt good, I bet."

"Dang good, girl. Felt dang good."

"Did you wanna keep it?"

"Get fired for sure if I kep it."

Bang.

The door swung inside. It was Martin Welles, the man Gussie had told her was the owner's brother, with the pencil still lodged behind his ear. He'd kicked the door open with force. His face was red with irritation.

"Gussie, what've you been doing? That kid's been in here for almost fifteen minutes. Is she sorting?"

"Yes, sir, Mista Welles. Eunice here's a good worker. Ya ought to tell your brother to give her a job."

Eunice blushed, then heard another voice from beyond the doorway. "Martin, you owe me two bits. She's already made it past fifteen. I'm heading over to bookkeeping before David gets back. Remember what you said—that you'd do the talking if he sees her."

Martin said, "All right, kid. You gotta get out of here. I'll give you that dime. You don't have to work the full hour."

"I need money, Mister. You said—"

"Don't sass me, girl. Now, come outta there and wash up."

"You said I can work the rest of the day if I don't puke. A dime and an extra nickel for every hour."

Martin took an angry step into the room but stopped when he encountered the smell. His lip curled, and he turned his head in disgust. "Suit yourself, kid. I'm going to the racetrack."

When the door closed, Gussie shook her head and said, "Ya something, Eunice. Ain't never heard nobody talk back to him like that. Ya see his face when he got a whiff? He about to puke hisself." Gussie continued to shake her head and laugh as she skated back to the pile. "All right then, Eunice, let's get back to work."

Not two seconds later, Eunice heard brakes squeal, then the sound of the rollers, then a crash as the truck's back door was raised in a rush. Next, the cover to the chute clanged, surprising her. Bags from the first sanitarium of the day hurtled down onto the smooth floor. The aroma registered before the color. Gussie grabbed a gray canvas bag and told Eunice it would be her next test.

Gussie stood the canvas sack in a teetering upright position, then pressed a knee into its side to balance it. She untied the drawstring and pulled its jaws open. As if intent on retrieving a hook from a giant catfish, Gussie thrust a hand inside its mouth. Then she leaned down, slid her other hand under the bag, and grabbed the canvas handle on the bottom. With a yank, she torqued her body and the bag followed in a somersault, its contents spilling out onto the floor. The odor assaulted Eunice, a stench far worse than that of the horse shit baking in the streets.

The lesson moved to the basin. No need to rinse out the sheets and diapers if only yellowed, Gussie instructed. If anything brown was caked on, she told Eunice to take it to the tub, where a drainpipe led to the sewer. The hole in the bottom of the basin was covered by a thin, flat, circular piece of rubber, a drain plate that sealed a corroded metal sieve. The rubber stopper was connected to the faucet by a rusty chain. Gussie called the sieve the "turd catcher" and snickered before reciting the rest of her instructions: Run water in the basin, scrub the dirty-dirties against the corrugated washboard, knock the gobs off into the water, feed the cotton in between the rollers of the hand wringer, turn the crank, guide it out, and drop it into the cart. When the water gets real bad, clear the basin. Pull the chain to remove the rubber stopper. Let the water and chunks drain down. If the water stops flowing, scrape the sieve with this metal brush. Don't get lazy and pull the sieve out. The gobs might clog the pipe, and then there'll be big trouble.

Before she turned the doorknob to the office, Eunice set herself. She knew that the big boss man did not want kids around. She swallowed, then opened the door and startled David Welles, who looked up from his blotter with a scowl. Blood rushed to his face. After badgering him all week, she did not talk. She stared into his eyes and waited for him to speak. It would be the first time she had heard his voice. The dismissive grunts did not count in Eunice's assessment.

"How did you get inside my plant?"

"The other Mr. Welles and a man he called Alfred brought me to the sorting room. Gussie's gone to do something in the big room, and I need some more work. I'm a good worker, Mr. Welles."

"What's your name, girl?" Welles asked.

"Eunice. Eunice Ritter."

"Well, Eunice Ritter, how'd you find the sorting room?"

"Didn't find it, Mr. Welles. Those two men took me there."

He stood, leaned over his desk, placed the heels of his palms on the blotter, and glowered down into her eyes. She did not flinch, only narrowed her own gaze in response.

"A standoff with a runt," he mused aloud. Welles smirked, then reset his stiff jaw. "What do you think about working with Gussie?"

"Gussie's a good worker. She showed me what to do."

"And the work?"

"It's hard work. But I'm strong. Ain't too hard for me, Mr. Welles."

"It can be disgusting the first time."

"Yeah, I can see that."

"Did you throw up?"

"No, sir. Smells don't bother me much," she lied. Welles rocked his head as he continued to stare at her. "Gussie said you do the hiring. Said if I make it all day without puking, you might give me a job. You think you might give me work, Mr. Welles?"

He laughed, which made Eunice wonder what was funny. When his grin disappeared, he said, "Head back to the sorting room, Eunice. Gussie'll be there soon. I expect some truckloads to arrive in the next couple of hours. Lots of sorting to do."

"I have a job, then?" Eunice shuffled her feet, which drew her eyes to both big toes poking through her worn-out shoes. She looked up to meet his answer.

"Maybe, Eunice. Let's see how you do the rest of the shift. I'll talk to Gussie and see what she thinks."

Eunice nodded up at the owner, still towering over his desk. "Fair enough, Mr. Welles." She swallowed and said, "Well, then, if you don't mind, I'd like to get back to work."

Eunice marched out of his office, closing the door behind her. She did not slam it, but the windows rattled. The women on the floor chattered as Eunice walked back toward the sorting room. No negative rumblings poured out this time. She heard one girl pass the word: There goes the skinny little kid that's been sorting with Gussie. Eunice felt her face flush when the girl said the kid hadn't puked. Gussie had said so.

Eunice was sitting on the floor when Gussie reentered. She apologized for having left Eunice alone for so long. Told her about a tangle of sheets that had gotten bound up in one of the washers. Said she was the one they always called to wrestle with anything that heavy. When she asked Eunice if she had been sitting there wondering if ole Gussie had up and left her, Eunice told her how she'd gone to Mr. Welles's office to see about getting that job. Gussie gaped. Then she laughed so hard she doubled over and gripped her thighs just above the knees. Eunice felt her own cheeks blush as her mentor gazed up at the ceiling and prayed out loud, giving thanks to her lord and savior for sending a devilish lil' angel from heaven to the sorting room to help ole Gussie.

Shaking her head side to side, the woman exhaled a dryer-size breath, then wiped her eyes with a clean rag and tossed it into the cart. Eunice liked Gussie more than anyone she knew. Even Ma when she was sober, which was most mornings. Unlike Pa, her mother saved her drinking for evenings. Gussie heaved and sighed, then let her arms fall limp. She kept shaking her head while beaming at her apprentice, whose own silent prayer was for Mr. Welles to give her a job in the sorting room.

Clang. The chute door flapped. Serial thuds whacked the floor —the first delivery Mr. Welles had promised. Still shaking her head and grinning, the giant hummed as she trundled to the pile. A hand the size of Eunice's two combined grabbed the next canvas bag and yanked it upright like it was a five-pound sack of beans.

The sorting progressed at Gussie's pace. Eunice marveled at how fast the woman's large hands moved through every task. Burly fingers belied their size, darting about with precision. There seemed to be no wasted motion. Eunice struggled to emulate her.

After sorting the contents of countless bags, Eunice's hands cramped. She paused to stretch her fingers backward. Over and over, both fists closed and opened. She wiggled her fingers like a burglar readying herself to pick a lock and then shook her hands to draw blood to her fingertips.

"Sorry, Gussie. My hands are cramping up."

"Go easy. Hands gotta get used to sorting."

Clang. Eunice panicked as they kept coming, each subsequent sack sliding down and colliding with its predecessors. She feared that Gussie would think she was being lazy. "Trying to keep up, Gussie. You're so fast. Sorry, I can't go like that."

"Not today, maybe. But if ya sort steady, Eunice, one day them hands ain't gonna cramp no more. Ya already a hard worker."

Eunice felt tears coming on. Fingers entwined and twisting, she stared down through moist eyes at the hands that had failed her. In a panic, she unloosed her grip and began massaging with violent thumb thrusts while alternating her palms, as if squeezing out poison from snake bites.

"Here, give me them hands, girl," Gussie said, as she took Eunice's filthy hands into her own. As the woman massaged, Eunice held her eyes on the brawny fingers working their magic.

Gussie was the first Negro who'd ever touched her. The first she had ever engaged in conversation beyond the simple exchanges necessary to negotiate random encounters: the gift of a bruised apple from Jefferson's stand; the boy her age who shined shoes a block away from her tenement; the old ladies who took her measure and sometimes offered a kind word. After hours side by side, Eunice had just received from Gussie a recognition that no one else—not Pa, not Ma—had ever hinted could be hers. She was a hard worker; Gussie had said so.

Gussie stopped massaging, lifted their embrace, and drew with it Eunice's gaze. Hands held by Gussie, Eunice crooked her head in order to wipe her tears on her own biceps. Averting her eyes from her mentor, she looked back at their hands and thought how tiny her own looked. Gussie did not tell her to look up. She simply spoke down to Eunice in a tender murmur as she returned to rubbing the cramps away.

"Child, I want ya to hear something—something I wasn't gonna tell ya unless ya was to come back here tomorrow 'n sort with me again."

No doubt the woman could have broken every bone in Eunice's hands with a single, forceful two-handed squeeze, but she released the cramps with a pressure sufficient for the task and no greater. Eunice's palms softened, and her pale fingers uncurled.

She wanted more than anything to come back here tomorrow and sort with Gussie. Waiting for Mr. Welles's decision was torture.

"I told them ya the best girl ever come help me sort. Best of the lot."

"Who'd you tell that to?" Eunice asked, as her moist eyes shot up to find Gussie's.

"Them in the big room. Them girls have to come in here 'n help sometimes. Mista Welles makes a few of them sort whenever there's too many deliveries." Eunice felt that her hands had unwound but did not want Gussie to stop rubbing or talking. "They always mopin' 'n complainin' about having to come help ole Gussie sort the dirty-dirties."

Their hands separated and fell to their sides. Eunice was shaking her fingers again when Gussie asked, "Better?"

"Yeah, for now. Thanks, Gussie. I hope they don't cramp up before we finish those bags." She had to pee and started to dance in place. Her eyes watered, but not with tears of failure this time.

"Eunice, ya better go. Wash yar face after ya clean yar hands." She winked and said, "Leave Mista Welles be. Come right back here after yar done 'n help me sort."

By the time Eunice returned, the room was vacant once more. Gussie had cleared the last of the dirties and must have made another run to the big room. Eunice was anxious but obeyed Gussie's command not to bother Mr. Welles again. Atop the smooth wooden floor, she paced in circles, shaking her hands to ward off a resurgence of cramps and biding her time until Gussie returned.

No sooner had Gussie appeared in the hallway, dragging two empty carts for the dirties, than another truck arrived. Brakes screeched, followed by the telltale *clang* at the chute. In addition to more gray canvas bundles, several green-colored bags joined the slide onto the smooth floor. The rush ended with the arrivals jumbled in a two-toned heap.

"Green bags are from the hospital. We gonna work them gray bags first."

Rather than grab the closest gray bag and dump its contents onto the floor, Gussie first set one of the green bags apart from the pile. It stood like a scolded delinquent against the wall, a special case marked with one long word in big, bold, red block letters a few inches below the drawstring. Molten rubber had been stenciled onto the canvas.

"What's that long word mean?" Dripped hot into the weave of the canvas, the rubber letters seemed a danger warning.

"Don't know. Any bag with them letters, don't touch. I sort all them. Hear me?" The branded canvas sack leaned against the wall; its red stencil was aimed at Gussie as she shuffled barefoot back to the heap at the bottom of the chute.

Eunice scanned the pile and did not see any others with red letters. Gussie grabbed the closest gray bag, pulled the drawstring, and yanked open its mouth. She reached inside, slipped her other hand underneath for the sewn handle, repeated her well-practiced maneuver, and dumped the dirties onto the floor.

As Eunice expected, the gray bag disgorged worn and faded white linens, yet among the sheets there were no soiled diapers for the basin. Their respite was brief. The next bag yielded several diaper-laden sheets, which were no worse than those they had sorted earlier.

Once the cart was filled, Gussie pushed it out into the hallway. An empty cart was rolled into the sorting room, and before she disappeared toward the big room, Gussie told Eunice to finish what was on the floor and instructed her not to touch any

of the green bags, and especially not the one with the red letters.

When the woman was gone, Eunice turned to look at the for-
bidden bag. She stood captivated until she realized Gussie would
be right back. Eunice wanted to clear the pile of laundry on the
floor before her mentor returned.

Without hesitation, Eunice worked feces off the diapers at
the scrub basin and fed the wringer. Gussie came into the room
just as the final piece left the rollers and fell onto the mounding
pile in the cart. She kicked her sandals off her feet, and they landed against the wall with a double beat. Gussie gave her apprentice a look of approval, then leaned over to grab their first green
sack. When its innards spewed out onto the floor, Eunice saw that
most of the articles were soiled green operating-room linens
splattered with blood, cascading out like rapids flowing down-
stream from a toxic drainpipe.

"Same as them shitty diapers. Scrub off the bloody gobs in
the basin, then run it through the wringer."

"Never seen so much blood, Gussie. Don't smell as bad as the
shit in those diapers," Eunice said as she sorted.

"Blood dry out better than shit. Shit smells even if ya hang
the sheets in the sun. But you gotta watch out for bits of people."

A small, downward-reaching hand stopped midair above the
pile. "Bits of people?"

"Fingers can roll out," Gussie warned. "One day I heard a
thud when I flipped a bag on its bottom. Knew right off something was wrong. When I dumped the bag, a bundle of green
linen hit the floor and didn't unravel, just laid there. I pulled one
end 'n out rolled a hand with all five fingers curled and its palm
aimed at me like I were some kind a fortune teller."

"Did it scare you?"

"Dang, girl! White man's hand about to grab ole Gussie for sure, I thought. Yeah, it scare me, but I had to pick it up anyway. Mista Welles had me take it out back 'n toss it in the incinerator. When it burn, it made a smell worse than any shitty diaper."

"Did you make the fingers move?"

"Child, what ya talkin' about?"

"You know. Like a chicken claw. Ain't you never pulled the tendons at the end of a chicken claw?"

"Why'd ya wanna pull on a chicken claw?"

"Makes the talons close like it's grabbin' something."

"Child, ya got too much time to play," Gussie said, shaking her head and laughing. "Though now ya got me wondering if I could've made a fist with that hand."

The plant whistle blew, signaling the end of the shift. Gussie's pace quickened. Eunice kept working to ensure it was not a false alarm. On the other side of the door, women were chattering as they sought the exit. Fading sounds—clinking, hissing, spitting—signaled that the machines were winding down for their night's rest. An eerie calm drifted into the sorting room.

Eunice and Gussie grabbed at the final piece from opposite ends. Gussie told her to let go, and Eunice released the sheet. As Gussie tossed it into the cart, she instructed Eunice to head to the lavatory and wash up with lots of soap and water, use the brush at the sink, get soap under her fingernails, make sure to scrub all the way up to her elbows. She looked at Eunice and told her that she'd "done real good" today.

Eunice walked to the exit, as directed. She stopped in the doorway, looked back, and asked, "You gonna work that bag?"

"What if I is?"

"I wanna see."

"Suit yaself, child."

Eunice stood to the side while Gussie's powerful hand crushed the red rubber lettering. Without hesitation, she pulled the drawstring. Before she stooped to address the pile, she snapped the bag flat, draped it over the side of the cart, then secured it as signage with a couple of wooden clothespins. The bag's bloody green linens were splayed on the floor. After one brief trip to the basin, Gussie looked at Eunice and said, "Nothing more to see. Wash up. Go to the office 'n get yar pay. See if Mista Welles gonna let ya work with me again tomorrow."

Gussie put her back into pushing the cart toward the big room, where Eunice guessed that no one else would touch it. The other women would shudder at its presence until Gussie returned in the morning to load it into a free washer.

As Gussie slogged past, Eunice craned her neck to keep her eyes locked on the red rubber warning. She repeated the twelve letters over and over, drilling them in tight formation like soldiers marching in her head. She vowed to recite them to herself as she walked home so she could write them down as soon as she found a pencil stub. Eunice wondered if the word was as important as it looked. Big word. Serious word. She would taste the pronunciation and repeat it to Gussie in the morning:

CONTAMINATED.

David Welles shook his head as he watched the girl he'd just hired exit his office, jiggling hard-earned coins inside her cupped hands. He had never before met a child like Eunice Ritter, the last person to leave the plant tonight except for Gussie and him. Still fuming about the wager that Alfred had confessed to, he brooded on the cruelty the two men had foisted upon a young girl, who had then beaten them at their own game. Not only had his younger brother ignored the policy, he had not had the nerve to stick around and admit his insubordination to David, man to man. Once again, Martin had delayed confrontation by escaping to the racetrack.

Years ago, when he had started the business, before he hired Gussie, David had not been able to keep anyone in the sorting room full-time. Whenever someone quit, he had sorted dirties himself with one or more of the girls from the big room. It took three hires to get one keeper for the washers and dryers in that damp hothouse. A girl who could handle the machines might quit after a stint sorting. More than one threw up on the floor of the sorting room, then just walked out of the plant.

It had taken a couple of years of building the business before he had brought on his brother and cousin. He wondered if either of them had ever even stepped inside the sorting room. Should have made them both start in there. *Never too late to right a wrong,* he mused. Let them take bets on how long either of them could go without vomiting. He sighed aloud, admitting to himself that it would only make things worse on the floor for his brother, who was already holding on to his authority as supervisor by a thin thread. Furthermore, putting either malcontent in there might push Gussie to walk out herself, and he couldn't afford to lose her.

The lights flickered out in the big room, and there was Gussie, appearing from the darkness like an army's bruised giant, a tired warrior, one of few survivors of a daylong, brutal battle. He watched her lumber toward the time clock. Tomorrow would be another busy day. David expected the plant to be jammed with deliveries early in the morning from three sanatoria and two hospitals; the afternoon trucks would almost double that. Gussie would need help sorting. Otherwise, the drivers would stack bags on the dock and the big room would fall behind schedule.

Eunice had caused him to reconsider his obstinate position on children at the plant. She'd worked all day in the sorting room and never thrown up, never complained. Maybe tomorrow, despite the peak volume, he would not have to assign any of the girls from the big room to sort after all. He had Gussie, who'd been sorting for more than nine years, and now he had Eunice Ritter.

CHAPTER THREE

E ricsson stood on the dock's slippery planks, staring down into the dark water that separated him from the bobbing vessel. At full mast, the Swedish colors flagged and snapped in the rain. The three youngest of his four grown sons—ages sixteen, seventeen, and twenty—looked back in his direction from the deck of the freighter, which was launching to sail across the Atlantic.

The old man was leaflike, flat-chested, tall, and thin, with veins unhidden beneath the exposed, translucent skin of his face. As he slumped, he held his wide yet shallow torso at a blade's working angle to cut the frigid breeze. Fat raindrops rippled the fjord's surface and pelted the slick wood around his feet. The downpour tempered the wind and cold; still he was numb.

Seldom had he visited this port, though his own fishing village rested less than twenty kilometers southeast along familiar shores. The fjord was a body of water he knew well. He had spent his entire life near its edge, married a girl from across the bay, run a small wooden ferry that he had built with his own hands, and raised a nautical brood that followed his footsteps into the family business.

Yesterday, his ferry had sunk, sent to the bottom by a storm and his sons' negligence. All but one of the children who were regulars on the morning run to the primary school across the bay had drowned. The surviving child—a boy—had made it to shore clutching a floating ring. The shivering youngster reported that while the captain stood at the wheel, the three foul-breathed brothers on deck—they smelled of booze, the boy said—were listless and began fighting with each other as the storm surged. When the ship capsized, the crew grabbed rings and abandoned ship. If the hungover men had not been Ericsson's own sons, he, too, would have called for their heads.

Late last night, Anders, his eldest and the ship's captain, had been ripped from his own bed by men of the village. Anders's wife had brought her in-laws the news, bursting through the door just past midnight. Certain the villagers had killed his oldest boy, Ericsson had felt his protective paternal instinct take over. He rousted his three younger sons from their sleep. "The men took Anders. Get up, get your boots on, and get to the skiff— move fast or die." Cloaked in a murky dawn rain, common advent of Sweden's flat sunrise, Ericsson had smuggled his three boys to this dock, certain that otherwise they, too, would be taken.

The rain had subsided. Unimpeded, the cold, shifting wind swept across the surface of the fjord, needling into the old man's woolen breastplate. He did not want to know the specifics of what had happened after Anders had been dragged from his home. Ericsson expected that soon a gruesome story of justice would reach him, then be retold again and again by eyes that would track him wherever he went along the shoreline. The forlorn father shook from his thoughts the image of his son's presumed death and tossed the nightmare into the sea.

The three Ericssons stood trembling shoulder to shoulder, huddled like soaked cattle, facing their father as the bleak water churned and the freighter departed for America. He stared at the steamer as it chugged into open waters, then let his gaze fall into the waves. Their escape seemed certain, if not warranted. Ericsson would not lift his head to capture one last look.

Drenched in mist and shame, the broken old man peered downward. Past the diving rays of the weak early sun, where gray met blackness, his doubts slipped deep into the water. The wake of the departing ship gave way to the fjord's uniform chop. He heard the shouts of his sons, but still he refused to look at them. Then he turned into the frigid breeze to walk off the dock. He hunched up inside his woolen collar and, in desperate defiance of a father's nature, told himself to think of them no more.

CHAPTER FOUR

—◦·◦—

Today was Eunice's sixteenth birthday. After four years sorting and growing physically stronger, she had been sent to the big room, a positive turn for the then fourteen-year-old, one that would not be in the cards for Gussie. Last week, when Mr. Welles had tapped Eunice for the mangle crew, it had caused a dustup among her coworkers, since she had been sweating at the washers and dryers for less than two years. Every woman in that steamy cavern wanted to get out. And from what the old-timers had told her, once a girl made it to the mangle, she was less likely to be tasked with sorting whenever the incoming dirties overwhelmed Gussie.

Before the plant opened this morning, Eunice was, as usual, waiting outside for Mr. Welles, who arrived each day at 5:30 a.m. The crew was expected to be inside, clocked in, and at their workstations by six o'clock sharp. Not even the supervisors, Martin Welles and Alfred Bittle, arrived until well after Mr. Welles unlocked the door and turned on the power; often they showed up after the operation was already in full swing. Alfred might sneak indoors a few minutes after six o'clock. Martin seemed to show up on his own schedule.

At lunch break, the word was out: Bags of dirties had started to stack up on the dock. It was the first backup since Eunice had moved to the mangle crew days earlier. The buzzing persisted throughout the break, including speculation about who would have to help Gussie. As the depression's grip held tight, the girls in the big room reserved their grousing for each other.

As soon as Eunice returned to her station, Alfred appeared at the mangle with a sheepish look. She guessed that, as usual, Martin had tasked him with selecting a girl from the big room to go sort. A week earlier, he would have assigned Eunice, who, during her time in the big room, had never contested his orders.

Now, before Alfred opened his mouth, she volunteered. "I'll go help Gussie if you get a girl to take my place." He grinned and seemed to float away, as if pardoned by a beat cop for a red-handed misdemeanor. When Alfred returned, Kathleen O'Bierne, a loud-mouthed bully, was at his side. Eunice would have selected someone else.

"Show Kathleen the ropes," Alfred said to Lillian, the oldest woman on the mangle crew. "Eunice's gonna help Gussie sort for a bit."

When Eunice stepped away to let Kathleen take her place, the stocky Irishwoman—the mother of a brood of unruly kids—bumped her hip against Eunice, sending her into the edge of the metal folding table.

"Fock ya, ya twig," Kathleen whispered into Eunice's ear. "I was due at the mangle, but ya took me job. Ya going back where ya belong, with that big nigga."

Eunice let the attack drop and pivoted away, rubbing her side where the table had proved less malleable. The malcontent's hip check had caused a painful bruise, but Eunice figured that Kathleen's victory would be short-lived. Tomorrow the Irishwoman would be back in the big room, sweating and muttering to herself in Gaelic.

By the time Eunice and Gussie finished the pile, the whistle had already sounded, and only Mr. Welles remained in the plant. Gussie turned off the lights in the big room; then the two sorters walked past the glass office on their way out. His head jerked. He must have registered their shadowy advance in his peripheral vision. Eunice saw him searching the penumbra through the glass. When Mr. Welles located the pair, he nodded at them, then lowered his gaze to the papers on his desk.

Gussie did not know her own date of birth, so Eunice never made a fuss about hers. Out on the street, after walking several blocks together, per their nightly ritual, she watched her friend lumber away, swaying back and forth under her great weight, in the direction of the boardinghouse where she took a room. Eunice was happy, having received an unexpected birthday gift. Gussie had been surprised to see her come into the sorting room. A broad smile creased her round face as soon as she turned from the basin. "Best of the lot" was all the woman said in salutation as Eunice stepped inside. Then, teary-eyed, Gussie started to sing in a murmur as the pair fell into their synchronized routine.

Prohibition had driven Pa to bathtub-gin makers, bootleggers, and speakeasies. The prior year, 1933, had brought an end to the country's futile attempts at forced abstinence and cleared the way for Pa's return to public venues in order to secure his alcohol. He frequented a legal establishment on Eunice's route home called the Pigeon's Post, so named for the white-stained eaves troughs of the alleyway that separated the saloon from a blacksmith's forge, the rafters of which housed a cooing kit of doves.

Ma was at the tenement building with Eunice's sister, Rita, younger by five years. Out of habit, Eunice walked to the Pigeon's Post after bidding Gussie goodbye. No one asked her to conduct her daily inspection. Although her parents had a common interest in alcohol, they each preferred the company of others when they imbibed—Ma at home and Pa in a saloon. As most evenings progressed, Ma would get sloshed at the kitchen table. Pa, on the other hand, might not show up until the next day, long after Eunice had clocked in at the plant. While she was working at the laundry, Uli was usually attached to Pa, who had been out of steady work as a laborer after the stock market had crashed. Since then, Eunice had not only paid the bulk of the family's expenses but had conducted her rounds after work to make sure her brother made it home at night.

When she arrived at the Pigeon's Post, she looked into the window and saw Pa sitting on a barstool with his back to the door. From outside, she scanned the saloon's interior, without fearing that he would notice her gaze. Amid the otherwise empty tables in the middle of the barroom, she located Uli, sitting by himself with his leather marble pouch. He was captivated by a single glass sphere that he was rolling back and forth on the wooden tabletop between his two cupped hands. She stepped to the doorway and grabbed the iron pull. When Eunice entered, she walked past Pa without interrupting his animated discussion with the patron on the closest stool.

Eunice assumed Pa would be as unaware of her exit as her entrance, so she paused to alert him. "Pa, I'm taking Uli home."

Two tall men entered, clomping past her to empty stools at the far end of the bar. They were arguing in a strange tongue she didn't recognize as one of the languages spoken in the plant. Kathleen O'Bierne had blasted enough Gaelic curses in her direction that Eunice was certain these words were not of the Emerald Isle. Other than English, she herself spoke only sparse German, but she recognized a few words of Dutch and had an ear for the cadence and inflections of Italian, as well as Russian and those languages that shared its Slavic roots. She sometimes heard other unknown tongues in the street, but the sounds these two newcomers made were as unfamiliar as the words themselves.

Both of the lanky men seemed like faded caricatures of Abraham Lincoln, although even more unattractive and far less intelligent looking. Given their wispy blond hair and pale complexions, she guessed they were Scandinavian, maybe Fins or Swedes. Their ears protruded from the sides of elongated skulls, a look reminiscent of mice. Their bulging eyes shone dull, more appropriate for a duo leaving the bar than one entering it. The unbridled nature of their arguing, along with a shared homeliness, suggested they were brothers.

"How old's your girl?" Pa's latest drinking partner asked.

Pa didn't hazard a guess and, without looking up from his glass, asked, "How old are ya, Eunice?"

"Sixteen, Pa. I'm sixteen and Uli's eighteen."

"I know he's eighteen. He had a birthday this year."

"Everybody does, Pa," she said, as she tugged on Uli's sleeve.

"When was his birthday, Eunice?" the stranger asked.

"Last month. March. The twentieth. Just like mine," she said.

"Yours's on the twentieth of which month?" he asked.

"April."

The man looked incredulous, then signaled the bartender. "Pour this young lady a drink. Same as us—whiskey." The barkeep pulled a glass from underneath the bar. He looked at Eunice, then at Pa, who in a start drained his own glass of amber liquid, then slid it forward in obvious hopes of a refill. Eunice had never taken a drink. She said nothing as the whiskey streamed into the glass set before her. The barkeep replenished the other two glasses after the stranger signaled that he would pay for all three pours.

"Why ya wasting yar money on a girl?" Pa asked when Eunice reached out for her glass. "Give me that, Eunice."

"You are one dumb kraut. It's your daughter's birthday, fool!"

Eunice pulled the drink out of Pa's reach, then smirked at him while she twisted the glass in circles on the bar top. The brim rose to her nostrils, and she reared back at the crisp odor, which reminded her of the harsh chemicals in the brick building that housed the dry-cleaning process. Pa grumbled and returned to his refreshed glass of whiskey. With that, Eunice took the shot in one gulp, in the family manner that she had witnessed over and over, day in and day out, since she could remember anything.

The cooing woke Eunice. Her head pounded. She smelled stale straw before she felt the stalks in her hair. Her lips tasted of the loft's dust that had coated her body throughout the night as she lay supine beneath the exposed roof decking. Sunlight flitted down through pinholes and illuminated swirling dust particles that resembled embers falling from the canopy of a burning tree.

She sat up; her shoulders and arms were covered in straw. *Where am I?* she wondered, as she gazed about. Then she panicked. *Where's Uli?*

Wings flapped. Two doves chased another to the attic vent. She watched their heads jut forward and back at the egress, and then, after a brief cooing exchange, all three were gone. Eunice leaned back, digging the heels of both hands into the straw and bracing her weight on her arms. Her headache overpowered the pains she felt elsewhere. She was achy, as if a lorry had hit her. When she stretched her legs out, she noticed the torn panties bunched around one ankle. The blood on her thighs told her a story she could not conjure. The strong stomach she had exhibited for years in the sorting room betrayed her now, and she rolled to one side and vomited into the straw.

She used the panties to wipe at the blood. It had dried. She would have to get to a washbasin to clean herself. After she stood, she shoved the ruined underwear into the side pocket of her dress. The pokes of sunlight hurt her eyes. She scanned the unfamiliar space and found the top rungs of a wooden ladder leaning against the open edge of the loft. Her body told of new aches when she moved forward to descend. A rustle from below stopped her.

"Who's that down there?" she asked, fearing that her rapist was still inside the building, waiting for her to wake up or for his lust to rise again. "I ain't drunk no more."

Low-volume grunting came from below. She heard clicks and thought he was walking across the barn floor to climb the ladder. She shouted out her lies: "I gotta iron bar here. Won't hesitate to crush your skull."

Click . . . click . . . click.

The sounds were not closing in. He seemed to be stopped in place, but she was afraid to look over the edge of the loft.

"Maybe you ain't the one that done this to me." The grunts seemed to come not from lifting or any type of work; they were not born of strain or even modest effort. "You the smithy?" All she heard was a muffled voice and the clicks.

"Hello down there?"

She held her breath and strained to decipher his words. His grunting had stopped. The clicking sounds seemed to be amplified in the silence. A gaggle of pigeons had collected on the outside of the vent and started to funnel inside. As each bird cleared the portal, it took flight above the loft. Their flapping wings made her shudder.

Click . . . click . . . click.

"Say something, goddammit!"

She scanned the loft for anything close to an iron bar. A hay hook had been abandoned on the wall under the pigeons' doorway. The worn wooden handle felt smooth as she took it into her grip. Eunice swallowed and, holding the hay hook high above her head, stepped toward the ladder. Before she reached the edge of the loft, from which she would be able to spot her attacker's ascent, she heard a familiar voice from below.

"Shoot for shooters, shoot for shooters."

CHAPTER FIVE

———·—·———

Eunice needed to confide in someone what little she could remember of the events at the saloon; all she recalled about the loft was waking up in a pile of straw to the sound of pigeons. After volunteering in the morning to help sort, Eunice had vomited at the basin for the first time. When the shift ended, as was their custom, she walked with Gussie partway toward their respective homes. They had traveled less than one block when she started to cry in front of the only person she trusted.

When the fuzzy story came out, Gussie was angry. She tried to comfort the girl with words that women have told each other forever but that provided Eunice scant reprieve, other than an understanding that she was not alone. Men were going to take what they could when the doors were left open and girls were unprotected, Gussie proclaimed. When Eunice told of Pa's presence in the bar, Gussie shook her head and drew a massive arm around the girl's shoulder.

They bade farewell, and Eunice walked away from Gussie, as well as from her friend's advice to tell Ma. In the weeks hence, her menses remained absent. She finally told Ma, who shrugged and asked if Eunice knew who had done the deed. Ma heard the tale of Pa's having encouraged his daughter to accept every round from two strangers, bug-eyed men who looked like brothers, so he could drink for free along with the birthday girl. Ma huffed, then walked to the cupboard for the bottle and a glass. Take it up with Pa, she said. It was his to fix.

Financial necessity, not paternal concern, drove Pa to drag Eunice back to the Pigeon's Post. Eunice had to work to support the family, and if some man had gotten her pregnant, then that man owed Pa, in Pa's estimation. She was mortified as he threw back a shot, then asked the barkeep about the two Swedes, the ones who had bought the rounds that night. The bartender looked at Eunice, then turned to Pa and indicated that she had been laughing and yakking about her head swirling. Announced that she needed some fresh air and was going to walk home. He said she almost fell over as she tugged on her brother's sleeve to get him to go with her. One of the Swedes guided the girl and Uli through the saloon door. The other one sat on a barstool next to Pa and bought a couple more rounds before his brother returned alone.

"Not surprised you don't remember shit," the bartender said, intimating Pa's inebriation that night. With her eyes averted, Eunice listened as Pa asked the barkeep if he knew which one of the Swedes had led her and Uli outside. The answer was meant as a joke, a distinction without a difference: the ugly one.

Pa told Eunice that he hadn't seen the Swedes at the Pigeon's Post since her birthday. By the time the brothers had finally returned to the bar, the night prior, three months had passed. Pa told her in the morning before she walked to the laundry that they'd confront the man together. She begged him to let it be. Pa said that she had no choice in the matter. Last night he had snookered the brothers into buying him a drink when he'd told them he would bring enough cash to buy them a couple of rounds if they met him there the next night—tonight.

Her stomach had not yet pooched out when Pa took her back to the saloon. The Swedes were already standing at the bar, and one punched the other in the shoulder when they saw Eunice. The pugilist, whose name was Gunnar, said that it was his younger brother, Jan-Petter, who'd gone outside with the girl and her brother. JP, they called him, tried to deny it, but when Pa showed him the hilt of a dagger, the Swede caved. He said the girl had not resisted. While they were in the loft, her brother had played with his marbles on the dirt floor of the forge.

The couple were married at the courthouse the following Saturday morning. Ma refused to come, citing that Rita would be rowdy and Uli was too feeble to understand why they were there. Another brother, Lars, the youngest of the three Swedes, was in attendance, along with Gunnar, who explained that the intake agent at Ellis Island had misspelled their family surname and altered it to Erikson. Eunice did not understand. It was a detail that seemed irrelevant to her. She wondered less about the history of her new last name than about the implications of the change forced upon her.

During the first six months of the marriage, Eunice's legal husband stayed with his brothers and found no invitation to her bed, which was the sofa she shared with Rita, while Uli slept on the floor behind the couch, where he seemed to feel safest. The baby was a boy she named Lete. She tracked down the father to inform him, but JP was indifferent and told Eunice to leave him be. All the better, she concluded.

Baby Lete slept swaddled in an open drawer in the pine

hutch next to the table that separated the kitchen from the front room with the sofa. Pa and Ma kept the bedroom for themselves, although Ma usually slept in there alone, as Pa was out carousing most nights. After the sun rose, the old man would stumble inside and fall across the bowed mattress in a stupor.

While Eunice worked at the laundry, Rita took the baby to and from a wet nurse who lived in their tenement building. Eunice hadn't seen JP in the month since Lete's birth, when Pa announced without warning that he and Ma, along with Uli, were going to move upstate to his older brother's farm outside the city of Geneva in the Finger Lakes region. Pa told Eunice that she and Rita and the baby would have to move in with JP or figure out something else. Pa said he had enough to handle with Ma and Uli.

She wanted to stay put in the tenement building with Rita and Lete, but the lease required a man's signature. Beyond giving Lete his birth father's legal surname, Eunice had seen no utility to her forced marriage until she faced eviction. Pa demanded that she send money to Geneva since—because of her—Uli would be as useless on the farm as a blind sheepdog. Married yet estranged, Eunice felt life's bindings constricting her, a young mother and sole provider for three.

In their second confrontation since the civil ceremony, Eunice chased JP down at the flophouse where he lived with Gunnar and Lars. Once more, she would test his indifference. When she stepped in front of him as he was about to enter the building, he seemed to search for any reason she might have chosen to bother him again. The baby had a surname, which JP and his brothers had declared at the courthouse was the purpose of the whole affair. Pa never got so much as a dime or a krona.

"You've never seen your son. You owe him a home."

"Fock ya 'n dat little bastard," JP scoffed.

"He ain't a bastard, remember?"

JP seemed stumped. Eunice gave him a minute to recall the Eriksons' familial proclamation on the day they had signed the marriage certificate. After what seemed to have been more than enough time for him to catch on, she dropped the distraction. She hadn't traipsed to the flophouse to debate semantics; rather, she had come with an offer of simple economics.

"Like living here, do you? Still sleeping on the floor?" Once more, she had to give the man time to gather his thoughts. He was a moron, a conclusion she had reached when Pa challenged him at the saloon. Eunice swallowed her disgust as she recalled standing there—at the Pigeon's Post—horrified that the simpleton was the man who had impregnated her.

"Ain't no room for no bitch 'n her brat. Find yar own place."

"I have a place. I need you to sign the lease. Has to be a man of age."

JP's face screwed up like he was being tricked. "Ya give yar money to yar pa. Stay with him. I ain't gonna pay ya nothing."

"Pa's heading upstate with Ma and Uli," she said, then stared. JP's mouth hung open. Waiting for him to consider the implications, she took a breath. "I'm going to send him a few bucks every month but keep most of my wages. I need you to sign the lease. If you sign, then, legally, it's your place, too. Give me what you spend now, and you can stay there."

JP glanced at the front door to the flophouse. He seemed to be puzzling over something. Eunice decided to help him reach a solution.

"You won't have to sleep on the floor."

His bug eyes inflated beyond their usual droopiness. An evil-looking smile formed between his protruding ears. *Let the idiot think what he wants,* she mused.

JP scratched his name with an X, and they took over Pa's lease for the one-bedroom flat she had known as home her entire life. When Eunice told him to sleep on the couch in his new abode, JP seemed baffled. She had commandeered the bedroom for herself, Rita, and baby Lete. Remembering Gussie's admonition, she had already installed a sliding bolt on the inside of the door.

After JP moved in, five weeks passed when the newlyweds were seldom near each other. Eunice settled into her life and became less worried about making ends meet. Each night she slept, panting with exhaustion, until Lete woke, demanding. Still in her teens, she had become a pragmatic woman who rebuffed any task or attribution someone else assigned her for the role of wife. Her name had been changed at no great social sacrifice. The Ritters were known drunks who'd moved upstate to mooch off the old man's brother.

Neither Eunice nor JP enjoyed an extended local family, much less a supportive community of friends and neighbors. Church was foreign to both. The depression had humbled, not emboldened, those other families who lived in the tenement building. As far as she could see, there was no one to lodge an opinion worth considering, unless she were to ask. Since the courthouse ceremony, Gussie had received the only requests for insight.

Eunice thought that JP did not seem the type to work high steel. He was tall and clumsy. It made more sense to her when she heard the story of how the Erikson brothers, upon arrival in New York, found employment with another Swedish immigrant—an ironworker. Their boss spoke few English words but had ferried his considerable skills with metal to America. She concurred when she heard that the old Swede had told the brothers that they were not the best or brightest of workers, but they had worked for him for years and understood what he wanted done and did it—for the most part. Soon after JP signed her lease, the brothers went to the old Swede as a trio and asked for raises. He told them that the depression had squeezed what he could pay and suggested that they look skyward if they wanted more money.

Gunnar and JP got on a crew that was about to raise a sky-scraper on Manhattan Island. Once Rita was old enough to earn her keep, Eunice could stop worrying that a hefty wind might toss JP off the building's skeleton and put a serious dent in her livelihood. Lars eschewed working above solid ground at dangerous heights and opted for bucking rivets on the George Washington Bridge, which would one day reach across the Hudson River. Eunice kept her mouth shut when Lars boasted to his older siblings that if he fell, the water would provide a merciful landing.

The lunch whistle blew, the crew scampered to the doors for fresh air, and Mr. Welles called for Eunice. Everyone knew that he used lunch breaks to meet with employees in private. He could fire a worker without disrupting the flow of the operation or, after conducting the necessary one-on-one business, send her back to her station before the break ended.

Eunice knew that she had slowed down even before Lete was born. Tired from work and lack of sleep, she suspected Mr. Welles had run out of patience. Martin Welles and Alfred Bittle were leaving the glass office as she approached. Martin huffed past. Alfred held the edge of the door for her and lowered his head when she took the knob in her hand.

"It's quietest in here during lunch," Mr. Welles said as soon as she stepped inside. She stared at him and wondered how long it would take him to get to the point. "Eunice, we got the racetrack business last week and, just yesterday, two new sanatoria—big ones. We're hiring more workers, and I'm going to need another supervisor. I want you to oversee the big room and run the mangle crew. Gussie, too. You'll be in charge of the sorting room."

She exhaled, just then realizing that she had been holding her breath. Not getting fired sunk in before she registered the promotion. She stared at him.

"Is that a yes? You want the job?"

"Yes, sir, Mr. Welles. Thank you," she replied. She hated that her lip quivered. The question she wanted to ask stopped on the tip of her tongue, and she looked down at the floor. Her shoes were sturdy, worn in but not worn out. Here was the very spot where she had stood as a ten-year-old, insisting she was a good worker, asking for a job, wanting nothing more than to return the next day so she could sort alongside Gussie. That little girl would not have hesitated. But that little girl had yet to fall under the family curse of alcohol and commit the error that would change her life forever. She swallowed the question, raised her eyes, and nodded.

"Good, Eunice. That's good indeed. I know you'll do a fine job."

"Yes, sir, I'll do my best."

"I've no doubt you can outwork anyone on either crew. Don't expect them to work as fast as you. Just move them along at a steady pace. Do you understand?"

"Yes, sir, Mr. Welles. You don't want me to lose them, or they might just stop."

"That's right. If someone can't keep up, bring it to my attention. Don't fire anyone yourself. Come see me if you think I should let someone go."

"Yes, sir, I get it."

"And, Eunice . . ." Welles paused. "Do you know what to do if someone challenges your authority?"

"Send her into the sorting room?"

Seeming pleased, he nodded. "That's right. Very well. Let's head to the big room and let everybody know that you're their new supervisor. Then we'll go back to the mangle and tell the crew about your promotion. Do you have any questions?"

These shoes should last another year, she thought. When, as a child, she had stood before him, both of her big toes had breached the leather and poked out a bit. She thought of Pa's taking Uli and Ma upstate to her uncle's farm. She thought of Rita and Lete. Wanting more financial insulation from JP, channeling her younger, bolder self, she cleared her throat, then said, "I do have a question, Mr. Welles."

Welles smiled and waited, triggering the courage she had displayed in his office years ago, the same spunk necessary to walk into an alley of hostile boys playing marbles in the dirt. "Do I get a rate bump?"

"Yes, Eunice, ten cents an hour."

"Thank you, Mr. Welles," she said. Ten cents an hour—the rate the cruel cousins had used to tempt the ten-year-old girl into the sorting room. When Welles rose to step away from his desk, she caught herself before she asked if she'd get an extra nickel if she could last a full hour.

As they exited the office, the lunch whistle sliced through the moist air in the plant. The workers in the big room took the news without a murmur, and then the duo set out across the cement floor toward the sheet mangle. Welles walked ahead of her and waved both arms to gather the mangle crew. He introduced their new supervisor, said that he would assign a girl to replace Eunice at the mangle, then pivoted and stepped away in the direction of his glass box. Once the man had turned his back to the crew, their eyes darted about the cluster as each sought confirmation of what they had just heard. Eunice stepped up to her station at the feeding table and said, "Let's get back to work."

Mr. Welles had promised more incoming business, but in the past couple of months, the volume of dirty-dirties had already spiked. For weeks before Eunice's promotion, the operation seemed to be running at full tilt. Sanatoria—human warehouses full of incontinent patients—combined with hospitals to flood Welles Laundry and Dry Cleaning with a river of grotesque linens. When the tide of dirty-dirties swelled, in attempts to keep peace across the plant, Welles spread out the distasteful sorting work among the women in the big room and, for the first time Eunice could remember, the girls who stood at opposite ends of the mangle.

Into the sorting room, two at a time, they joined Gussie, whose only respite came with a call to lift something too heavy for anyone else, even Kathleen. Eunice worried about Gussie, who, exhausted and scared for her job, no longer muttered protests as she trudged back through the plant, past the truck bays, to the room where odiferous canvas bags crowded her workspace and encroached upon the scrub basin.

In cities throughout the country, a diaspora of rural laborers exacerbated weak job prospects. Used to pitching manure, girls straight off the farm soon discovered that human evacuation lacked the relative sweetness they'd left behind in straw-covered barn stalls. Streams of vomit spewed onto the worn wooden floor of the sorting room, yet even the city girls with the weakest stomachs took their turns at the basin without threatening to quit.

Mr. Welles told Eunice that, in addition to her new responsibilities, she could spend an hour or so each day learning the sewing machines. It was the skill she'd long coveted. As Mr. Welles had explained, now that she was a supervisor, he was less concerned that she would learn the craft and leave his employment—a scheme that she had never considered. Regardless, given the impending deluge of dirty-dirties, Eunice guessed that she would not sit with the seamstresses anytime soon.

Welles had selected Kathleen from the big room to take Eunice's old job. She entered the mangle room with a smug look on her face and, as if she owned the place, stepped to the end of the machine, where Eunice and two other women stood feeding sheets into its jaws. The red-haired brute of a woman was eclipsed in the plant only by Gussie's dominant presence.

As Eunice backed out of her station, Kathleen swung her body in an attempted repeat of the hip check that had once sent her into the edge of the feeder table. Eunice stepped out of the bruiser's way but said nothing. Kathleen rocked side to side as she settled into her new post.

"I know the mangle already, remember? Ya can go sort dirty-dirties with yar darkie, Missy Supervisor."

"I'll watch you feed in the first few sheets, then leave you be, Kathleen."

"Ain't nothin' to shovin' the sheets in this end. Yar nigga needs yar help, Missy Supervisor."

"Call me Eunice."

Red-faced, the Irishwoman turned with a scowl. Powerful,

freckled hands gripped the air, as if holding the ends of a phantom branch; then Kathleen leaned in toward Eunice. The big-bodied bully brandished her imaginary stick, mere inches from the face of her new supervisor. With a quick plunge of her hands, she broke the invisible branch over her raised knee. "Yar a twig, Missy Supervisor, 'n I could snap ya in two just like that."

Lillian, the oldest woman at the table, stumbled out of the way. She pulled a single warm sheet from the cart and rolled it into a bundle in order to hold it up off the concrete floor. She pressed the bunched sheet to her chest. With the modest payload braced under her chin, she shuffled back to the tabletop. She was bent so far over by a curled spine that staring at her shoes seemed a requisite for walking. Lillian had performed this simple transfer to the feeder table countless times, but the tension Kathleen had wrought proved discombobulating. The old woman began to pitch over, but Eunice's hand caught her before she slid to the floor.

"Thank ya, Eunice," Lillian said.

"Dead weight," Kathleen muttered, snarling. Her contempt for Lillian and the rookie supervisor hung in the hot air. Eunice locked eyes with her, then took the warm sheet from Lillian and snapped it above their workspace without looking away from Kathleen's glare. The sheet fluttered before the women, then floated down upon the metal tabletop, where synchronized hands slid the flattened linen into the mouth of the mangle.

Once more, Eunice stepped away from the table. "Okay, Lillian, take back your spot."

Kathleen's side brushed Lillian, who struggled to withstand the modest hip check. The Irishwoman chastised her elder, laughing and saying, "Ya have to do better than she did. I had to smooth out a wrinkle Missy Supervisor missed before we fed it in.

She already forgot how to keep the mangle from ironing creases into the sheets."

Eunice stepped up behind Kathleen's broad shoulders and said, "You got a problem with me, Kathleen?"

"No problem at all, Missy Supervisor, now that yar outta the way."

"Call me Eunice."

"Sure thing, Missy Supervisor."

The fact that only yesterday Kathleen had spent time sorting with Gussie did not affect Eunice's decision. She issued a threat that she would enforce without qualm. "Call me that again, Kathleen, and you'll spend some more time sorting."

"Me arse," Kathleen muttered.

Before Eunice's promotion, the two women had been equals. Eunice thought of her new position and opted to take the high road. She did not want to antagonize Kathleen further, so she turned in the direction of the other end of the mangle, where she would inspect the pressed sheets exiting into the waiting hands of the folders. But as Eunice started past her, Kathleen reached for the one-meter-long steel rod that the crew used to align the mangle guides. With a white-knuckled grip on the shaft, she raised the rod toward the rafters of the old livery. She held her breath inside cheeks flushed red and aimed the bar at the bun tied tight on Eunice's head. The wide-eyed crew, trapped by anticipation of a horrible bludgeoning, froze at the sight of Kathleen in her murderous stance.

Eunice moved on her attacker. Before her assailant could yank the bar downward, she wedged her hand, the one that moments earlier had caught Lillian, into one of Kathleen's exposed armpits. Her other hand snagged the Irishwoman's smock, which she twisted into a handle. Leverage from beneath gave Eunice an advantage, and she drove Kathleen backward, shattering her pelvis against the feeder table.

The steel bar flew out of Kathleen's hands onto the tabletop. In a loud series of clangs, the rod skittered toward the open, chomping mouth of the mangle. Eunice yanked the machine's emergency brake in the instant the monster's jaws clamped the steel bar. The machine ground to a halt, the rod sticking out of the mangle's bite like a toothpick.

Kathleen lay moaning in a heap on the floor as Eunice walked stiff-backed toward Mr. Welles's glass box. After she repeated her account, he complained about the shutdown and the repair costs to get the mangle back into production. Mr. Welles steamed out to the floor to inspect the damage and confront a shocked crew. He was followed by Eunice, who assumed her brief stint as supervisor had come to an end.

The iron rod protruded, clamped in the molars of the mangle. Mr. Welles calculated aloud that it would take the mechanics and welders all night to repair the equipment. He told the crew that if not for Eunice, it could have been much worse. He sent them all to the big room and told Eunice to go get Gussie to help lift Kathleen. The moaning woman bellowed from the floor, "Don't let that nigga touch me!" And then she passed out.

CHAPTER SIX

—·—

Joseph swung from the branch and dropped to the ground next to Jackson, his fifteen-year-old cousin and senior by less than a year. The boys were late. Every morning they were expected to visit Grandfather and help the old man with simple tasks he could no longer handle.

The tree was the tallest perch in their village. If either of the boys had troubles, or simply sought solace and perspective, he would climb high in the canopy and sit alone. When one found it necessary to share worries in confidence, they scaled their tree together, as they had done today at Jackson's request.

Last night, Jackson's older brother, Ellis, had returned to the reservation, as he'd promised, in time for summer's powwow. Before the first snow, he had gone on his solo journey from Idaho to Seattle. Ellis spent his seventeenth birthday there in the midst of strangers and the city's constant drizzle. The two youngsters had been excited for Ellis's homecoming as a boy turned man—a brave. Instead, their hero had returned a drunk.

When Ellis arrived home, he was disheveled. Grandfather was angry and refused him an audience. This morning, the boys had climbed their tree before going to Grandfather because Jackson wanted Joseph to help intercede. He explained how distraught Ellis had been, when, after midnight, he had stumbled into the room they had shared as kids, in order to sleep off his liquor. The rift between Grandfather and his eldest grandson was not the only dilemma Ellis's return posed. Jackson had planned to follow his brother next year. After seeing Ellis arrive in shambles, Joseph doubted that his oldest cousin would be wont to leave the village again anytime soon. There would be no one to follow when it came time for Jackson's solo journey.

They ran to the shack and Grandfather's bedside. He had no sons of his own and had long told his three grandsons that they should honor the old ways. Grandfather had instructed the boys to study those village men who had tried to walk the line between modernity and tradition, only to lose their balance and stumble onward in a drunken stupor—the fate that had shriveled their fathers. Now Ellis had cast his lot with the bottle, as had the two men who had married Grandfather's daughters.

"Grandfather, can we make you tea?" Joseph asked.

"Yes, Jackson. Tea would bring me peace."

The boys exchanged glances. It did not matter that the old man confused them—he always had. Glaucoma compounded the challenge, and he had not yet calibrated his faint hearing to Jackson's cracking voice, the result of exiting pubescence. The two cousins were of similar short stature and, when viewed from behind, they were often mistaken for each other, thanks to their matching long black hair. Both were acrobatic, well known for scaling trees and scampering atop the highest beams of the wooden trestle at the nearby railroad bridge. Joseph did not tease Jackson about his verbal squeaks. He envied his older cousin. Between them, he would be the first boy turned man.

Grandfather sipped, then coughed with a gurgle. A droplet trickled down his chin. With labored effort, he raised a wrinkled, ruddy finger and wiped the bead away. They knew he was dying.

When the snow had melted and green shoots had pierced the dirt to seek the sun, the old man had declared that he hoped to see Ellis return for powwow. Now Ellis was home, the leaves full in the trees, and yet the old man might die without having embraced his first grandson.

"Will you see Ellis today, Grandfather?" Jackson asked. Joseph thought his cousin was fighting against his will. When they had sat high in the tree, they had vowed not to plead too hard on Ellis's behalf.

"Did he send you two in his stead?"

"No, Grandfather. He was very sad that you wouldn't see him yesterday," Jackson said.

"Was he sad or inebriated? He might be a sloppy drunk like your father. Always moping and staggering around. Useless. Never a brave."

"He'll be okay when he wakes up, Grandfather. Will you see him?"

"Asleep still? Ellis did not come back a boy turned man." The tea rose once more. Grandfather took a sip and let his head fall back. He winced with pain. "A brave must speak for himself," he muttered.

Joseph reached out to touch Jackson's forearm. Grandfather once again brought the porcelain mug to his lips, sipped, then closed his milky eyes. Joseph shook his head at his cousin. He was a proud man, and Ellis had injured him.

"I'll tell him, Grandfather. He'll come to you soon," Jackson said.

The old man grew agitated and started to cough again. Tea sloshed over the brim and onto his weathered skin. Joseph took the cup and wiped it off with a towel hooked over the bed's headboard. He dabbed wet stubble on an unshaven chin. After drying his grandfather's hand, he placed it onto the old man's heaving chest. Joseph wanted to let him rest, but he sensed Jackson felt trapped in the gap between two whom he loved. He leaned closer and said, "Grandfather, you always told us that there were two wolves inside every man, one good and one bad."

He coughed, then sputtered, "Yes, two wolves. Always fighting."

Joseph watched the old man shift his weight to assist his breathing. The ancient head, draped with long white hair, fell back against the headboard, above the pillow. Grandfather aimed his clouded eyes at the ceiling before he said, "Tell Ellis to come after he feeds his good wolf. It needs sustenance that does not come from the bottle."

"Can one wolf kill the other, Grandfather?" Jackson asked.

"No, but their struggle is constant. One might hide, cowed by the stronger wolf who wins the day."

"Which wolf is stronger, Grandfather?"

"The one the man feeds the most."

Joseph bit into the dried jerky and tore off a strip. He stared at the railroad tracks and thought of Grandfather, dead now for more than two years. He took a swig from his canteen. Swallowing the water, he folded the rest of the jerky in the brown paper, then wrapped it in his other shirt and rolled it together with the canteen inside the woolen blanket. He tied it all into a tubular bundle with two red bandannas. The train slowed, approaching the bend. Among the boys of the village, Joseph had hopped on at this spot more than any, except Jackson. Holding the small pack at his chest, he waited for the slow-rolling engine to pass.

He bit hard on the knot that linked the two bandannas, then

lunged for the bar. Grabbing hold, he pulled and then scrunched his legs up into a tuck until his feet found their familiar perch. Knees bent, hamstrings pressed against calves, he realized that his grip was too low and gasped with panic. Beneath his buttocks, he felt the fast air skimming the rocks of the railbed. The train's thrumming reverberated in his rib cage and drowned out his racing heartbeat.

Joseph had a few seconds to decide whether to jump off before the train rounded the bend and accelerated. The soles of his shoes pressed against the rattling iron crossbar. Foot-high grass waved from the bank. He could push away, roll through the softness, and try again tomorrow night.

Muscles from his neck to his feet were locked in painful contortion. He gazed up the side of the boxcar at the full moon. Over his shoulder, up ahead, the black locomotive disappeared from view as the engine pulled the cars through the bend. The train unfurled into a straight line, then picked up speed. The sweeping wind bent blades of grass. Drawn back to the railbed, he saw the gray rocks blur and knew it was too late to abandon his attempt. His grip remained strong and his feet secure, yet his buckled legs burned as he rode. He had told his mother that, like Jackson, he would send money, never suspecting that he would have trouble hopping the train that would take him off the reservation.

A weaker boy might have rattled loose, fallen to the rocks, and bounced under the grinding wheels. Sure of his left grip, Joseph released his right hand and tugged the pack from his teeth. Underhanded, he tossed the rolled blanket into the open boxcar, grabbed for the vibrating bar, then brought his forehead to his fists and panted.

He inched himself up, alternating his hands as he would climb a rope. Bouncing in a vertical stance with his knees flexed, he stood just outside an arm's reach of the gaping doorway. Side to side the boxcar shook like a wet dog coming out of a creek. Joseph swung his feet toward the exposed floor. His toes clawed for traction as the train reached top speed. The wind hit him full force in the back. He looked down and squinted at the rocks, which streamed past like rapids.

Sweat compromised his hold, and his cramped hands began to slip. He released one to wipe it on his shirt, then dried the other. With a single, powerful surge, he torqued his body, released his hands, and fell inside. After spinning halfway across the pan of the boxcar, Joseph rolled onto his back, breathless.

With a start, he sat up to search for his bundle. It had skipped across the empty, vibrating floor to the back wall of the car. After crawling on all fours, he clutched the blanket and sat against the wall with his knees bent and the soles of his feet planted. The boxcar rattled, and remnants of cargo dusted the air. His gaze turned toward the rush coming from the opening. The distant sky was clear and filled with stars that sparkled like rain suspended. The moonlight, which had made the night boarding possible, bathed the distant hills. He knew the car was moving while each star held its place. The train whistle blew. After a rough start, his solo journey had begun.

A steady wind brushed the right side of Joseph's head as he sat facing out. The loose denim of his pants flagged around his legs, which he dangled over the edge of the open boxcar. The muscles he had used to rescue his boarding pulsated.

The full moon exposed the reservation's flora. If hidden fauna ventured out, they'd risk the clear vision of waiting predators. An owl swooped down and, while searching for prey, sailed alongside the train until the locomotive left the bird to its hunting. The moonlight's brightness reminded Joseph of the night Jackson had left last year. His letters reported how he had seen the rounded foothills, outlined by stars, and how each jagged mountaintop had clued his location.

No longer anxious, Joseph smiled at his awkward mount. He wondered if any of those who preceded him had had similar trouble hopping the train when their time came. All had practiced like Jackson and he had. No one had confessed to such failure when they returned for powwow as boys turned men. The drunks divulged only what the whites had done to them.

Whenever a boy went missing, the words that buzzed around the village were "Portland" and "Seattle," the assumed choices of destination for any absent would-be brave. Some jumped off early, ending their solo journey after a brief ride. Joseph planned to slip from the train when he reached Sandpoint, where most had continued west. He told his mother that he would find his cousin in New York City. No other Nez Perce brave from their village had traveled the continent as far as Jackson, the first to see the Atlantic shore. As he had promised, Jackson sent his mother money. Joseph's own mother's fears about the journey and its distant terminus had grown in the past weeks as Joseph prepared to follow.

Jackson's trip had been mapped out in detailed letters to guide Joseph, who dropped off the train in Sandpoint, then jumped onto another, heading east. The papers highlighted which trains to catch at rail yards all the way to New York. At the end of the last letter, in bold print, was the address where Jackson worked and the name of his foreman: Tom Burke.

Jotted down in clear, feminine script were the instructions Jackson could not have written himself, sentences that Joseph struggled to read. Jackson had asked his scribe, Mrs. Burke, to write in a private letter to Joseph that he would work in the sky with him. They wanted Indians, braves, to walk the high steel. Joseph should tell his mother not to worry and that he, too, would send money. Don't tell her about working on tall build-ings—Jackson's own mother did not know. Everyone in the village thought Jackson worked on the docks, loading ships larger than any building they had ever seen.

CHAPTER SEVEN

————

In the early morning, one day after Joseph found New York City, the cousins arrived at the construction site together. They had braided each other's long black hair and tied off the tails with leather from broken bootlaces. As had been his custom on the reservation, Joseph wore one of his two red bandannas around his forehead to capture sweat and kept the other stuffed in his back pocket. After Jackson left to ascend the lift, Tom Burke put Joseph to work atop the hard-packed dirt floor of the yard near the perimeter of the fall line, inside which, closer to the rising iron framework, debris from above might dent a skull or tear a shoulder. He was to labor below with two brothers, William and James, from South Carolina, which he remembered from the map of the United States pinned to the wall in the reservation schoolhouse.

Joseph had never seen a Negro in the flesh up close and recoiled when Tom Burke introduced him to them. When he reared back, James elbowed his big brother and said to Joseph, "William here took a step away—just like you—when we met Jackson. I thought William was going to run off. Never seen an Indian before. Me neither."

William nodded and laughed. Then he held up his bare forearm to Joseph's and said, "Your skin's a different hue, but almost as dark as mine."

Together, they unloaded trucks and filled buckets to send up to the men. As the morning wore on, the duo talked to Joseph, not past him. They volunteered that both of their grandfathers had been slaves and that their father was a sharecropper.

"How come you two aren't working on the steel?" Joseph asked.

"I'd be up there right now if Tom would let me," James said.

William, on the other hand, said, "I don't trust the whites. Better to be down here, where I can defend myself. Just in case, you know?"

"You mean run away?" James chided his older brother. He turned to Joseph and said, "William wouldn't go up there if he had wings and only Negro angels worked the high steel." Angels aside, Joseph remembered stories on the reservation about what whites had done to his people. Seemed to him that having dark skin made many a man cautious, for good reason.

After their lunch break, Tom pulled Joseph from the brothers to try a brisk walk atop an I beam laid out on the ground, waiting for the crane. Tom kept his own feet on the dirt, following close behind. Joseph crossed the steel at near a sprinter's pace without looking down at his feet. When he made it to the far end of the beam, rather than hop off, he stopped and turned to face his approaching boss, who was already huffing after he'd covered little more than half the distance. Joseph inched his ankles backward past the steel's edge and stood with the balls of his feet holding his weight, while letting his heels drop to stretch his calves. It felt good after carrying loads all morning. Smiling, Tom stopped, took his cap off, and shook his head.

⌐•⌐

Late in the afternoon, Tom brought Joseph up the elevator to get a sense of the building's height, which he said would rise in the weeks ahead at a rate faster than corn grew in Idaho. Then Tom admitted with a laugh that he'd never been west of Pittsburgh, which Joseph also remembered from the white teacher's map.

As they neared the top, Joseph noticed that Tom held the railing of the elevator with a rigid grip. Tom said that if Joseph were half the natural Jackson was, he'd work up there full-time. The foreman said he just wanted to make sure Joseph understood the job of a runner, who delivered, along with tools and other materials, red-hot rivets to the ironworkers.

Before they headed down, Tom pointed to a tall building several hundred yards in the distance, its windows glistening in the afternoon sunlight. "We'll be looking down on its rooftop in less than three months," he said.

The lift made a hard landing at the bottom. After exiting, they stepped outside the fall line, then turned together to gaze up to where they had been and saw Jackson walking on top of the I beam that laid the foundation of the fifth story. Joseph wanted to get up there and step out of the cage into the open air.

"You did well today, Joseph. Let's go to the shack so you can meet the missus. She'll get you squared away and help you with that letter to your mother."

They climbed the roughed-out staircase, and before they stepped into the shack, he said to Joseph, "Edith handles the paperwork. I can't read my own scribbles." As they entered, Tom brightened and said to the woman at the desk, "Darling, here's our new man, Joseph. Wants to get a letter off to his kin. Told him you'd get him set up for pay and then help him write that letter."

"Ma'am," Joseph said, as he sat on the stool Tom had pulled out with his foot.

"Pleasure to meet you, Joseph," she said, then sent her husband a playful look as he stopped at the door on his way out and turned back toward the desk. Tom winked at her, then glanced at his new hire and said, "I'll come back with Jackson when he comes down. Tomorrow we'll take another ride up the lift, like you asked. I'm gonna keep you working down in the yard for a few more days, but it won't take long—promise."

"Thomas, wait! I almost forgot to ask you. Were Gunnar and JP up there all afternoon? I want to log their time correctly."

"They were." He glanced out into the yard and then returned his frown to her.

"How'd it go for them?"

"A little skittish, but they know the tools and what's got to get done. I hope they find their legs soon. It ain't gonna get any easier." Tom winked at his wife once more, then turned and said, "All right, Joseph. I'll be back with Jackson in a bit."

Mrs. Burke smiled as she reached for the inkwell. "Give me a minute to finish these couple of entries, Joseph, so I don't forget."

His eyes did not leave the pen as it traveled from inkwell to page. After recording the figures, she placed the pen in a horizontal tray on the front of a pewter base that held the glass reservoir. Pursing her lips and leaning over the open book, she blew a soundless whistle to dry her numbers, then moved the open register to the edge of the desk. "That one's the time log." Mrs. Burke drew a sheet of paper from a drawer. "But let's write that letter first, Joseph."

In a tender voice, she asked simple questions in order to clarify his message. When she stopped writing, she showed him what she had written to make sure it was correct. He deciphered most of the words, although he couldn't have built the sentences or written them with such flowing script. He could print the entire alphabet, but drawing the loops and sweeps of cursive remained a puzzle.

Hazel eyes—set in a pleasant, narrow face—looked straight at him in the way of his aunt or any woman of their village. Mrs. Burke did not curl her lip like the other white women in the city, who seemed disgusted by his long hair and ruddy skin and the scent of a hard journey on his ragged clothing.

"Jackson took great care to have me put down all the important information about his trip from Idaho. Amazing memory for detail. He had a few scraps of paper and a pencil stub, yet he remembered every turn, every number. Wanted it to be clear, so you could find him without getting lost along the way."

Joseph nodded but remained reticent.

"Will you teach me your tribal name?" He looked at her, then blurted out syllables in his native tongue.

"Like a melody," she said. Her lips moved in silence; then she looked at him and said, "Well, it's a lovely name, Joseph, but I won't attempt to repeat it aloud until you write it down for me. Maybe we can practice before Tom and Jackson get here." She smiled and said, "Now, let's get you set up in my log."

She retrieved the open register. Joseph watched her eyes scan the page and then settle. "We've added several new men since Jackson." The pen rose from its tray, and before she dipped it into the inkwell, she asked, "What's your last name, Joseph?"

"I just use Joseph, ma'am."

"Do you have a full English name?"

"I use Joseph with the whites," he said, with fleeting confidence. Young at being a man, he shifted his position on the stool and steadied himself.

"Joseph, you know from Jackson that life's difficult here." She returned the dry pen to the pewter tray and sat back. He remained silent but held his eyes on hers. "If you don't use a full name, it'll make things harder for you."

He studied her slender face, with its open, equine smile. In some ways, she reminded him of the teacher's wife who lived with her husband and children on the reservation, although Mrs. Burke sat with broader shoulders and straighter posture; her facial features were sharper and more symmetrical. The hazel eyes were far livelier than those of the teacher's dowdy wife, yet the two women shared a gentleness and alabaster skin so unusual it had caught him off guard, twice. Jackson had told him that Tom Burke and his wife were two of the few whites who would be kind —who would give him a chance.

"Ma'am, my grandfather refused to use what the renamers gave him. He wouldn't respond when it was spoken. He'd walk away." As boys, their broken fathers would shrug or belch out loud whenever they heard the old man admonish his grandsons never to forget their tribe's true name, Nimíipuu. When they were of an age for school, before they met their white teacher, he made them repeat back to him in English that it meant "we the people."

"Does your father use his rename?"

"Yes, but I don't."

"Why, Joseph? Doesn't that hurt your father?"

"My father doesn't feel anything, ma'am. My father's always drunk." She seemed shocked and waited for Joseph to continue. "It's the name of a horse thief, ma'am. The renamers thought it was funny and laughed at my father."

From a second desk drawer, she pulled a canvas bag and extracted from it a well-used Bible, which she opened on the blotter. She made an entry, then turned the book toward him.

"A wedding gift from my parents. I already wrote 'Joseph.' Please write your tribal name under where Jackson put his." Mrs.

Burke handed Joseph the pen, which would bring him, as he knew himself, forever into her family Bible.

On the left side, the top half of the page was covered in the woman's handwriting. Each entry was placed on a horizontal line that had been drawn with a pencil and ruler. Probably the names of her relatives and Tom's, he thought. They all contained a date of birth, and a few had the date they had passed. He assumed her grandfathers and Tom's were recorded there.

To the right, on the next page, names had been scrawled by multiple hands, occasional scribes not practiced at writing on straight lines. Near the bottom, scratched in his cousin's rough handwriting, was Jackson's Nimíipuu name. Next to it, written in her script, was the English moniker of a famous rodeo man from their tribe.

"You and Jackson are two peas from the same pod, I swear. He also refused to use his father's rename."

Joseph smiled at his cousin's choice of the eminent roughrider and said aloud, "Jackson Sundown—of course."

With labored precision, he wrote his Nimíipuu name. He stared down at the page and then handed the pen back to Mrs. Burke. She took it and spun the Bible toward herself to inspect what he had logged.

"Thank you, Joseph. I'll work on the pronunciation of your tribal name." Mrs. Burke looked up at the wooden rafters of the shack. After tapping rolling fingertips on the desk blotter, she lowered her eyes and paused until he gazed at her. "Joseph, what if you also use Sundown?"

"No, ma'am, I can't take it from him. I'll be just Joseph."

"If you have no last name, I fear that someone will give you one, like the renamers did to your father. You don't want that, do you?"

"No, ma'am."

Mrs. Burke seemed to spin in circles in her head. Her eyes widened, and she said, "Your tribe is also called Nez Perce. What about Perce?"

"It was given to our people by Frenchmen. *Nez perce* means 'pierced nose' in their language. My grandfather taught us always to speak our tribe's true name: Nimíipuu."

Her eyes returned to the opened Bible, which Joseph knew was the book the infamous renamers used. As her finger traced the handwritten entries, she seemed to drift off, murmuring an audible hum that stirred him in his seat.

"My brother-in-law was born upstate in the Finger Lakes. His hometown is Canandaigua, situated on the northern shore of a beautiful lake by the same Indian name. He said that as children, he and his friends would hunt for arrowheads, searching the land where the people of the Six Nations—known also as the Iroquois League—had lived for centuries. Do you know of these tribes, Joseph?"

"No, ma'am."

Mrs. Burke closed the book and let her hand rest on the worn leather cover. "Joseph, would you consider a name that isn't offensive, a name your grandfather might have approved?"

"Canandaigua?"

"That might be a bit difficult. I'm thinking of one of those Iroquois Nations—the Seneca—whose Anglicized name the elders tolerated when trading with the European fur trappers. You'd have a proud name that no one would mistake for a horse thief's."

"My teacher taught us about the Roman Empire. Seneca was a famous philosopher." He paused and looked at her. "Ma'am, do you know their true tribal name?"

"Onöndowága, which means 'people of the great hill.'" She

smiled and said, "That'd be even more difficult than 'Canandaigua' for English speakers, Joseph."

He nodded, then repeated aloud, "Onöndowága." Then he whispered, "Great hill people." Joseph recalled how he had felt earlier, standing with Tom in the elevator's mesh cage, overlooking Manhattan Island as if they, too, were standing on a great hill.

He reopened the Bible, found "Joseph" on the page, spun the book for her, then pointed to the blank space below her writing of "Sundown." Mrs. Burke drew a peaceful breath. She picked up the pen, dipped its tip, and wrote "Seneca" in the same feminine script that he had followed across the continent. After she returned the pen to its tray, the Bible spun back toward Joseph, who stared down at the simple moniker that his ears must know in a strange world. Glancing up from the page, he nodded his acceptance of her gift.

Mrs. Burke beamed and said, "It's a pleasure to know you, Joseph Seneca."

CHAPTER EIGHT

—•—

J oseph was making his way back to the village and about to switch trains in Sandpoint once again. Unlike on his eastbound journey, less than six months ago, Joseph had not slipped into empty boxcars unnoticed at various rail yards across the country. Passage for his entire trip home to the reservation had been purchased in New York. On the platform, the conductor inspected his ticket, then handed it back to him. His final destination was Lapwai Station, where he would be met by his mother and aunt, and Ellis, depending on his condition.

The locomotive roared to life, readying to pull the train farther south through the panhandle of Idaho, where tracks had been laid atop Nez Perce territory. Joseph climbed the metal stairs to board the passenger coach. He was cautious and spoke little to the other riders in the cabin as he settled into a seat, one with a window to his shoulder.

The wavy glass distorted the passing images. As the train picked up speed, his resting head bounced against the windowpane. Traveling amid crowded passengers made it seem a much longer trek than when he had rattled toward the Atlantic alone. Soon he must face the questions from his aunt—Jackson's mother. Crossing the continent had not provided the answers he knew she would seek. He himself still had many of those same questions.

Tom Burke never lied, never told Joseph that Jackson's fall was a freak accident, which was what the papers said and what the cops had concluded after talking to the crew. Joseph didn't need anyone to confirm it had been murder, a crime that had been Gunnar Erikson's alone, a crime of hatred against the best man on the crew, a man who, Gunnar often railed, was not human—a danger. No one on the crew thought the Eriksons would survive raising four more floors, much less reach the planned top of the building. Blaming Indians could not hide their unsurety or mask their tentative steps in the open air. Long before Jackson fell, to every man on the crew, the Swedish brothers had posed the real danger.

When the steel rose on that fateful day, as always, Jackson was the first man out on the I beam that had been set to start the new floor. Gunnar had ridden the elevator to the top with Jackson, but the Swede must have held back in the cage. Working far out on a beam below them, Joseph heard Gunnar shout at Jackson about some mess he'd left at the lift's exit. He accused Jackson of setting a trap to trip him. Then Gunnar seemed to lose all control and started screaming in Swedish. No one on the crew heard Jackson reply to the one-sided argument as Gunnar continued to squawk like a crow, as if bluster might disguise his obvious fear.

Joseph didn't see Jackson walk back toward the cage, or what Gunnar then did. He knew not to divert his vision without caution, so he sat down to secure himself. But before he could twist to gaze up at the man's hysterics, Jackson fell. As the train rumbled forward, Joseph thought of how he had spotted Jackson falling, as now, out of the corner of his eye, the passing Idaho scenery disappeared behind him in blinks.

Heavyhearted, he stared out across the landscape. He wondered if Ellis had continued to decline; then he thought how little

space was left between his oldest cousin and the bottom. Had Ellis
been able to drive the wagon, or had he sat drinking while one of
the women guided the horse?

Familiar landmarks entered Joseph's view, and the train
slowed. The whistle blew as they crawled toward the platform.
Through the window, he saw them and recoiled at the sight of
Ellis, slumped in between his mother and aunt. He was propped
up, bookended by the stoic, gray-haired sisters.

As the train ground to a halt, its brakes screeched. Steam
blasted through the brass whistle again. Joseph saw the two startled women jerk, while Ellis seemed unfazed. Not even twenty
years old, and his cousin wore the rotting face of a tired old man
close to death after a crushing life. His clothes were filthy from
wallowing in the mud. Joseph wondered if his broken cousin
possessed the strength and coordination for the task at hand.
Without Ellis, he would need the grieving women to help slide
Jackson's casket onto the bed of the wagon.

On the ride to the village, Joseph's mother did not utter a word,
though he knew that she wanted to ask many questions. When
they were alone, after they had unloaded Jackson's coffin, Joseph
was certain she would beg him not to return to New York.

A depleted whiskey bottle rolling back and forth, tinkling
against Jackson's pine box, interrupted the rumble of the wagon.
Next to Joseph on the wooden bench seat, Ellis twisted toward the
women who sat in the back beside Jackson. The reins snapped as
Joseph coaxed the horse into a quicker pace. His cousin reeled
from the mare's jolt, and Joseph grabbed his sleeve to prevent him
from sliding off and under the spinning wheels. Wavering, Ellis
followed the tug, while his head continued to point backward.

Drunken burps and hiccups jiggled the broken man. Joseph glanced at Ellis again as he stared down into the bed of the wagon, focused not on his brother's coffin but on the rolling empty bottle.

With a flat hand on her son's casket, Joseph's aunt broke the silence as if she alone had license. "One letter said he fell." Joseph crushed the reins in his hands. "The teacher read the letters to me. He said one was from Joseph and one was from the man, Burke. The scratches were the same. One hand wrote both letters?"

"The boss man's wife, Mrs. Burke, wrote what I told her and what he told her."

"The boss man can't write letters?"

"He writes like I write. His wife made the marks so the teacher could read both letters to you, so you'd understand."

"Boss man's letter said Jackson fell. Did he fall?"

"Yes, he fell to the ground from very high. He died instantly, felt no pain."

"How did he fall? Jackson could climb anywhere, like a squirrel. He never slipped, so how did he fall? Was he drunk?"

"No. He was never drunk or careless on the high steel. Jackson was the best man on the crew."

Throughout the entire train ride across the continent, Joseph had anticipated—dreaded—this conversation with his aunt. No one in the village would believe that Jackson had misstepped and fallen to his death. Nor could they comprehend the extreme height, or how powerful the wind could be at the top of a reaching skyscraper.

"Don't tell me about the wind, Joseph. You had the woman write about the wind in your letter. You didn't have her write that Jackson was blown off the steel. You just told her to write about the wind."

"I didn't want to lie to you," he said, then snapped the reins again to rush the horse forward, away from his torment. Jackson had fallen on a cloudless day when the air was calm.

"Who did this, Joseph? Don't tell me the wind."

"Someone on the crew, a white man."

"Do these whites, with their many laws, not punish their own? Why do they protect this man?"

"No one saw the man push or trip Jackson, but they were alone up on the steel. The crew knows that Jackson never lost his balance. I heard them talk. They, too, believe the white man killed him. But they can't prove anything. All they saw was . . ." Joseph's words stalled in midair, as he wished Jackson could have.

"What did they see? What did *you* see, Joseph?"

"I saw Jackson fall past us to the ground. He was above us, up top with the white man. We seldom look up, unless . . ." Joseph stopped as he recalled the image of his cousin falling like a shot bird. Already seated, Joseph had dropped at that instant to hug the girder. His gaze never left Jackson during his descent. Tears washed onto the cold steel as Joseph's cheek pressed against the I beam. He strained to see any life in his cousin's contorted body far below on the ground. Joseph got to him on the first elevator to descend. After seeing Jackson up close, he wished that he had never come down.

"From what tribe is this white man? What people would do such a thing?"

Joseph had asked himself that question, though he knew that no tribe made a man good or bad. Each must become master of self. Grandfather had taught them that inside every man, re-gardless of his tribe, were two wolves who were always fighting for control of the man. One wolf was good; one wolf was bad.

"Swede."

On the train ride back to New York from Idaho, Joseph did not take a window seat. He had no ticket. It was early autumn and still warm enough to jump the trains, as he had in the spring when he was a would-be brave on his way east to rendezvous with Jackson.

He rode the floors of empty boxcars as homage to the two dead men whose presence he shared as he traveled eastbound. Grandfather once more told the boys the familiar tale of his own solo journey—a long hunt—when he became a boy turned man. How he had changed from hunter to hunted, and then back. How, bloodied under the hide of a mountain lion, he'd walked into a camp of braves from his tribe and fallen on his knees at their fireside. Only one survives such a contest, Grandfather said. Kill the cat and wear it, or pass through its stomach.

"I didn't expect you back, Joseph. I mean, not so soon. Edith'll be glad to see you. She's been worried." Joseph looked at Tom and waited. "You looking to get some work?"

"Yes, Tom, I'm looking for work."

Tom swiped the toe of his boot across the ground, as if he were tongue-tied and looking for words in the dirt. "Want me to help you find another job? You know, maybe on a different crew?"

Joseph shook his head. "Tom, I came back to work for you," he said, half full of the truth.

"Well, that means a lot to me. You're one of my best men ever, Joseph." Tom averted his eyes once more. Joseph suspected his old foreman didn't trust him around Gunnar, who'd claimed that Indians would take every white man's job on the crew before the year was out. Tom was right to assume that Joseph was not among those who believed justice would prevail in another life. Yet Joseph wanted Tom to see that his intense anger had passed. It had been prominent at the train station when Tom had helped load Jackson's casket onto the boxcar for the ride west.

Joseph's restraint felt unforced, as if nothing Tom might say could stoke the heat of his anger. Now he understood Grandfather's cool composure, which had at times sent chills through him as a boy. Joseph's solo journey, too, had become a hunt, he told himself. If Tom hired him back, on his next climb, he would track Jackson's killer. Tom's eyes lifted with a cautious look that signaled he expected from Joseph a blast, not ice.

A passing shadow crossed over the structure, which looked like giant steel fingers clawing the sky to snag such clouds. Joseph's neck craned until he spotted the crew, who had continued to reach higher since he had left with Jackson's body. The sun's rays were like shiny needles being dropped from the sky. Thumb to temple, Joseph shielded his eyes with a flat hand and squinted to locate Gunnar. The crew looked like ants. From so far away, the Swedish brothers' sticklike statures and cautious movements did not betray them.

"Gunnar up there?" Joseph asked, with the calm of a hunter.

"Joseph, he ain't up there; neither's JP."

"You fire them both?"

"Just one," Tom said, his toe sweeping and his eyes searching the hard-packed dirt.

"You firing me, too?" Joseph's heart sank. Why would Tom keep JP and let him go?

"You can be working tomorrow, if you want. I got a friend over at that site right there. See the steel just starting to poke up above those buildings? He'll take you on, on my word. I'm sure of it."

"Firing me, then?"

"Gotta get things settled down around here, Joseph, you know what I mean? I've lost another man since . . ." Tom's voice trailed off. He grabbed a handkerchief from his back pocket and dabbed both eyes. "That makes three in so many months. The authorities been poking around every other day lately."

"All right, Tom. I get it."

"You want me to go see my friend about getting you on his crew?"

"Please. I'd appreciate it, Tom." Joseph felt stabbed by this man he thought as fair as any he'd met—on or off the reservation. Then he wondered if James would ever get the chance to climb. "Tom, why didn't you fire JP, like me? Because he's white?"

"I did fire JP. Wouldn't've mattered to me if he was purple. Just gotta get things settled down around here."

"You didn't fire Gunnar?"

"He fell, Joseph. On his own. A couple of days ago."

CHAPTER NINE

B esides a few wispy clouds, the sky was clear when Eunice headed out on her mission. Thunder sounded as she hurried down the last block. The deluge came on just as she arrived at her destination. She stepped through a sheet of water and squeezed forward under the inadequate awning. The cascade sliced downward, inches behind her already wet shoulders, as she drummed her knuckles on the door to Gunnar's apartment. His widow, Monika, pulled the door open a slit and peeked out with widened eyes at the sight of her sister-in-law. Eunice hunched in closer to keep the awning's runoff from hitting her in the back.

"Monika, I'm sorry to trouble you while you're in mourning. I just came for the suit I let Gunnar borrow." Monika held the door open the smallest of cracks and did not invite Eunice inside. "I'm getting soaked out here, Monika. Hand it over, and I'll be on my way."

"I don't got it."

"Gunnar told JP that he left it for me. Said it was right there—behind you—on the coat rack."

"Told ya, Eunice, I don't got it."

Eunice pressed the door open and charged into the entry. A woman's ratty coat and a few sweaters hung on the row of hooks. "What'd he do with it, Monika?"

"Nothin'... He's dead, remember?"

"Yeah, I know he's dead. But that suit didn't walk outta here by itself, now, did it?"

"I gave it to the funeral man. He came to pick up clothes to bury Gunnar in."

"McClean? Billy McClean took it?"

"That's what I said, ain't it?"

Eunice sighed, thinking Monika was dumber than her dead husband. "That suit's my property, Monika. My boss gave that to me from the pile of items people don't pick up. I mended it, and now I need to sell it."

"I don't got it, I told ya."

"You don't have any money to bury Gunnar. I'm selling that suit to help pay for the funeral."

"It's on Gunnar. That man took it for the funeral, just like he's supposed to."

"Who said McClean was supposed to take it? It's my suit, Monika. Not yours. Not Gunnar's."

"Gunnar told me ya give him the suit for the funeral."

"That was for Lars's funeral, remember? You think I'd tell a man I was giving him a suit for his own funeral?"

"Well, how's I supposed to know that?"

Straight as a bell tower rope, Eunice walked through the doorway and descended the wet stairs toward the street. Rain smacked her face. She bowed her head as she walked toward the mortuary. Her tight hair bun started to lose its shape as she darted around swelling mud puddles. By the time she arrived at McClean's funeral parlor, the bun had unraveled and her saturated clothing was matted against her skin.

After shopping for Lars's burial, she had chosen the mortician William S. McClean. She thought he had an odd name for an undertaker, but, name aside, Billy was the man for the job. He proved her correct. McClean stuck to her instructions, made sure the unpleasant business was completed fast, and got it done on the cheap. She didn't shop around when Gunnar fell.

No hearse in the driveway, no rigs or automobiles waiting outside. Eunice marched toward the front of the funeral home alongside a hedgerow that lined the drive. She stomped up the stairs to the front door. Under the protection of the porch roof, not pausing to brush the beads from her hair or clothing, she worked the brass knocker as if she intended to wake the clients draining in the basement.

The face of the man who seemed to her always ready for tragedy filled the open doorway. "Mrs. Erikson, you're soaked! Please come inside. Let me get you some towels."

"I don't need to get your floor wet, Billy. Do you have that suit Monika gave you by mistake?"

"Mistake?"

"She gave you a suit that's my property. I lent it to Gunnar for his brother's funeral, and I need it back."

"The suit I put on Mr. Erikson? His wife told me that was what he wanted to be buried in." Blood rose past Billy's thick neck. His round face flushed up to his receding hairline. Built like a man who'd put a few people into undertakers' hands after bar fights, he hadn't struck Eunice as a mortician—more like the street toughs she had grown up among.

"Monika isn't the brightest candle, Billy. It wasn't hers to give you."

"Mrs. Erikson, I'm very sorry for the confusion."

"No problem, Billy. Just give me the suit, and I'll be on my way."

"The wake starts in less than an hour. Under the circumstances, Mrs. Erikson, would you consider donating the suit?"

"I wouldn't."

He looked incredulous. She had thought morticians were taught to hide their feelings better.

"Well, Mrs. Erikson, would you consider leaving him in the suit for the wake, at least?"

"Is he leaking on it?"

"Impossible. Mr. Erikson's body was drained last night." Billy took a deep breath and shook himself as he exhaled. "We might be able to work something out with his widow. You know, maybe she can buy the suit from you?"

"That woman doesn't have two pennies to rub together. That's why I hired you myself. And I need to sell that suit to help pay for the funeral. You want to get paid, don't you, Billy?"

"Well, maybe you and I can come up with a solution after the wake. I can't bury him naked. That wouldn't be right, would it?"

"He ain't complaining, is he?"

"Mrs. Erikson, please."

"You change your mind about getting paid, Billy?" Eunice could see the man was stymied, so she sighed and said, "All right, keep it on him for the wake. I'll stick around after everybody leaves."

"Mrs. Erikson, please understand that the wake's about to start. I doubt I'll have replacement clothes until the morning. The burial time is early, as you know, but I'll do everything I can to switch him out of your suit before we have to drive to the cemetery."

"Let her think he's going into his grave like he is. I'll go get you a change right now and bring it to the wake. After she's gone, you get my suit off him. Just don't tell Monika."

"Understood, Mrs. Erikson. I'll have your suit ready to pick up after the burial."

"I'll get the suit tonight, Billy," she pressed. "When will you have it off him?"

"Midnight, Mrs. Erikson. I'll have your suit ready for you at midnight. Come to the back door, please. I'll wait for you in the kitchen."

Glass in hand, Billy sat alone in the dark long after closing down his second Erikson wake. Family members and the obligated had left hours earlier. The house was quiet, yet the collar around his bull neck was still pinned tight for business. He had dreaded the morning's burial, and, despite the late hour, he was desperate to replace the mineral water in his glass with whiskey. His oldest, Sean, had already missed curfew. He hoped Mrs. Erikson would be here and gone before the lad arrived.

The bottom plank of the back-porch stairs creaked, and Billy snapped to attention. She was prompt. Despite the woman's modest weight, the treads' nails strained in their wooden channels as she rose. He shuddered, visualizing her rigid posture and firm grip on the banister.

Billy heard Mrs. Erikson's sharp knock on the door as if it were high noon, not midnight. He stood, pushing the chair away from the kitchen table with the backs of his legs. Lapels tugged into symmetry, he downed the glass, thinking forward to the whiskey, and scooped up the soft package.

Rapid knuckles rattled the porch door again. Fearful she would soon pound the door with the heel of her fist and disrupt the sleep of his wife and their five youngest children, Billy hurried across the kitchen. He had assumed she might want to inspect her property. She did. With practiced hands, Mrs. Erikson placed the brown paper on the kitchen table, untied the bundle, clutched her possession at the shoulders, then snapped the suit coat so that it hung open before her. She spun it around in the light, then grabbed the slacks and repeated her inspection, as if she wanted to ensure no new stains had been added by either process—Billy's embalming or Gunnar's decomposition.

Mrs. Erikson seemed satisfied; she rewrapped the suit in the paper and retied the twine. The other bundle, which she had brought to the wake, sat untied on the marble countertop.

"Haven't put it on him yet?"

"Uh, not yet, Mrs. Erikson," Billy said. When she had stepped up with the package after the wake, he had thought the parcel too lightweight, maybe just a simple cotton work shirt and pants. Mrs. Erikson had not waited for Billy to inspect the contents. Once alone, he'd unwrapped the bundle and understood why. One size fits all—a single, threadbare bedsheet. Billy would not have buried a stray cat in that stained and tattered shroud.

"Wake's over, Billy. The box stays shut, right?"

"Yes, Mrs. Erikson. No one'll see the body again."

"All right, then," she said. He was exhausted and struggled to retain his professional decorum, and she called him out on it. "You look like that sheet bothers you, Billy."

Every mortician practiced a poker face, but the moment gave away his hand. Billy fought the temptation to tell her about Mrs. Zorn, the widow of a wealthy man he'd escorted into the next life, three weeks prior. When her husband died, she brought two clothing options to the funeral home; she was perplexed, vacillating about her man's dress code for eternity. She called Billy the day of the wake, having decided on Mr. Zorn's favorite blue suit, the one he wore to church every Sunday. She left behind his tuxedo, saying she would drop by to pick it up when she felt up to the task. After Gunnar's wake, Billy called Mrs. Zorn to tell of the poor young widow who possessed only the laborer's clothes of her late husband. Honored to help a fellow Swedish immigrant, Mrs. Zorn insisted on donating the tuxedo. He guessed that Gunnar, from the neck down, had never looked so good.

"I'm sorry, Mrs. Erikson, it's late and I'm expecting my son home soon. He's past his curfew, and I don't want him to think he can slip upstairs without an explanation. Is our business finished for tonight?"

"I've got my suit, so we're done." His grimace betrayed his thoughts. "You can judge me if you want, Billy. Gunnar wasn't a good man. They say he killed a man. He died owing me money, and he won't need a suit where he's going."

Mrs. Erikson pivoted, walked to the back porch, and slapped the screen door into an outward swing. Billy stopped it from crashing back and let the rattle slow before the door settled into its frame. At the top of the back-porch staircase, she cast back over her shoulder a final, terse comment: "Sheet's clean, Billy."

The bottom step creaked under Billy's weight when he went to dump the sheet outside in the trash bin. She was walking down the driveway with the package at her chest. Before Mrs. Erickson rounded the corner of his property, she passed his sixteen-year-old son, Sean, who was hunched over, with his hands on his knees, vomiting into the hedgerow that trimmed the long, sweeping driveway. The boy turned as she walked toward him. Billy saw him recoil. Despite poor lighting, his son must have caught a glimpse of those ice-cold blue eyes. Billy knew from experience that her stare could dart into a person like a hooligan's knife. Dressed in black, her hair in a tight bun, the straight-backed woman breezed past Sean in a glide, as if she were sailing just above the ground.

Billy climbed the stairs, then turned to watch his son, who

did not notice his father. Sean struggled to stay on track. Held upright by one shoulder scraping along the hedgerow, he lurched up the driveway. The mortician entered the house and let his long-anticipated whiskey slide into the glass. He sipped, then glanced at his pocket watch, wondering how long it would take his son to make it inside.

Billy sat at the table with his eyes aimed at the porch and a pour of his finest Irish whiskey in hand. He listened to the quiet. When the door finally opened and the boy appeared under the lintel, Billy was impressed by the lad's drunken stealth. Somehow the teen had prevailed over each tread that Mrs. Erikson had made screech.

Gape-mouthed, spewing breath in a mixture of cheap bourbon and puke, Sean swayed as he tried to freeze in place. Billy returned his glass to the table and cleared his throat. "Sean, I'm disappointed in you, but I'm glad you're home safe. We'll talk in the morning. Do you need help getting upstairs?"

"No, sir."

"Be quiet, and don't wake your brothers."

"Yes, sir." Sean paused. "Pa?"

"Yes, son?"

"I think I saw a witch."

"And where might you have seen a witch, boy?"

"Just now. Outside, by the street. She wore black. And her eyes were like nothing I've ever seen. She looked into my soul, Pa. I'm not sure I can get to sleep."

"Whiskey'll do that to you, boy. We'll talk in the morning. Try not to think about the witch."

Billy watched his son take hold of the banister and pull himself up the back stairs, alternating shaky hands one over the other. As Billy drained his glass, his thoughts turned to Eunice Erikson.

He poured another drink to the echo of his own advice: *Try not to think about the witch.* Billy brought the whiskey to his lips. He shook off a shiver that curled up his spine as he muttered aloud to himself, "I'll do the same, boy. I'll do the same."

CHAPTER TEN

Squirrels scrambled atop the shack's roof as if they'd been startled by a cat. The envelope with the money for Jackson's mother was wrong. Edith removed the cash, then tore the envelope in half between the words "Jackson" and "Sundown." Opened to its front pages, Edith's family Bible offered inscribed names like prayers in the uplifted palms of the devout. She padded her eyes again with the moist handkerchief. Before retrieving her pen from the inkwell, she turned the Bible on an angle in order to catch the light. Crying harder, she dabbed the tip into the pool of blue ink. Onto the face of the fresh envelope, she copied Jackson's Nimíipuu name. She blew the words dry, then spread the sides apart and inserted the bills.

Joseph entered the shack; he had cleared the steps undetected by Edith. The kerchief went to the corners of her eyes in quick succession; then she crushed the hanky in her hand and brought it to her lap.

"Tom told me to pick up my pay. And Jackson's, for his mother."

"Joseph" was all she could eke out.

"Is Tom here?"

"No, at the cemetery."

"They putting Gunnar in the ground?"

"Yes. The wake was yesterday," Edith said. Wondering if Joseph would confront JP, as Tom feared, she watched for the telltale signs of pent-up anger so clear to her when she had accompanied Tom to the train station, where he had helped load Jackson's casket into the boxcar. Today, Joseph seemed calm. Too calm to betray his resentment. Edith worried that the cool efficiency for which he and Jackson had been well known as workers might soon again be on display toward a different end. *Revenge served cold* came to mind as she thought of an old saying that had always made her shiver.

"Any word from Tom's friend?"

"Tom talked to him last night. You made a good impression, Joseph, when the three of you met over at the site. You're on the crew, starting Monday morning."

"Please tell Tom that I'm thankful, ma'am."

Maybe it's all for the best, she thought. Tom had fired them both. Out of sight, out of mind, her own mother would have said. That alone might leave vengeance to separate graves—one here in New York and one on a reservation the better part of a continent away. Edith counted out his back pay onto the surface of the desk. After he stuffed the folded wad of money into his front pocket, he held Jackson's envelope in view, then sighed at the sight of the tribal name she had copied from her Bible with care.

"Joseph, I'm so sorry."

Boots stomped on the steps. An ebullient man burst into the shack, barging in on their private sadness. Frank Lawrie was the longest-serving member of Tom's crew. Together, he and her husband had raised several buildings on Manhattan. When complete, the current project would be their tallest.

"Joseph! Thought I seen ya walk into the yard. How long ya been back, boy?"

"Frank," Joseph acknowledged. "A couple of days."

"Well, good timing. Let's go!"

"Frank, leave him be. That isn't a good idea. Tom wouldn't approve. You know that, right?"

"Now, Edith, don't be mothering the boy. The crew's gathering right now." A loud whistle pierced the walls of the shack, and squirrels scurried across its bonnet. "Come on, Joseph. We're going to the Pigeon's Post. Having a little sendoff for Gunnar."

"Guess I'll be heading back to the boardinghouse, ma'am," Joseph said, as he stuffed Jackson's folded envelope into his back pocket, opposite the one with a red bandanna. He nodded to her, then to Frank, with what looked like a forced smile, and left the shack. Lawrie snorted a giggle, then turned to follow him outside.

"Frank! Leave him alone, hear me?"

Tom had told her this morning that he'd be glad when the day was over. Be glad that he wouldn't have to worry about JP taunting Joseph and what the boy might do to defend his honor—or Jackson's. He told her that Joseph had a look he hadn't seen since the army—since the war. Some men snapped; more boys did. Some men focused; even the rare young one.

"Joseph and JP got no beef," Frank said over his shoulder. "Little drink'll settle everything." She heard Lawrie call out at the top of the steps, "Hey, Seneca Joe, where ya going? Slow down, Injun!"

Edith closed the cash box, then slid the tin container into a desk drawer and hurried to the doorway. *He's only a boy,* she thought, frantic with maternal worry. A crowd of men with broad smiles gathered around Joseph, foiling his attempts to escape. Frank's arm squeezed his neck, and the crew slapped Joseph on the back. They whisked him through the yard and out of her sight.

Eunice seldom drank in JP's presence and never stood between him and a drink. She paced herself and held her booze better—and drank him under the table whenever it served her purposes. Once lubricated beyond his natural orneriness, he was as easy to control as a sleepy lamb that she could tie to a fence and collect later.

Burke's crew had already gathered when she and JP entered the Pigeon's Post. The men raised glasses to acknowledge their arrival. "Down the hatch, JP," Tom ordered, as he offered the glass jigger. "Eunice, here's a shot for you as well."

Without hesitation or feigned demur, she accepted the whiskey. She reached for a clean tumbler from the row stacked upon the bar top and poured her shot into the larger glass. It would give her something to hold while she endured these men. She'd nurse the drink until she thought she could leave JP behind, harmless. The first taste slid down her throat with a familiar warmth. In one hand, she held the tumbler to the bar's countertop; she would let the sip settle before considering another touch. Devoid of outward emotion, JP tossed back his shot and brought the glass down to the bartender for a refill.

She took in the surroundings. It was here, three years back, on her sixteenth birthday, where she'd dropped her guard. On the next barstool sat the man who had led her to the smithy's loft across the alley. JP gulped his second shot, then stared straight over the bartender's head into the downward-slanted mirror. She wondered if he'd spotted the Indian standing at the back of the crowd. *That's the other boy—the dead one's cousin*, she realized. Maybe a year or so younger, he was about her age and seemed out of place. Better get JP sauced, she thought, as she tapped his empty glass toward the barkeep, who held the whiskey bottle at the ready. JP polished off his refill, then gaveled the shot glass onto the surface of the bar for another pour. He settled in on the stool for the duration. He belched out loud. The crew noticed and cheered.

She guessed that the married men on the crew had invoked the fallen-comrade rationale in order to avoid any hassles at home. *Hope none of them are mean drunks like the brothers Erikson,* she thought, having no appetite for a fight to break out.

With an amber residue on the inside of her glass, she turned it over in her hand for inspection like a prized marble shooter. Uli had spent many an afternoon in here, rolling his marbles on a tabletop while Pa drank. She couldn't conjure the color of the shooter that she had returned to him after bludgeoning his head in the alley. Yellow, she thought, but maybe it was more of an amber after all.

Eunice slipped off the stool to let the tide of soon-drunks splash against her husband in name only, a man she despised. She stepped toward the stand-up piano placed against the long wall opposite the bar.

From a safer distance, she monitored the reflections of the animated crew in the angled mirror. With an elbow braced atop the piano, she observed the men unleashed. They drank with abandon, unworried that the saloon might pitch and cast them overboard. With severe hangovers, they would wash up on their respective home shores by morning. Unbound—liberated for the night from their family moorings—the men were free to drink without restraint; a coworker had died.

"Funeral?" the piano player asked, as he lifted the keyboard cover. The musician sat down, cracked his knuckles, and ran the scales.

"Yup, my brother-in-law," she replied sideways.

"My condolences," he said into the sheet music. Then he

glanced at a small, framed mirror on the wall above the piano. Eunice, too, could see the bar and its rowdy clientele from their shared vantage point.

"That little mirror gives you eyes in the back of your head, huh?"

The piano man smiled as he intertwined his fingers, swung his hands—palms out—into a conjoined stretch, and cracked his knuckles again. Then he lowered the tools of his trade to a second, light landing on the keys. Ignoring the sheet music, he played while alternating his gaze between the mirror and two doorways: the entrance from the street and a back door to the alley.

"Any requests?" he asked her.

"Don't play any Swedish songs."

She considered the piano man a bit of a dandy. He was skittish, poised for urgent escape, with his legs set like springs and his bottom just catching the edge of the piano bench. Eunice thought he would bolt at the first sign of trouble. Needed his hands to eat, like the rest of them.

"What?"

"Just keep it upbeat."

"Got it," he said. Before he struck the keys again, he checked his little mirror.

Eunice favored her position. Because of the angle of the outsized mirror above the bar, none of the patrons' reflections were blocked from her view. The bartender had a pink bald spot in his dark hair. Facing the entryway, the Indian stood off to the side of the crowd with his hands shoved deep into his front pockets. He also appeared ready to break free. JP and Gunnar had spat their contempt for the two Indian cousins, who, she knew from the Swedes' invectives, could flit like birds and run like squirrels across the I beams, no matter how high the steel climbed. Glass at her mouth, she watched him. Indian or not, he was far better-looking than any Erikson. Scanning to JP, she scrunched her nose and curled a lip.

Frank Lawrie bought a round for the men, although she noticed the Indian did not pick up his shot glass from the bar along with the others. Lawrie demanded everyone's attention before they drank, then lifted his glass and said in a loud voice, "To Gunnar Erikson!"

"To Gunnar!" returned the chorus, and then they tossed back their shots while JP shouted out a string of Swedish words ending with "Gunnar." He then drank his shot and slipped halfway off his stool.

Stopping in place like shocked gophers, the crew turned in unison toward JP. Most had been standing with a hand on the shoulder of their closest drinking partner. They traded stares and fought to control their laughter, which only made most of them turn to the side and double over. JP had never embarrassed Eunice, but ever since the night Pa had confronted the man in this very saloon, he had always disgusted her.

She didn't know these men or their wives. Burke, she had met at Lars's wake. He and his nice-enough wife had come to show their respects, given that Gunnar and JP—recent hires—were on his crew. No one else from the construction site had attended. Remembering her sixteenth birthday, Eunice took in her surroundings, cringed, and concluded that not only was JP disgusting, he still frightened her.

Poking fun at the Erikson family's trait of protruding ears, Frank shouted, "To JP—the last of the wing nuts!" As if the slur had put a flame to JP's shirtsleeve, he turned with a start and, this time, slipped off the stool altogether. He reached his hand back toward the wooden bar and, with considerable effort, returned to his stool like a blind man. Frank had a fresh pour sent to JP's glass, which caused the Swede to shift his attention. "A little drink'll fix everything. Ain't that right, Wing Nut?"

Eunice had planned to corner Tom Burke tonight. JP had told her that the Indian had gotten another job straight away because Burke had vouched for him. Meanwhile, he'd told JP he should try the docks. Didn't think he was cut out for working high steel. Burke was right, she knew, but still she was hoping he might know somebody who'd hire JP as a simple laborer like Pa, if not a riveter or welder, which were the skills the brothers had learned when they had first come to America. Maybe the old Swede would take him back. She needed to keep him working and bringing in money. If he were jobless, he'd be drunk earlier in the day. Then nobody would hire the man whose name was on her lease, and she'd have a tough time making ends meet, much less sending cash upstate to fulfill her obligations. Pa could go to hell, but she knew in her heart that Ma was Ma because of Pa. And Uli was Uli because of her.

Elbow on the piano, yet to take another taste of her first pour, Eunice took in the crowd. She didn't know how many of the assembled were on Burke's crew. The way the patrons acted made it appear as if everyone in the saloon had come in tribute to Gunnar. JP had worked with men she didn't know, men who now seemed to be using Gunnar's death to get pissed like a war had just ended—one they hadn't fought.

In the mirror, she took stock of JP's progress. He had started to rock in place, but she could tell he might still get enraged. From her current viewing angle, his protruding ears did give him the look of a huge wing nut. She shook her head at the lanky goon as he struggled to hold his balance on the barstool. Tom

Burke might have done her a huge favor by firing JP. He wouldn't have lasted much longer up on the skyscraper, and she still needed him to bring in some money beyond whatever he spent drinking every night. What in the world had made those gangling Swedish ogres think they could work on anything higher than a stepladder?

Eunice saw JP scowling into the mirror, where he had spotted the Indian at the back of the crowd, inching his way toward the door. Tom Burke peeled away from the cluster surrounding JP at the bar just in time to intercept the young man at the exit. Eunice stepped into earshot, in hopes of grabbing Burke when the Indian left.

"Tom, I better be going. Thanks again for helping me get on over there. I'll do you proud."

"I know you will, Joseph. I'll check in on you in a couple of weeks. The missus and I want to make sure you're doing okay," said Burke, who then hiccupped and batted his eyes. When the foreman lost his balance, the Indian grabbed his arm and said, "You okay, Tom?" Burke stood, wobbling. He looked into the young man's eyes and then down at the floor. He teetered once more. The Indian guided Burke to the nearest table and slipped him into an empty chair. He laid his hand on the foreman's shoulder. "You and Mrs. Burke been real good to me and Jackson."

"Hey, Seneca Joe, you got no drink in your hand, boy. What the hell's wrong with you?" Frank Lawrie asked, as he approached the table.

"Frank, let him be," Burke protested.

"Tom, we ain't on the job. Celebrating the fallen, ya know. We never did have a drink with Seneca Joe here, in honor of ole Jackson."

He almost escaped, Eunice thought. Yanked away at the elbow by Frank, the Indian they called Joe or Joseph looked back to Tom. The edge of the crew's cluster swarmed around Joseph, pulled him toward the bar, and pressed him onto a wooden seat. He was separated from JP by two other men, who, hunched over in conversation, elbows on the bar, were standing between the adversaries' stools and talking to the bartender.

Frank Lawrie pressed a shot glass into Joseph's hand. "To Jackson!" Frank shouted.

A cheer went toward the ceiling. "To Jackson!" echoed the crew.

"Fock dat Inyun!" JP shouted.

Joseph didn't take the bait. To Eunice, the Indian seemed self-possessed beyond his years. He stared at JP with no change in expression whatsoever.

She shook her head and started back toward the piano. When Lars and Gunnar were alive, the three brothers were notorious for causing bar fights. In spite of no longer possessing safety in numbers, JP could be volatile all on his own. Once she was sure he was too drunk to start something, she'd leave. She envied Monika. If only she didn't need JP's X and his earnings, she mused, as she took her second modest taste.

Frank lifted Joseph's elbow, raising the glass to the young man's lips. She had heard that some Indians were like Pa; that first shot of whiskey might trigger a rush for the next, and then the next one after that.

"Come on, Joe. This one's for Jackson." Joseph drank it down, then tugged in vain to free himself. "No ya don't, Injun," Frank scolded.

Eunice noticed the look of desperation on Tom Burke's face and approached him. He was slumped in his chair. "What's the matter, Tom?"

"Can't stand up to help Joseph. Can't stand up right now," he muttered. He looked up at her and shook his head. He closed his eyes and gritted his teeth, as if his mind had suffered a violent collision of contradictions. He opened his eyes and looked at her, as if for the first time, and then, slurring his words, asked, "How did *you* end up with JP?"

She'd been around drunks for as long as she could remember. They could blurt out the questions everybody else wanted to ask. Tom Burke had hired Gunnar and JP a few months ago. He'd had time enough to form opinions of the brothers. Looked like he now had an opinion about Eunice, too.

"I need him to find a job, Tom," she said, feeling as if she had nothing to lose. "The depression ain't giving no breaks. He knows the tools good. Could you put in a word?"

Burke didn't seem to have picked on up her plea. He looked at Joseph while speaking sideways to Eunice. "Neither of them cousins ever drank with white men. Too dangerous, they said."

Tom grabbed a corner of the table and shouted at Frank Lawrie, "Leave him be, Frank, for chrissakes!"

Burke attempted to stand. He pulled himself halfway up, tottered, then crashed back down onto his chair. He waved a hand at Lawrie, not in a futile effort to grab Frank from too far a distance, but to dissuade. Then Burke dropped his hand. He looked like a man who'd let go to drown.

"The men don't know what they're doing to Joseph. Long time ago, he told the missus that once he started, he never stopped drinking; the drinking always stopped him."

The crew's shared excuse had been fading into its own fresh grave. The men now seemed to be avoiding JP, which Eunice

guessed was how it had been any given day on the job before he
was fired.

A tenor's rich voice cut through the crew's levity. Frank
Lawrie sang out. She thought they seemed surprised by their mel-
lifluous coworker. The crew jostled him, laughed, and rolled into
a new surge. Undeterred, Frank raised his voice, singing over the
hysterics of his mates. Drinks in hand, they joined in with rau-
cous voices and spilled onto the island surrounding the piano
man. If he'd wanted to escape, he no longer could.

The musician had spotted the trouble too late, and Eunice
was not interested in being his mediator. Her elbow came off the
piano top. She stepped away with her glass and left him to fend
for himself. His subsequent attempts to stand were met by several
hands on his shoulders, forcing him back down onto his bench.
With a desperate look on his face, he called out to the tender, who
shrugged from behind the protection of his bar and shouted, "I'd
keep playing if I were you."

The boisterous crew had gathered around the piano and left
JP and the Indian sitting with no one between them at the bar.
Cursing in slurred Swedish, JP jerked his head around toward the
ruckus. After accepting a steady stream of amber shots, the Indian
was drunk. He stood faltering in place and called out for Frank,
who didn't hear him. Joseph pushed away from the bar. When he
reached the nearest table, he climbed onto a chair, stood straight,
and yelled, "Frank!" over the heads of the crew.

"Seneca Joe!" Frank shouted back.

Joseph steadied himself, then cupped his hands around his
mouth, bent his head backward, and let out what Eunice took for
a war cry. He continued ululating until JP screamed, "Fock dat
Inyun!"

She watched as the lanky oaf stumbled off his barstool in

attack, lost his balance, and, with a loud grunt, collided into the chair, causing Joseph to jump before he fell into space. Eunice marveled at his impressive landing; the soles of his feet found the floor like the paws of a cat and stuck in place; his knees were bent, his arms flexed, elbows out like he owned the orchestra with his baton. She watched as the hapless crew mates attempted to subdue JP. A violent crash brought the Swede to the floor near the wooden table where Tom Burke sat, defeated after several failed attempts to stand.

A few of the men fell in a heap on top of JP. Frank was laughing and splayed himself atop the Swede, as if trying to pin him in place. "We better hold you down, Wing Nut, until you cool off. No fighting today—it's your brother's wake, for chrissakes!" The moaned protests in Swedish caused Eunice to cringe, step farther away, and pull the last taste of relief from the whiskey she'd been nursing.

"Did ya see ole Seneca Joe land on his feet?" Frank Lawrie beamed from the top of the scrum.

"Get dat focking Inyun outta me sight," JP cried. Joseph swayed in place and gawked down at him. "Quit staring at me, ya little bastard."

"Get him outta here, Tom," implored Frank Lawrie, rolling in laughter. "Don't know how long we can hold JP! If he gets up, he's gonna try to kill that boy."

"Come on there, Joseph, let's get some fresh air," said Tom, standing in a wobble, erect for the first time in more than an hour.

In what looked to Eunice like a move meant to steady himself more than to steer Joseph toward the front door, Burke placed an open hand on the young man's shoulder. Joseph calmed at Tom's touch, and the pair turned away from the mash holding JP in place on the tacky floor. Shoulder to shoulder, incapable of synchronizing their steps, the duo staggered to the front doorway. The door slammed hard behind them.

As the crew stood, they raised JP like a sunken barge, docked him back on his barstool, and then spun him around toward the bartender. Garbled Swedish curses flew across the bar with spittle, and the bartender backed away. After swinging his head side to side and slurring more unintelligible words, JP succumbed and lowered his forehead onto his folded arms atop the wooden bar.

Far afield of the cluster, Eunice smirked. Now she was free to go home and check on Rita and Lete. Before she left, however, she walked to the far end of the bar and jerked her head to signal the bartender. She'd have a second pour while she made sure JP was out.

From the bar, Eunice watched Tom Burke topple back inside the saloon by himself.

"What happened to Seneca Joe?" Frank Lawrie asked.

"Told me to leave him be," Tom said, finding his table and slumping down into the empty chair. "Said he'd pull himself together and head back to his boardinghouse."

Thunder clapped, startling the revelers. Frank glanced toward the street and said, "Look out the window, Tom. It's starting to rain. Boy could drown in a puddle, as drunk as he is. Shouldn't we go check on him?"

"The kid'll be fine," Burke said, as he hiccupped.

Eunice had had enough, and, despite the downpour, she left her unfinished drink on the bar top and headed out. The storm surged. There was no awning, so she backed up against the front door to assess her path home. It was foolish to walk through the deluge, but she had no intention of going back inside the Pigeon's Post. She hunched her shoulders and stepped into the rain.

With her head lowered and angled to stave off some of the downpour, she squinted as she hurried forward. Before she reached the blacksmith's entryway, she looked down between the two buildings and saw that his alley door was flapped open. Maybe it was morbid curiosity. Maybe it was a better alternative of shelter in the storm than rejoining the drunks. Another thunderclap—she turned into the alley and scampered to the door, which was swinging on its hinges in the rain. She stepped inside and found the blacksmith gone. Rain pounded the roof. Her eyes started to adjust to the dimness, and she soon saw that the forge was cold.

Eunice thought it best to let the torrent pass, so she searched for the lantern where it had hung before, just inside the doorway. At the fire pit, she found the smithy's flint and sparked a finger of straw to light the lantern's wick, then lowered the glass globe. A dull yellow radiance hung like fog above the dirt floor and thinned out as it rose to the rafters. Holding the lantern out, she shuddered when her gaze went to the ladder leaning against the edge of the loft. The storm no longer seemed a deterrent; she wanted out.

In a panic, she turned from the forge toward the swinging door and, guided by the lantern's light, passed several vacant stalls. Before the internal combustion engine gained its dominance, each pen might have been occupied by a beast of burden, either standing in new iron shoes or waiting to be fitted. Out of the corner of her eye, she caught movement on the straw-covered floor in one of the pens. The pounding on the roof crushed any sound the gurgling Indian made as he lay supine. He was vomiting on himself and had started to aspirate. She had seen it before and knew Joseph could choke on his own puke if she didn't flip him onto his side.

Eunice untied the red bandanna from around his neck and started to wipe the mess clinging to his long hair and mottled clothing. After spreading the muck into wider swaths, she stopped rubbing. The clothes required a basin, and she needed to soak the bandanna to address the slime on his hair and skin. Joseph protested when she pulled off his boots. Undeterred, she also ignored the nonsense that he babbled as she took his clothes.

A wooden tub sat adjacent to the workbench docked at the forge. She imagined the blacksmith pounding his hammer against a red-hot horseshoe braced atop the anvil, then turning with his tongs to dip the iron into the tub, causing a sizzle. She could hear the hiss and see the rise of steam.

The water level was too low. Lantern in hand, she searched for a bucket. One hung on the wall within arm's length of the hand pump that crowned the well in the corner. She hooked the empty pail's handle over the spout and then pumped as she had, less than two years ago, when trying in vain to flush the Swedish seed from herself.

After several trips, she had enough water in the tub to work Joseph's clothes. Eunice tossed his shirt in and thought of how, on her first day sorting, Gussie had told her to puke on the floor, not on the pile. When multiple girls were sent inside to help sort, they might be okay with the blood and shit until one threw up. Then Gussie would stand there, shaking her head, as the dominoes fell. Eunice thought of her friend as she scrubbed the vomit off the Indian's cotton shirt, wrung it out, and then hung it to dry.

Before soaking the denim jeans, true to her profession, she checked his pants pockets. A second red bandanna she tossed into the basin, where it floated with the one she'd taken from around his neck. In his other back pocket, she found an envelope with gibberish printed on its face; there were greenbacks stashed inside. She held the envelope under her armpit as she shoved her fingers into the first of the front pockets. It was empty, while the second bulged with more cash. Gussie's fox stole came to mind and made her smile. Eunice would tell her in the morning. Into one of Joseph's boots she shoved the envelope; into the other went the separate wad of bills.

Eunice wrung out the jeans by hand, thinking that Gussie's wringer would have saved time and removed more water. Draped to dry over the slatted wall of an empty stall, the pants dripped.

She placed the boots on the workbench with the heels hooked on the anvil. The wet leather toes pointed at the dormant forge. Even next to dying orange embers, they'd be dry in no time. She wanted to light a fire but would not risk a disaster.

Moans drew her attention. Joseph wriggled in a curl, like a baby abandoned. His long hair, matted with vomit and mud, clung to his skin. She wrung out the two bandannas, tossed them into the empty bucket, and returned to the hand pump.

Mumbled complaints accompanied every swipe. When she had finished as best she could, she sat him up against the wall of the pen. He was tottering when she walked back from the pump with another bucketful. She knelt with a horse brush, which she drew from his crown down his mane, coaxing away most of the mud, puke, and straw, while yanking out only a few strands of long black hair. As he groaned, she wiped the ruddy skin of his face with a wet bandanna.

She stood to inspect her work. Standing over him, she concluded that he wouldn't get much cleaner until he took a proper bath. Joseph wavered, and she crouched down to put her hand on the outside of his shoulder before he pitched to one side. Once he was righted, she let go and he fell to the opposite side. Her other hand stopped a hard crash; then she guided his descent to the floor, where he drew himself inward, as if fetal. Eunice went to another stall and returned with her arms full of dry straw. It took four trips to build the mound that would be his temporary mattress.

Teeth chattering, naked, and wet from her cleaning, Joseph was in a full shiver. The horse blanket she found would do the trick while she left him curled on the mound. She'd go tell Tom Burke to get in here to take care of his man. The foreman wouldn't be up to the task for some time, but she'd make certain he knew that Joseph was in need. Hoping to avert her eyes from the sight of JP, she'd go back into the Pigeon's Post one last time.

Lantern in hand, Eunice paused at its hook by the door and looked from the trembling bundle up to where the ladder faded into the darkness of the loft. Hand flat to her chest, she slumped, unable in the moment to hold up her shield of anger. *About that age*, she thought, as she turned back toward Joseph. The horse blanket trembled. He could freeze to death if Burke didn't come soon. *Can't let that happen*, she told herself, and she slipped under the blanket to warm him.

CHAPTER ELEVEN

———◦•◦———

Weeks after JP lost his job, Eunice realized that she was pregnant again and that Pa had done her no favors by forcing the marriage. She wanted to get away from JP before she started to show. He was dumber than a post, but he would know that it wasn't his child on the way. The man was violent by nature, and she felt anxious to keep herself, Rita, and Lete outside his reach.

The laundry kept her busy six days a week. One Wednesday, Mr. Welles let her off for a few hours to attend to some "family business," as she called it. Eunice waited on the marble stairway for the courthouse to open, and when the locks turned, she marched through the doors to be first in line at the counter. Wanted a divorce, she told the clerk. After listening to Eunice, the man said she had a high hurdle to clear. He looked her up and down and then intimated that she would need to hire a lawyer to press her case. When he suggested that her best chance for resolution was to bring her husband to the courthouse, she slumped. Her thoughts roiled as she trudged to work. Gussie just lowered her shaking head when Eunice told her what she had learned from the clerk.

Later, not knowing what else to do, Eunice begged JP for a divorce. The old Swede took him back on at his metal shop, where he earned more than enough money to be self-sufficient, but now that his brothers were dead, he had nowhere else to go. He could afford room and board, as well as his daily allotment of booze. Yet he scoffed at her suggestions to divorce. Said he wouldn't leave, either. Falling onto Eunice's sofa each night in a drunken stupor was the path of least resistance. Ruing her words, she cringed when he repeated that his X on the lease made it his home, too. Her legal status was one of the few things he seemed to control other than a shot glass.

Once again, Eunice asked Mr. Welles for some time off during business hours. She went to the library, at Gussie's encouragement. Her friend couldn't read, but she knew that women like Eunice didn't have any easy way to leave a marriage. The librarian concurred and explained that for many a woman without means, a marriage contract seemed to hint of indentured servitude and could be as difficult to escape. Eunice didn't understand. She read what the librarian selected about the history of early immigrants to America, those who had fallen into such predicaments. When she returned to the desk, Eunice asked the librarian if those were fancy words for slavery.

The bookish woman shook her head and shepherded Eunice to an aisle in the back of the cavernous room. She took down an unwieldy volume and carried it to an open table, where she flipped through thick, glossy pages until she found what she was looking for: a 1863 photograph of an escaped slave named Gordon, whose back was covered with keloid scars from the slaver's whip—scars so thick that they looked like fat banana slugs crawling just beneath the surface of Gordon's skin.

The next day in the sorting room, Eunice grew somber as she reported her encounter with the photograph. Gussie didn't want to see the picture of the man they called Gordon. When she was a child in Alabama, she'd seen such marks on the backs of shirtless old men bent over in the fields. Then she said that she had never told anybody in New York what she wanted Eunice to hear. Told her how her own great-grandmother had been sold away from Gussie's grandpa when he was a little sprout. "It different for sure, girl. But ya ain't free, neither," Gussie said.

David Welles had never seen Gussie enter his office. When she kicked open the door, the glass on all sides rattled. Neither had he ever seen such fire in her eyes. As she screamed, he assumed that it was the first time in her life that she had yelled at a white man.

Standing with Eunice—unconscious and cradled in her arms— Gussie shouted, "She fainted! I couldn't leave her in there, Mista Welles. Help her, please."

"Gussie, set her down over here," he said, as he grabbed his coat from its hook and spread it on the floor. "Is she in labor?"

"Don't think so."

Eunice moaned as she started to come around. Welles went to his water pitcher and poured her a glassful. He knelt and raised her into a sitting position as she gathered her senses. Gussie stood back, hands held together at her breasts.

"Gussie, help me get her up into the chair."

They sat Eunice down and positioned themselves as sentries on each side. Her hands went to her rounded belly, as if she wanted to apologize for whatever her unborn child had endured in the fall.

"Mista Welles, Eunice can't be sorting no more until after that baby comes. She bigger than with her first. Might be twins, even."

"Yes, Gussie, I can see that. You can go back now. I'll tend to Eunice and then send a girl in to help you."

Gussie stood firm. When Eunice regained her composure, she looked up to her guardian and said, "It's okay, Gussie. I'll be fine. Thank you."

David watched his giant lumber across the threshold. She pulled the door behind her. It settled in its frame without a sound.

"She's right, don't you think, Eunice?"

"Afraid so, Mr. Welles. I got light-headed, then started to pitch over."

"Are you injured? The baby? Did you hit your head on the floor?"

"Don't feel hurt. Last thing I saw was a pile of bags in front of my face."

David leaned back and sat against his desk. Weeks ago, he should've overridden her stubborn insistence to sort in her condition. When her first baby was born, her water broke in the sorting room on a Saturday. She was waiting for him to unlock the plant Monday morning. Of course he realized that she was not the invincible woman that she portrayed. Still, he should have known better.

"Eunice, I wanted to talk to you today," he lied.

"You can put me back on the mangle. I can fold sheets, no problem."

"No. I've been thinking that now's a good time to switch up some responsibilities among the supervisors."

"I know how to run the sewing machines. I can sew, Mr. Welles."

"Yes, you've got that down. But I want you to train in other departments, too." He stepped past her and returned with the pitcher of water. "Keep drinking, Eunice. After I train you, you'll supervise purchasing and bookkeeping."

David watched her absorb his words, which suggested that

she would step into the bastions of his relatives—men. He was aware that she had little formal schooling, but she knew her figures and could read better than Alfred, if not Martin. She seemed puzzled as she took a sip of water.

"Don't worry, Eunice. I know you can handle it. Once you're trained, I'm going to add the seamstresses to your remit. More than one of them has asked me if you could supervise their room, too." As much as he relished that several women from the sewing room had spoken to him, David understood it had less to do with their comfort approaching him than it did with their discomfort with his brother and cousin.

"You talk to Martin and Alfred yet?"

"I'll talk to them next. Wanted to make sure you accepted the changes first. You agree with my proposal?"

"That all sounds real good, Mr. Welles. Thank you." In the past, whenever Eunice had received a compliment or any good news from him, she had lowered her gaze to her feet and waited for him to speak again. Today, her eyes dropped to guide her hands rubbing slow circles on her belly.

"Any questions before I talk to the men?"

"I can still go help Gussie when the bags back up, right?"

"Not until after you have your baby. Then, if you have time, you can work with Gussie when she needs the help."

Martin was angry, as David had expected. He and Alfred would together take over Eunice's former responsibilities overseeing the big room and the mangle crew. Martin knew without asking that the sorting room was part of the deal.

"What's next? You going to teach her to drive, for chrissakes?" Martin asked in a surly tone.

David cut him off. "Grow up, Martin. You still have the drivers. You and Alfred will keep packaging and dry cleaning, as well as all the hand ironing and steaming. The seamstresses will stay with you until I'm done training her on the paperwork and she delivers her baby."

"Why don't you let me train her?"

David recoiled at his brother's suggestion. It was out of character for Martin, who shirked any task and had never volunteered to do anything. David guessed that Martin thought he could browbeat Eunice about her lack of education and push her to quit. She wasn't easy to intimidate, but David wouldn't let her suffer needless humiliation at the hands of his ne'er-do-well brother.

"I want you and Alfred to focus on your new duties. See if you can make these departments more efficient."

"Eunice steps in all over the place whenever those girls slack off. Doesn't supervise for shit. Just does the fucking work for them."

"Then you'll have ample opportunity to improve things, right?"

"I'm not going to step in like she did. They're going to have to do their damn jobs!"

David fought not to throw Martin's words back in his face. Without assistance, his brother was yet to do any job David had given him. Keeping Alfred by his side would insulate Martin somewhat, but they'd struggle to replicate the way Eunice kept things humming along. Between the two men, Alfred would suffer her absence the most. Such was the family pecking order.

Martin turned at the doorway and grumbled, "Gussie's going to miss her in the sorting room. And those girls in the big room are in for a surprise. Don't expect *me* to help that damn nigga sort!"

David was not surprised to see how fast she picked everything up. Eunice had known the particulars of the business long before she had ever seen the books. At one point, he grew embarrassed when she ran the numbers in her head faster than he had finished his own calculations. All week long, she had asked basic questions in attempts to reconcile the records with her knowledge of the plant. By the end of her last day of learning the bookkeeping, Eunice exposed a puzzle, which she herself solved before David even understood the conundrum. Much more than Eunice's water broke on her final day of training. Action was required and would be left up to him, since his relatives had done the skimming.

Martin and Alfred must have thought that they had covered their tracks. All the purchase orders matched the paid invoices. But Eunice knew the operation hadn't required all that was bought and paid for, at least in the amounts depicted on the books. The money went out, but the stuff to run the plant was nowhere near what the records reflected as purchases. Eunice said she was certain, and David didn't question her beyond his initial shock.

Clever penmanship had bumped up the volumes on selected purchase orders and their related invoices. David did the banking, but Alfred checked off deliveries, and then Martin paid the vendors, in person. He had always been happy to get out of the building with the excuse of settling accounts. David preferred his glass office.

As with the purchase orders, all the receipts that Alfred tabulated matched the doctored invoices. David knew, because he ticked and tied the registers before he went to the bank each week. When Eunice estimated the gap between expenditures and needs, it appeared that Martin had lost more money at the race-track than his big brother could have imagined.

After Eunice gave birth, Gussie was the only one at the laundry whom she told about the result of her hours of labor. This time, there would be no wet nurse. Too risky. Along with a toddling Lete, Rita stayed at home. Eunice had explained to Mr. Welles that something was wrong with her newborn. He didn't pry and allowed her to shuttle back and forth on foot the few blocks between home and the laundry in order to nurse.

Gussie knew that Eunice had misled Mr. Welles and everyone else at the laundry. She had had twins—identical twins. Identical red-skinned, black-haired boys with round faces, high cheekbones, and deep-brown eyes. When Lete was born, there was no mistaking his resemblance to JP. The twins also looked like their father. Gussie told the young mother that she and her newborn babies would suffer if she kept them. She told Eunice about the nuns. "Gotta get those babies to the orphanage," Gussie had said. "Take them before word gets out, and before you can't bear to let them go."

It had been less than three weeks since the births, and this morning Eunice was about to lose her confidant, her mentor. The train steamed toward the two women standing on the platform. Gussie's carpetbag was at her feet. Her massive, fleshy arms surrounded Eunice, who, with her head cradled in Gussie's bosom, sobbed. Passersby didn't withhold their loathing. The two sorters ignored the repetitious epithet aimed at the white girl in the embrace of a Negro. Neither jerked at the underlying truth: "Lover" was the right word to describe Eunice. Gussie reciprocated without her usual reserve in public.

"Can't your mama come up here, Gussie?"

"Mama don't know no place but Alabama. I got to go to her."

Eunice knew that Gussie had traveled to New York with her auntie, who had died soon after the two arrived. She was her mother's only sister. Mama was to follow with Gussie's little brother, Henry, but those plans died with her auntie. Gussie then made her way to Welles and found a room in a boardinghouse, where she had resided until this morning.

"Gussie, isn't there someone who can take care of your mama for a day or two?"

"Henry was the last one. She all alone now. She sad—tired and scared."

"I don't blame her, Gussie. I'd be scared, too."

The locomotive pulled several railcars past them. They stood where the last passenger car was supposed to stop, the one every Negro would have to move into once the tracks crossed an invisible line farther south. Gussie didn't care to move later. She understood why some folks might prefer to ride up front for several hours. Raised in Alabama, she simply wanted to find a seat that would take her all the way to Mama.

"Well, here comes the end of the train, Eunice. Wish I could stay longer, but I got to get to Mama straightaway. She can't take no more waiting."

"I thought her church ladies were stopping in."

"Those women are too old. And the men around there are too scared to do it."

"Scared to do what?"

"Cut Henry down from the tree where them white boys strung him up."

Looking up from his paperwork, he saw his brother coming. David dropped his pen and exhaled through clenched teeth as Martin stormed through the open door. When he reached to shut it from the inside, David held his hand up and asked, "Did you wash your hands?"

"For chrissakes, David. I wash 'em before I blow my nose. Look at my fucking hands, would you? They're more wrinkled than Lillian's face."

"So, you've met Lillian, I see. Been working here the last twelve years."

"Yeah, well, she can't sort worth a damn."

"Speaking of sorting, why aren't you in there with Alfred right now?"

"I came to lodge a complaint."

"Complaint? All right, Martin, what've you got to complain about?"

"It's about my supervisor."

"Eunice? You've got to be joking. She's been going in there to sort alongside you two laggards several times a day. Doesn't have to. You know that, right?"

"She left the plant. Just walked out. Keeps walking out every couple of hours."

"She's got my permission."

"If she's gotta go home to feed that damn brat of hers, she shouldn't be a supervisor."

"You're really full of it. That woman outworks everybody in the plant, even though she goes home a few times a day to feed her son."

"She should be home with her kids. Shouldn't even be here,

much less taking up a supervisor's job. Taking a position from a man."

"Like you, maybe?"

"How about Alfred? He's got kids and all."

"She's got kids—two of 'em."

"Yeah, and a husband."

"Her husband isn't working here."

"Well, I hear he isn't worth a shit. A drunk that got himself fired, and now his old lady's taking up a supervisor's job."

"You and Alfred are lucky I didn't fire you on the spot."

"It's the principle of the thing, David."

"Martin, enough! Eunice is holding the plant together, not tearing it apart. Now, get back to work," David ordered.

"You don't know, David. People are distracted. Talking all the time about that damn baby of hers."

"People talk. As long as they get their jobs done, I don't care." David knew about the rumors. He hadn't probed, just asked her if there was anything he could do. She had requested only that he let her go home a few times a day to feed the infant and make sure that her younger sister, Rita, was handling the kids okay while Eunice was at work. The older boy, Lete, was a handful on his own and wasn't taking to his little brother. Eunice had told David that she didn't trust her toddler around the baby.

"They're talking, all right. Can barely hear the machines, they're talking about her so much."

"Get back to work, Martin. Quit stalling."

"David, you've got to face facts, is all I'm saying."

"Doesn't sound like you have any facts."

"One of the girls on the mangle knows her sister, Rita. Says that before this baby came, Rita always had the older boy out and about. Kid's uglier than sin, our girl said. Saw him more than once herself. Looks like his daddy, she said. Eunice's own sister calls the kid Wing Nut because of his big ole ears."

"And what's your point, Martin? Still stalling?"

"My point's that Rita said something real bad's wrong with that new baby. Worse than just being ugly like his big brother."

"Martin, enough! Eunice is getting her work done and more. She has my permission to go attend to her baby until he's weaned."

"You've got two grown men doing women's work!"

"You two still don't amount to one Gussie. That's why Eunice goes in there all the time. Whenever she sends one of the girls in alone, you two stop and let the girl do all the work."

"Like I said, you've got to face facts, David. Quit defending her when she's causing a ruckus out there, is all I'm saying."

"You're not making any sense. What kind of a 'ruckus' is she causing by feeding her baby?"

"Everyone's saying that the kid's retarded or shaped like one of those circus freaks. Remember how huge she was? You've seen pictures of those Siamese twins, right? Two heads attached to one body? Maybe she's had a couple of babies all jumbled together."

"Martin, stop it. You shouldn't be spreading such rumors."

"How about what the drivers are saying?"

"Trying to get a couple of drivers fired, are you?"

"Tar baby. Saying the kid don't look like a wing nut—like the old man and the big brother. Natty-haired, black-skinned tar baby."

"That's ridiculous!"

"Yeah, well, it sure seemed pretty ridiculous the way she fussed over Gussie."

"Shut up and get back to work."

"Drivers could hear 'em talking in the sorting room, you

know. One of 'em stood listening at the top of the chute on the loading dock. Said that ole Gussie was telling Eunice about how she shouldn't keep the child once it was born. Eunice must have known something was real bad. Gussie gave her the right advice. Said to get rid of the baby."

"Martin, you'll keep your mouth shut if you know what's good for you. Seems like you're the one trying to cause a ruckus."

"All I'm saying is, no white woman can keep a tar baby—that's for sure."

Every evening from Monday through Saturday, after working all day for the old Swede, JP would head straight to a bar. On the nights that he got paid, he brought home a few bucks to complement the booze on his breath. Eunice had given him a wide berth since the babies arrived—twins with hair as black as a moonless night in the dead of a Swedish winter.

Eunice still sent money upstate to Pa. If not for Lete, Rita would've been in the sorting room months ago. Instead, Eunice had fed her sister piecework as a seamstress, tasks she could accomplish whenever Lete wasn't tackling her or throwing at her head whatever he could toss. After the twins were born, Rita seldom wielded a needle and only mended those articles Eunice left for her in the rare moments when the babies were settled and Lete was asleep.

Pa wanted Rita to leave the city. He said that he hoped to prevent Eunice's fate from befalling his younger daughter. Wanted to keep Rita out of the bars and someday marry her off to a churchgoing farm boy. Eunice wondered if Pa planned to make the match or just send Rita to church while he got drunk on Sundays like he did any other day of the week. Pa's pressure on Eunice had been mounting. And each day she felt the threat of JP hovering near the ruddy twins.

A reluctant father to Lete, a danger to the infants, JP stayed out past dinnertime most nights. Eunice welcomed his absences. Even if she could get by without his money, he still wouldn't give her a divorce. She often fantasized about letting the lease go, kicking him out of her life, and heading upstate with Rita and the kids. JP wouldn't follow her, wouldn't demand that the police chase down his lawful wife. He was simply too lazy.

One night, JP came home early and slammed money down on the kitchen table. Not a trace of booze on the man; he'd come straight from work. The last time he had arrived sober, he had demanded that she execute her plan soon, or he'd follow through on his threat: a few bricks in a burlap sack. Get the babies to her parents' upstate and out of his sight, like she'd said she would, or he'd drown them both in the Hudson River.

Eunice sat at the table, breastfeeding one of the baby boys. The child sucked in blissful rhythm while his twin slept in the bedroom. Under a narrow, chin-high window, the faucet leaked a steady drip into the sink. Next to the icebox, the two-burner stove completed the floor plan. A water closet down the hallway housed the one toilet that all tenants on the floor shared.

With single-handed aplomb, she placed in front of JP a glass with a couple of shots of whiskey. "Made some good money to-day, I see. That'll sure help around here," she said, not trusting why he had chosen to share any of his wages beyond their stark agreement.

The hyperactive toddler Lete flew around the tight room with his ears sticking out like matching halves of a broken saucer. Buttoning her blouse, Eunice tried to shush him with a stern look, which he ignored. Like a bored steer watching a farm dog dart about a pasture, JP followed his son through a dull gaze. As the boy shot past, Eunice caught his arm with her free hand and pulled him to her without rousting the baby dozing in her arms.

"Sit here with your father till I get back," she ordered as she rose.

"Vere da fock is Rita?"

"Don't say that in front of the boy!" She scowled at him. "Rita's out." Then she glanced down at the greenbacks and her suspicion mounted. "What's that money for? Just helping out?"

"Is for Rita, for the bus. I vants her and them Inyun brats gone. Ya gotta send them to yar pa, like ya promised."

"They're not weaned," she said. She scooped up the bills, then stepped away with the sleeping infant and headed toward the bedroom. "I'll keep this safe till it's time."

Two dresser drawers, pulled halfway open, served as makeshift cribs for the twins.

Kneeling, she placed the cooing baby into the open drawer below his sleeping brother. Eunice closed the bedroom door without a sound. The whiskey bottle now sat on the table in the spot where JP had slammed down the money. She searched for Lete, who signaled with a loud fart and a giggle that he had crawled behind the sofa.

"Your boss found some good work?" she asked, not out of interest, but to gauge JP's disposition.

He grabbed the bottle and refilled his glass. She wondered if he was choosing to ignore her question. Soon he'd be so drunk that he'd start babbling in Swedish.

"Ya miss dat focking Inyun?" he asked, sending spittle across the table with his insult.

"Why would I be missing him?" Eunice replied, not flinching or otherwise signaling that he had landed a blow. After one look at the babies, she had admitted to JP that he was not the father but refused to tell him who was.

"He poked ya, goddammit!" he shouted. A violence in his esophagus sent his fist to his sternum and his chin toward his chest. He coughed, then, somewhat subdued, finished saying what had seemed so crucial to get out: "Vether ya admits it or not." He took a swig, slammed the glass down on the table, coughed again, and then mumbled something in Swedish.

Dumb as he was, Eunice knew she would never convince JP that the twins' father was anyone but Joseph Seneca. A lousy liar, she hadn't even attempted to make up a story. She had kept her explanation short and to the point, told him the truth: She saw the man only once and never laid eyes on him again. As far as she was concerned, it wasn't any of JP's business.

Veins on his face pulsed purple beneath his translucent skin. He seemed to her to be much more aggravated than usual, and nothing was worth the ire she might trigger with more questions. Better to hear him snoring than espousing nonsense in either language. Eunice poured him more whiskey, nodded at the glass, and willed him to drink. He grabbed the refill, drank the contents in a gulp, slammed the glass on the table, then rubbed his palms across the wooden surface.

Another pour, and she nodded again. He threw back the drink, lifted the empty tumbler, and stared through its thick bottom at the tabletop like a bored and gemless jeweler through his loupe. Garbled Swedish words, laced with more spittle, flew toward Eunice. She wiped her face with the back of her hand, gritted her teeth, then contemplated as a silencer the iron skillet soaking in the sink, its inviting handle within easy reach.

Cries came from the bedroom. Lete farted again, his laughter an indication of his premeditation. Her firstborn—an unruly, unsympathetic child, and an unnerving replica of his father—provided a painful mnemonic of her misfortune. The handsome twins reminded her of her third grave mistake, which had crushed forever the what-might-have-beens that had flirted with her imagination since puberty. Gussie had been right: Wanted or not, her babies had to go.

Pushing the skillet's handle under the water—out of sight and temptation—she left JP stammering. With a silent turn of the doorknob, she scurried to lift the crying baby from his drawer in order to keep his just-fed brother asleep. She brought the hungry twin fast to her breast. The baby pulled hard on her nipple as she returned to her chair at the table.

"I hate dose lil' shits!" JP declared. He teetered, batted his bug eyes, and yawned. *Should be the end of it for the evening*, she mused with relief. As if gravity had doubled on the planet, his head crashed down.

Overlapped wrists supported his brow as he babbled at the tabletop in Swedish. JP no longer presented a threat. She cuddled the infant, stroking his smooth, soft face with her free hand as he suckled.

Lete had fallen asleep behind the couch. As soon as she placed the baby in his drawer, she would come back for the toddler and bring him into the bedroom where he slept on a plush, child-size mattress that she'd sewn. She'd leave a note for Rita on the outside of the apartment door so her sister wouldn't enter and wake JP, who would find the sofa on his own or not. Eunice didn't want him to find her sister. She knew what she'd write. She had done it before.

JP is here. Tap bedroom lightly. I'll let you in.

Holding the baby to her chest, Eunice turned the doorknob with her free hand. Everything inside the dark bedroom was close—skinny pathways ran along the wood floor from door to bed to dresser to window. The narrow dresser comprised five drawers. Two were pulled open; one waited for her delivery. She placed the baby under the soft, folded blanket and pulled it up around him. She then knelt on the same spot where, less than an hour before, she had placed his brother inside the lower drawer.

The infant was silent. A sign of warmth and a full belly, she thought, as she felt for the edge of his blanket, which proved elusive. She flew her open hand palm down at low altitude over the floor of the drawer, then landed it flat upon the cool slats of bare wood. Empty. Baby and blanket had both disappeared.

Gussie had been right, the babies had to go, but this made no sense. No newborn could roll, but, on instinct, Eunice slapped her hand against all four sides, then raked the drawer's floor with frantic fingers. Through the weak lighting, she peered down onto the space where she had set her sleeping son. Nothing. She saw nothing, as if staring into a deep well. Muffled snoring from the other room was the only sound.

Fire found the wick; then she set the height of the flame and lowered the globe. With the lantern raised, she spun, scanning the room. From the occupied drawer, her baby's face beamed his innocence. The emptiness of his brother's makeshift crib left a hollow intrigue. Down on her knees again, she brought her cheek flat and level, close to the floor. She swung the lantern like a fog light warning seamen of impending reefs. The room's floor met all four walls; only the legs of the furniture—like derricks rising from the ocean—disturbed the sea of worn wood. There was no infant under chair, bed, or dresser.

The lantern's light swept across the bedroom walls as she

stood spinning once more in disbelief. There'd been no noise. Listening, smelling, and straining her eyes, Eunice searched the room for clues. Tears came as she thought of her dreams to be rid of the twins. She recanted all previous acts of self-pity, wanting only to hold her lost son.

Practical if nothing else, Eunice shook off her indulgence. Some trick by JP when she wasn't looking? Had Lete slipped inside and shoved one of the babies through the window onto the fire escape? That nightmare sent the beam toward the pane of glass, where the light ricocheted into her eyes. She lowered the lantern and shielded her vision, then captured a telltale clue wedged in the corner of the sill. It hung abandoned, snagged by a sliver in the wood, pulled unnoticed from the seat pocket of the kidnapper's pants. A red bandanna draped from the window.

CHAPTER TWELVE

O ne look at the delicate newborn, and Edith Burke knew
she held Joseph's son. Her breath halted when he admitted to the kidnapping. "Why?" was all she said, as she shook her
head and stared into his worried eyes. Joseph told her about the
stranger who had called himself Martin Welles. "Just trying to
help a colleague," Welles had told him. Edith cooed at the infant
as she listened to the story—how Martin claimed that he worked
with the baby's mother, the wife of JP Erikson. The mention of JP
caused Edith to look up and find Joseph's eyes once more.

Martin had told Joseph about rumors that the child was illegitimate, the product of an extramarital dalliance. After having
heard about JP's temper and the insinuations that he meant to
harm the baby, Martin said that he was motivated to intervene.
He met JP in a saloon, where Martin plied him with whiskey.
Once his tongue was loosened, the Swede confirmed he wasn't
the father. Blamed an Indian. Martin said that, still, he needed to
verify the physical threat, and JP soon bragged how easy it would
be: burlap bag and a couple of bricks, then a short walk to the
Hudson.

Edith cringed at the image of the baby being murdered as
her arms cradled the sleeping infant. The thought of JP as perpetrator did nothing to dissuade her worries. She knew the man's

temper, a family trait. No one could prove what Gunnar had done to Jackson, but she could see why Joseph had not dismissed any threat JP posed.

"Martin said the cops wouldn't do anything if he reported JP's bravado. The bluster of a slighted drunk, they'd say."

"Joseph, how did this man find you?"

"He asked JP if he knew the Indian. JP told Martin that Tom had helped me get on at a new construction site. A couple of days ago, Martin approached me in the yard after my shift ended."

Martin told Joseph that he had been beside himself with worry and that he had tracked him down out of compassion for the child. Said that if it was his young son in danger, he'd want to know. Would want an opportunity to save the baby from certain harm. At the bar, JP had vowed to remove the evidence of his wife's infidelity in a matter of days, one way or another. Time was of the essence, Martin warned.

Edith had always thought of herself as a bit naive. Tom said so, too. Her Bible was in the drawer near her hip. Jackson Sundown and Joseph Seneca. Remembering the boys who would not take their fathers' renames, Edith smiled. She believed Joseph had been hoodwinked by Welles, who she assumed wanted money, not justice.

"And then what happened, Joseph? Was the kidnapping your idea?"

"No. I thanked Martin and told him that I was going to confront JP. Would tell him that I'd kill him if the baby was harmed."

"No! You didn't threaten a white man! What did JP say?"

"Martin talked me out of it. Said it wouldn't prevent the crime, and that if JP killed the baby and I followed through, it would be murder on top of infanticide. He said he had a better idea."

Asking Joseph if there was someplace far away where they could move the baby, Martin had counseled the young father toward a safer solution. The reservation, a small village. Yes, Martin had responded. Idaho would provide more than the necessary distance from New York. JP would never find them. Still a dangerous plan, but it was better than letting the poor child perish. And superior to fatal revenge, which wouldn't bring his son back to life and might land Joseph a seat in the electric chair.

The baby started to wriggle. Edith brought him to her shoulder and patted his back. *He's getting hungry,* she thought.

"Joseph, this baby will need to eat soon. Have you thought about that?" The hospital was only a few blocks away. If he left the baby with her, she could get his son to safety within minutes. Her only decision would be whether to unveil the mother's name or not. Eunice Erikson must have been frantic about the missing child. She was so young. Already a mother and now with a newborn that had lived under the hazard of JP. Edith wondered if the whole story about JP's threats was but a fabrication by Martin Welles to prompt Joseph to action. Thoughts of the brothers Erikson sent a chill though her, as if dusk's breeze had found a breach in the shack's wall. As she pulled her sweater around her with her free hand, she wondered if Eunice Erikson was in danger.

"Martin said he knew a white woman, a wet nurse, who would travel with the baby to Idaho. I'm heading to meet her next."

"Why did you come to see me, Joseph?"

"I need your help, Mrs. Burke. I didn't know where else to turn." He reached into his pocket and pulled out a thick wad of bills. "Will you hold this for me? I don't want to pay Martin until my son is safe in Idaho."

"Pay him for what, Joseph?"

Martin had told him that the moral act of saving his son

would still be a crime in the eyes of the court. The risks for the two strangers—both Martin and the wet nurse—would be extreme. He quoted a price for his services and the woman's, then offered to handle the money for both.

"I paid him half of his price up front and gave him enough money for the woman's train tickets to get her to Lapwai." Joseph explained how he'd already booked passage for himself and would pay the wet nurse the rest of her fee, including her return fare, when he took the child from her in Idaho.

"When Martin asked me how he could be certain that he would get paid in full, I told him that I'd leave the money with you, Mrs. Burke, and that once I got back to Idaho, I'd telegraph you to pay him." Edith frowned, and Joseph reared back. "I mean, if you'll do that for me."

Robbed of the chance to counsel the teenage father against the desperate acts he had already taken, Edith became his accomplice. If she had refused to help, she would have doomed both father and son. Her only demand was that he not mention any of it to Tom. With that, she handed Joseph the baby, pulled the cashbox from its drawer, and stored the roll of greenbacks destined for a man named Martin Welles. She took off her sweater and wrapped it around the baby's blanket. With her hand on his shoulder as they walked to the door of the shack, she offered Joseph only the tailwind of urgency, no chastisement for having sucked her into a crime of complicity.

Joseph's confidence in the scheme had fallen with the drop in temperature. The despair he had seen on Mrs. Burke's face haunted him as he made his way through nightfall toward the railroad station. Her words of warning had become the greater ghost:

"You've kidnapped a delicate newborn, Joseph. Keep him dry and warm. If the wet nurse doesn't show up on the platform, take him immediately to the hospital and leave him inside, where they'll find him as soon as he cries. You alone can't take him to Idaho. He won't last the journey. You'll be your own son's murderer if the child dies in your arms."

Upon arrival at the station, Joseph sought shelter from the steady drizzle. As he stepped out from the back of the main building into the lamplight, everywhere he looked, people appeared to be staring at him. Hunched over, he kept his eyes averted, walking along the platform to where he was to meet the wet nurse.

Small as the infant was, Mrs. Burke had told Joseph that the newborn would be difficult to conceal—not from the eyes, but from the ears, of passing mothers. Nestled in Joseph's arms, the son he sought to save began to stir, no longer sated by a full stomach.

The baby awakened, wriggling for the breast and a dry diaper. Amid meddlesome white people milling about the station, the infant would soon draw interlopers who might disrupt their escape. Martin Welles had said the wet nurse would appear just before the train's scheduled departure; "a large woman with a limp" was the only description he had provided.

The approaching locomotive's whistle pierced the night, startling all atop the raised platform. White clouds surged about the iron wheels, and billowing steam rolled onto the platform. Like cattle, the travelers followed each other up the metal stairs to their cabins.

Passengers waved through half-opened windows to those who had watched them board. Well-wishers who were afforded no further view of their people—passengers without window seats—disappeared back inside the station to escape the weather.

The whistle blew again. Rambunctious youngsters began

agitating. Parents begged caution, knowing their excited children would chase the caboose to the end of the platform, from which the train would be launched into darkness like a ship slipping from its moorings to pass into open sea in the dead of night.

Among the dwindling crowd, the conductors strolled along the platform, encouraging the last of the intertwined to pull apart and bid their final farewells. A bulky woman, hobbled with a severe limp, approached one conductor, who looked at her ticket and then pointed several cars forward. She tottered in the direction of the rumbling locomotive gathering its strength to pull the long train of cars into the night. A weathered carpetbag in her grip, the woman rocked in her stride past her appointed car, waddled through steam that blasted her skirt, then strode beyond the engine to the end of the platform, where, hidden in the shadows with the baby, Joseph watched and waited.

In a whisper that wouldn't frighten a deer, Joseph called out, "Mrs. O'Bierne! Over here." The night's breeze shifted, and the woman's odor met him before she turned to offer a ventilated grin—several of her teeth were missing. Narrow, deep-set eyes hid inside a face so freckled that her pale skin appeared infected.

"He's hungry," Joseph said, as he handed her the traveling money. "I'll be riding in the back car and slip out when we change trains. Walk to the rear of the platform. I'll find you."

"Ya's a worrywort, ain't ya?"

"Long journey, and I don't know who we'll confront."

"Yeah, well, ya're smarter than ya look. Red baby with a white woman's gonna be tough to explain."

He recounted what Mrs. Burke had suggested. "Tell anybody who asks that you're a wet nurse working for a rich man who lives in Seattle. Say that his wife died in childbirth in New York."

"A rich Injun?" she scoffed.

"Spaniard. Ship's captain from Madrid. Dark people there. Just say that's all you know. Can you remember that?"

"Yeah, yeah, I can handle things."

"It's important that you have your story straight."

"Don't want me telling them he's a lil' half-breed been stolen by his Injun daddy, huh?"

The calm of a hunter met her insult, as his grandfather would have advised. The treasure left his arms for hers. His empty hands grew cold. Joseph rubbed his fingers in his palms, worried that he had just passed his son to a devil. The waving lantern pierced the steam and drew their gazes. A conductor's authoritative voice cut through the cold air: "All aboard!"

The crooked woman stepped with his baby out of the shadow and into the light. To avoid detection, Joseph slunk alongside, tight against the side of the building, hidden in a narrow penumbra as he escorted them toward their car. The baby cried out, then grew quiet.

"Yeah, he hungry. Take to the teat real good." She flashed a grin of sparse teeth. "Ya give him a name?"

"Jackson. Keep him warm, Mrs. O'Bierne."

"All aboard!"

"All right, Injun. Jackson here's in good hands. Got a brood of brats meself."

"Remember, Mrs. O'Bierne, I'll find you at the end of the platform when we change trains."

"'Mrs. O'Bierne.' That's funny."

Losing his whisper, Joseph spoke in a frantic voice: "Martin Welles told me that's your name—Mrs. O'Bierne, right?"

A thick, freckled hand gripped both the worn leather handle of her carpetbag and the iron railing on the stairs. In a quarter turn, she paused on the first step of grated steel. Without looking at him, she tossed her answer back into the shadows with a laugh. "Yeah, 'tis. Ya're an Injun, so ya betta call me that. Kinda funny, though. Most everybody just calls me Kathleen."

David Welles seemed preoccupied as he unlocked the door and brought power to the darkened plant. Not wanting to trouble him with news of his brother's recent hooky, Eunice went straight to the sorting room to work down the backed-up pile of bags. When the lunch whistle had blown yesterday, Martin had disappeared. Alfred had worked like a snail until the end of the shift.

The days since Gussie's departure had brought a consuming loneliness to Eunice; the kidnapping of one of her twins compounded her sadness. After discovering the cooked books, she had been distracted by the constant need to bail out her two lazy sorters—grown men who whined like motors needing the oilcan. Soon, the whistle would signal the start of the shift and their complaining.

The peace and quiet of laboring by herself offered poor consolation for the dual absence of her child and her best friend. She was desperate to talk to Gussie. As she worked through the pile, the solitude tormented her. One of her babies had disappeared, kidnapped by the Indian. Was the child safer than his twin? If she went to the police, would a father who cared enough to risk his own life be tracked down and sent to the chair? Would she bring that baby back within JP's lethal reach? The unopened green bags from the hospital taunted her with brutal possibilities that might befall either or both of her newborns.

The shrill morning whistle cut across the plant and flew through the open door of the sorting room. Five minutes passed, and still neither of the men had arrived. Eunice worked until the backlog of bags stuffed with dirty-dirties had been depleted enough to expose the wall opposite the chute.

A silent presence stood watching her in the doorway. She turned, expecting Gussie, and shook herself at the sight of Alfred. His sleeves were rolled down, and he grinned with the look of an alley cat that had just raided a teeming rats' nest.

"Whistle blew a while ago. Time to roll up your sleeves, Alfred."

"Well, you're about done, so why should I bother to roll up *my* sleeves?"

"Don't test me, Alfred. I covered for both of you yesterday. I'm not doing it again today."

"So you did, Missy Supervisor."

"What did you say?"

"Just agreeing with you, Missy Supervisor. That's all. Can't get mad when someone agrees with you, can you, Missy Supervisor?"

"The last fool that called me that lost her job and got some broken bones to boot."

"Yeah, I remember."

"Then knock it off and get to work. Where's Martin?"

"He's talking to David in his office. Don't think he'll be sorting today. And neither will I."

"We'll see about that," she said, walking toward the door. Alfred backed up to let her pass. With obvious theater, he raised his open hands near his ears and pressed his back against the wall, as if he wanted to ensure she wouldn't brush her filthy hands on his clothes as she stepped toward the lavatory.

After she rinsed the lye away, she dried her hands, pausing with the towel. She thought of JP and Lete and wondered again if the stolen child had been the luckier of the two infants. She wished she at least knew whether he was safe.

When she exited the lavatory, Alfred was standing there, smiling. She straightened herself and said, "You're supposed to be sorting, Alfred. I don't like being a snitch, but I have to tell Mr. Welles."

"I ain't sorting for you no more, Missy Supervisor. No more!"

"Do you want to hear what Mr. Welles thinks about that?"

"Sure do, Missy Supervisor."

"Follow me, then."

"Right behind you, Missy Supervisor."

The door that years ago had proved a poor defense against a ten-year-old girl looking for work stopped the grown woman. Mr. Welles was alone, sitting at his desk, staring at the entry as if his next breath first required the door to open. When she had walked through the building, chased by a near gleeful Alfred, she had wondered why he was so cocky. Why, when they passed from room to room, did it seem as if the voices of the crew fell to soft landings like sheets flapped at the mangle? The whole way to the office, the humming of machines and humans had met her ears.

"Alfred, why aren't you sorting?" David asked.

"Eunice thought I should hear something."

"Nothing for you to hear, Alfred. This is a private matter between Eunice and me. Understand?"

"Where's Martin?" Alfred asked, alternating his gaze over each shoulder as if his absent cousin might be lurking.

"From what he told me, he's on his way to the racetrack," David said, with unmistakable disdain.

"Can I go, too?"

"Sure, Alfred. It's a free country."

"Okay, then. Be here in the morning to take back my old job, right?"

"No, that's not right. That's not even close. If you don't get back in the sorting room within the next five minutes, don't come back tomorrow, or any other day."

"What about Martin? You let *him* go to the track. Ain't fair, David. Just ain't fair."

"Free country, remember? He made his decision, and I accepted it. After what he did, I've no respect for him, or you, or that Kathleen woman who used to work here. Alfred, now you've got four minutes to get back to sorting."

Eunice had recoiled at the mention of Kathleen's name. Alfred acted unsurprised and challenged his cousin: "You fired Martin? For telling you the truth?"

"I gave him the same option that I just gave you. He took the racetrack over sorting. It'll take you a couple of minutes to make it past the loading dock, Alfred. I don't think there's enough time for any more of your questions."

With a bang that shook the glass in the adjacent windows, Alfred slammed the door. The owner pointed to the two chairs that faced his desk, their backs aimed to the doorway and the mechanical songs of the plant.

"Sit down, please, Eunice."

Mr. Welles tapped the desktop as he rounded its perimeter. She watched him like she was one of the condemned, staring unblinking at an approaching executioner. He moved his papers out of the way, and the edge of the desk propped him up as he sat back to talk to her.

He had never looked so sad, Eunice thought. Today, he appeared broken, as if his anger had fled and he would rather work alongside his loathsome cousin, sorting dirty-dirties, than continue the conversation with her.

"My brother and I had a serious falling-out this morning. He's done around here. I'm very sorry. Really I am, Eunice."

"Did you catch him stealing again?" He averted his eyes. "I'm sorry, Mr. Welles. Nobody likes a family fight," she said, while sensing that the problem had less to do with his family than with her own.

Holding his gaze on his feet, his shoulders slumped, he shook his head and said, "Martin's always been a problem for me, Eunice. He's jealous and lazy. I gave him a job he didn't deserve, and I've regretted it every day since. He embezzled that money from me, and now this. Can't pick your family—isn't that what they say?" The knuckles on his hands whitened as he squeezed the desk harder.

"Yes, sir, Mr. Welles," she said. Family—she had never been offered a clear choice, either.

"You remember Kathleen O'Bierne, of course," he stated, without looking away from his shoes.

"I do. Seems Alfred remembers her, too." The quiver in her voice felt like a shock wave that might send the Brooklyn Bridge into the East River. This could end only one way, she thought. "Are you firing me?"

When he released the desktop, blood returned to his hands, which he folded into a cup in his lap. "No. But you might want to quit this place, Eunice, after you learn what my brother has done. Martin and Kathleen have stirred up a hornets' nest inside the plant." Then he raised his head. "Eunice, I know your infant has red skin and that his father was an Indian."

No reason to deny the facts, she thought. She swallowed and stared into his eyes. "I need the money, Mr. Welles. You know that, right?"

"Yes, I do. And if you want to stay, you can." He averted his eyes again. "But if you want to leave, I'll do everything in my power to help you get another job someplace. A good job. You deserve a good job, Eunice. And I'll help you make ends meet until you get paid."

Then he raised his gaze once more and said, "I'm so sorry. Martin thought he could get you fired and take back his old job if I knew you had an Indian's baby."

"Well, seems like Martin's right."

"No, as I said, he's gone and you can stay if you want. But everybody in the plant knows. You'll be dealing with their comments and slurs from this day forward."

"Like you said, can't pick your family. I've got what I've got." Eunice stood, tugged her smock, and grew straight with a conviction to move forward. "Always paid my way. So I'll suffer the talk until I get something else. If you know where I might find some good work, that would help me get outta here."

"There's a laundryman I know who I'm guessing would be happy to have a hardworking, experienced supervisor like you, Eunice."

She recalled the request she had once made of Tom Burke on JP's behalf. "Can you put in a word for me, Mr. Welles?"

"Of course. It would be my pleasure."

As her boys grew, so would the difficulty of protecting her red-skinned son. JP would pose a constant threat. When Gussie had suggested taking the twins to the nuns, Eunice had thought that at least they would have each other. But she could not countenance the orphanage now that one of her babies had been stolen. Her best alternative was to have Rita serve as the boy's mother and move them both to the farm upstate. The infant could be somewhat hidden in the rural setting of the Finger Lakes, while Eunice worked to provide the money.

"Do you know any laundrymen upstate?"

"Whereabouts upstate?"

"Rochester or Syracuse. My parents and brother live with my uncle on his farm outside Geneva."

"I can check with some of our suppliers. A lot of them sell to plants like ours all over the state." He seemed to inflate with the chance to help her. "I can certainly ask around, if you like."

"Thank you, Mr. Welles."

He pursed his lips and exhaled what seemed a long-held breath, which she thought was expelled in unconscious relief. "Eunice, I'll do what I can."

When the door settled against its wooden jamb, no part of the glass box rattled. Heading in the direction of the sorting room, she heard the crew's murmurs and realized that she might have just walked from his office for the last time.

PART II

CHAPTER THIRTEEN

M arie Ritter, pregnant and nauseous, snapped back from her trance to address the eight-year-old twins fidgeting in the back of the station wagon. "Leo, give her back the doll—*now!*" She often told people that her kids traveled well. After only two hours in the car, it already felt like a long trip as they drove westbound on the New York State Thruway, the Empire State's swath of Interstate 90.

Rita reacted to their mother's intervention with a smirk for her brother, Leo. Marie knew her daughter could have liberated her Raggedy Ann without any assistance. Torqued into an insolent twist, Rita yanked the cotton doll back. She flared her eyes, then showed Leo her shoulder and snuggled Raggedy Ann to her cheek.

"Rita, don't be smug! I saw you taunt Leo with that doll," Marie white-lied. She had blocked out their bickering for several miles, until the volume of Rita's goading had spiked and invaded Marie's relative peace as she rested her head against the vibrating passenger window.

Late to the escalation—apparently lulled by his own thoughts and the zing of tires on asphalt—Henry Ritter scrambled to his wife's aid. "Rita, Mommy doesn't feel well. If you wave Raggedy Ann at Leo one more time, she rides in the glove box until we get to Gramma Eunice's house. Do you understand me?"

"Yes, Daddy," she mumbled.

The return of the freckle-faced doll allowed the whir of the road to dominate the atmosphere inside the blue-and-white '55 Chevy Nomad. Leo sulked, and Rita was subdued after her short-lived triumph. Marie's persistent morning sickness had subsided somewhat when they found the smooth surface of the thruway. She welcomed the relief that would end when they exited I-90 and resumed a jostling drive through turns and curves on graveled access roads and uneven side streets as they neared their destination. Staring out the window, she watched the rippling landscape of upstate New York. The spring-green fields were set on rounded hills that pitched in cadence with the butterflies in her stomach.

Before they had piled into the station wagon, Henry had folded down the backseat, creating a flat cargo space so the kids could spread out during the drive. Détente imposed, the twins reclined out of sight, their heads hidden from parental view by the back of the front bench seat. Over her shoulder, Marie saw the twins' stockinged feet stretched in the direction of their hometown, Schenectady. She pulled herself up to steal a backward glimpse of the kids, who looked away from each other into their respective sidewall windows. The sunlight warmed the cargo space. The hum of rubber tires and the Nomad's low-amplitude vibrations combined to rock the twins to doze.

The rolling farmland seemed to undulate beneath working tractors and grazing cattle like a tranquil sea that lifted idle boats and birds at rest. Over the years, Marie had enjoyed their drives through the countryside, where she often fantasized about raising her kids in such a rural environment. "Bucolic" was the word she'd shared with her husband to describe her dreams. Henry—the lonely farm boy—was conflicted. "At least the kids would have each other," he'd said. Each other and chores that, as kids from

Schenectady, they might find far less pleasant than "bucolic" implied.

Mesmerized by the verdant expanse, Marie perked up when she spotted one of her favorite sites on the familiar stretch: a well-kept farm with a tire swing that hung from an ancient oak tree in the front yard. She never saw a child playing on the swing and wondered how long ago some farming father had tied the rope there for his children. With its trunk's gnarly burls and twisting branches that draped near the grass, that oak was, to her, straight out of the Brothers Grimm. It must have been there before the first homesteaders—more than a century ago—had planted tree barriers around the house and barns. On their first Mother's Day drive to the farm, she had asked Henry why farmers planted so many trees when they had to clear their fields of the same. He laughed and chided the city girl. Without those plantings, he told her, there'd be nothing to stymie the full force of winds and winter that pounded the infamous Snow Belt. He said he'd shiver just remembering the whistle at his bedroom window and the flakes of snow drifting against the inside of the sash.

Last autumn, Henry had looked like a ghost after he had taken the call from his paternal grandfather, Pa, who reported in a matter-of-fact tone that Ma—his wife of over sixty years—had died. Marie had known them both, but she'd never met her mother-in-law, Rita's namesake, who had gotten pregnant as a teenager. As the story went, when Henry was four years old, his mother abandoned her son to be raised on the farm by his grandparents.

Henry remembered that Aunt Eunice would always visit the farm on Mother's Day with her son Lete in tow. Pa told him that cousin Lete was the spitting image of his father, who they called JP, which made Henry appreciate the man's absence. He had never even seen a photograph of JP.

Every year since they married, Henry asked Marie to accompany him to the farm on Mother's Day in order to visit Ma, who had always seemed indifferent to the ritual. Pa took advantage of Henry's presence to get some work out of him, which left Marie to fend for herself with Ma. After the twins were born, they, too, rode to the farm every May for the occasion, yet Ma had little to do with Marie and kids.

When the news came, Marie expected the twins would go with them to Ma's funeral and she wondered why Henry seemed shaken by the prospect. That's when he told her the full account of what Pa had blasted at him over the phone line. Henry's *mother* was not his actual mother, she was his aunt. *Aunt* Eunice was Henry's birth mother and the cruel boy he had known as cousin Lete was his half-brother. Pa told Henry that Eunice could not have kept him, the result of an extramarital dalliance, in the same household with JP.

Pa went on to say that *Aunt* Rita had insisted that Henry learn the truth before she would attend Ma's funeral. She hadn't seen her parents, sister Eunice, or brother Uli, much less her alleged son, since she escaped her rural imprisonment as Eunice's surrogate. After a baffling goodbye hug, she'd kissed four-year-old Henry and told him that one day he would understand. Then she'd hopped into a traveling salesman's sedan and left Henry on the farm with his grandparents and Uncle Uli.

This year, with Ma gone, Marie assumed she would enjoy the day of honor at home in Schenectady, where Henry could play with the kids rather than submit to Pa's bidding in the spring fields. However, Henry lamented that the annual Mother's Day visit was the sole family tradition that he held over from his youth. Marie didn't press him to admit that it was the only time he could remember being near his actual mother. Visiting the farm was out, but Marie had agreed to Henry's plea to stop by Eunice's home in Rochester today—Mother's Day.

The almanac's standard prediction was that by early May, the region would pass from harsh upstate winter to its muddy spring. This year's forecast was no different. As the Nomad cruised on through more familiar scenery, Marie held her breath when they drove past the exit sign for Geneva. Henry craned his neck to follow a dilapidated silo as it faded behind them to his left. It was covered with bright green leaves of crawling ivy, another of spring's clues.

"Just passed the farm's exit, Marie. Took it every Mother's Day since we were married."

"I thought the car might turn on its own, Henry."

Marie marveled at the final throes of winter. Dark, crud-crusted ice—the last to melt—huddled in the shadows of the ditches, hidden from the sun. Grass and weeds shot up, and emerald buds on the tips of tree branches sprouted in view. In the fields, tractors held their lines as farmers took advantage of the lengthening days—no time to waste in the brief Northeastern growing season. She rolled down her window to sip the fresh air, then turned to the farm boy behind the steering wheel. "Spring has sprung, as they say. Do you miss the farm?"

"Pa must be peeved that I'm not there pitching in this weekend. He said that after I got out of the Marines, it was the only reason to look forward to Mother's Day. I'd come back and help out a bit. Now that Ma's gone, I really should drive up next weekend to give him a hand."

A hand Pa didn't deserve, she thought. "Darling, we'll be there soon. Do you want to talk before we arrive? The kids are asleep."

"No, not particularly, I guess," he said.

"That's okay, Henry," she said. "It's only been a few months. Still pretty confusing, huh?"

"Here we are, driving on to Rochester instead of getting off for the farm. Guess it's all sinking in. My long-lost *mother* returns for Ma's funeral, and I see her face-to-face for the first time since I was a little kid, right after Pa tells me she's not my mother after all. Yeah, it's pretty darn confusing."

"Lete didn't know either, right?"

"Not till Ma died."

"Wonder what's going through his mind. His younger cousin turns out to be his half-brother."

"He thinks Eunice is his mother, and his alone, and that I don't count. Lete's been talking to JP, most likely."

The signs made clear the remaining distance, less than an hour drive. The closer they got, the more she wondered how much of her intensifying nausea came from being pregnant. No one in their little family, not even Henry, had ever been to Eunice's house on the outskirts of Rochester.

Despite their annual journey from Schenectady to the farm, they had seen JP only once—at the cemetery on the cold day Ma was buried. For reasons unknown until Ma died, JP had never visited the farm. Marie had cringed when she saw him staring— bug-eyed and gape-mouthed—at her children. His mien at the gravesite had reminded her of photographs of hungry hyenas.

"Marie, how're you feeling?"

"Sick to my stomach."

"Maybe that's a good sign?" Henry asked, without taking his eyes from the road. "You know what I mean?"

"Yes, darling. A little morning sickness is a small sacrifice for a healthy baby."

When the couple had learned that Marie was pregnant, they had agreed to name the baby Eunice if it was a girl. Marie hoped the gesture might herald a stronger bond between Henry and his mother. She took a deep breath and rolled up her window.

The station wagon's cabin grew quiet except for the tires and the rushing air that whistled at the vent window cracked open on Henry's side. Marie shimmied across the bench seat and snuggled against him. They rode like that until the exit. Marie turned to inspect the sleeping passengers, whose heads rocked in tender rhythm as the station wagon accelerated beyond from the toll booth. Eyes closed, the kids' faces still pointed away from each other. Leo had a bubble of drool at the corner of his mouth.

"They're out," Marie said. Henry hadn't spoken a word since they were on the thruway. She nudged him and said, "You never told me about your conversation with Pa after the funeral when he asked you to take him to that bar. Pa can be pretty blunt, I know."

"Same old story, except there was a different sister who got pregnant by the Indian."

"Did he say anything about why your aunt Rita left the farm when you were little?"

"Oh, yeah," Henry said, shaking his head. He checked the rearview mirror, then the side mirrors. His gaze went to the speedometer. She wondered if he would repeat what Pa had said. Then he eked out, "Sorry, I meant to tell you. He was sort of vulgar about it."

"What did he say?"

"Said Aunt Rita didn't have sex with 'no Injun,' but she 'got fucked' anyway. Couldn't believe he said it, but he did. Are you sure the kids're sleeping?"

Marie swung her left arm over the bench seat to get eyes on their children. "Still out, though bouncing a bit too much. Can you slow down, please?" She returned to face forward, then said, "You want to switch subjects or just enjoy the scenery? It's pretty over here this time of year, isn't it?"

Insects rose into the warm spring air to end their brief lives on the Nomad's windshield. "Look at all those bugs!" Henry shook his head. "Oh, Marie, I've wanted to talk to you about it every day since Ma's funeral. Just been putting it off."

"I don't want to upset you even more," she said.

"No, I'm going to have to deal with Eunice in a little while. And Lete, of course, not to mention those boys of his. And this year, JP, too. Probably a good thing to talk it out before we get there."

"Henry, you were quiet the whole way home from Ma's funeral. All that day, Eunice seemed cold to us. She must've been pretty embarrassed."

"Pa told me that Eunice always came to the farm on Mother's Day because he made her. I said I thought she was coming to see Ma. He laughed at me and said, 'Ma didn't give a damn about seeing her on Mother's Day.' It was his decision."

"His decision?"

"Yeah, he said that he made Eunice come so she'd have to see both me and Uncle Uli at least once a year. Thought it was important for her to remember that she turned Uli into a pet, then threw a red stain on the whole family."

Pa, Marie mused, disgusted. She'd just learned that he'd been there the night sixteen-year-old Eunice got pregnant. The man who should've been protecting his teenage daughter was too drunk to care that she'd stumbled out of the bar, led away by JP. How could a man as good as Henry have resulted from that cluster of negligence and abuse?

"A red stain, Marie. Took me a minute to get that one."

Marie stroked her husband's arm. She remembered the stories of her own Italian ancestors who had immigrated to America two generations ago. The taunts about their olive skin caused her to bristle. It didn't require a genealogist to determine that Henry and Lete possessed different heritage. "Why do you think your aunt Rita went along with the story in the first place?"

"You know Pa. He made the decision. Wanted Eunice to keep sending money, and her younger sister didn't have any choice. At least, not until someone came along to offer her a way out. Then she ran away from the farm and let her parents raise the unwanted child on their own."

"Henry, don't say that!"

"Got it straight from Pa."

"What do you mean?"

"I should've known better. Led with my chin."

"Henry, you're upset and talking in code. Your chin? I'm confused."

"In the Marines, we all did a little boxing to blow off steam, and sometimes the non-coms would have the guys put on gloves to settle disputes."

"What's that got to do with Pa?"

"Just that I was trying to explain, in boxing terms, that I 'led with my chin.' Dropped my gloves, let my defenses down."

"How so?"

"I was referring to Pa's 'red stain' comment. Look at me, Marie, and then look at my family. I asked him why Eunice didn't want me. Why Aunt Rita ran away from me, too. He threw back his shot of whiskey, slammed the jigger down with a smack, and started to choke with laughter. Laughed so hard, tears flowed into his eyes—eyes that were dry the whole time we were burying Ma. Took him a minute to compose himself so he could get it out. He wiped his eyes, shook his head, then looked at me like he would when he was about to hit me with the razor strap. He jeered and said, "Cause ya're a lil' bastard, that's why.'"

Asleep on her husband's shoulder, Marie was shocked awake by
Leo's frantic plea. "Mommy, I gotta pee!"

"Can you hold it until we get to the next exit?" Henry asked.

"No! Mommy, make Daddy stop! I gotta pee, real bad!"

"Henry, pull over, please. He can go in the trees," she said,
pointing to the nearest island of pines, oaks, and maples.

A couple of doors swung open, and two bodies sprinted down
into the ditch and up the other side, toward the woods. Marie registered spring's humid breeze crawling inside the Nomad, then
turned to check on her daughter. Tousled hair splayed across one
side of Rita's face. Frowning, eyes still closed, Rita brushed at the
strands as she rose into a kneeling position. The girl's cheek was
sweaty, and Raggedy Ann, serving as pillow, had pressed pink ruts
into her skin. She stretched her arms up and out as she yawned.
Marie smiled and turned back to watch Leo rush to the trees.

Eyes on her husband and son, Marie rested her chin on the
crease of her arm, which she'd folded atop the rolled-down passenger-side window. It was going to be a hot Mother's Day. There'd
be no hidden ice left in the ditches by the time they drove home.
She wondered if the unusual warmth might also help to melt the
cold heart of her husband's mother.

"He's always got to pee," Rita announced, as she lowered her
arms. Then, as she knelt, she patted about the back of the station
wagon for her doll.

"Boys are that way sometimes, dear," Marie said.

"I heard you whispering to Daddy."

"Honey, I thought you were sleeping."

"I did fall asleep, but not right away."

"Did you hear him talking about Pa?"

"No, just about you being sick. I think I fell asleep after that."

Marie sat up and ran her fingers through her own, shoulder-length brown hair, then checked her image in the rearview mirror. She had expected to see her thick curls in a wind-blown jumble. But she was shocked to find her complexion shining as white as the floating clouds. Since her teen years, she'd been told she was the duplicate of the Italian great-grandmother she'd never met. She sighed, thinking that right now she looked more like her pale in-laws than like her own family.

"Well, I'm fine, dear. Just a little tummy ache." Her hand stopped on her belly before she reached into her purse. Hairbrush in hand, she sent it several times through her own locks, then turned to address her daughter, "Come here, baby, and let me comb out those tangles."

"Ouch!"

"Sorry! You're sitting so still—my fault." Marie held the brush and glanced through her open window. She watched as Leo stepped behind a skinny tree. Henry turned back to the car to grant the boy some privacy. "Here, Rita, I'll go slow, I promise."

"You're going to have another baby?"

Marie questioned when her curious little girl had fallen asleep. "Yes, dear, I'm pregnant. Can you keep it a secret from Leo for now?"

"Why can't Leo know, too?"

"We didn't want to tell either of you just yet. As soon as my tummy pooches out, we'll tell him, all right?"

"Because you don't want Leo to get scared like last time?"

"That's right. Let's wait a few weeks."

"Will you tell Daddy that I know?"

"Maybe it's best if it's just our little secret. Would that be okay with you, Rita?"

A stubborn knot of hair resisted the brush. Rita's head was dragged downward, but this time she didn't protest. "Mommy, why's Gramma Eunice so mean to Daddy?"

"She's had a very hard life. She's tough—I'll grant you that. I'm not sure she's trying to hurt anybody, though. I suppose she doesn't know how people see her at times."

"She doesn't care, Mommy. Why would she pretend to be Daddy's aunt if she cared?"

"Times have changed, Rita. Folks didn't used to talk about some things back when Daddy and I were kids. It's the nineteen sixties now. People are different. Maybe Gramma Eunice will change, too, but that's her decision. Right?"

"I guess so. I think she should decide to be nicer, that's all."

"Well, let's remember to think about how Gramma Eunice might feel. That'll make it easier for us to be nice to her."

"I think she feels mean!"

"Well, I think maybe she feels sad. Sad and embarrassed."

"Why do we have to call her Gramma? Does she even want us to call her Gramma?"

"Your daddy does. He's called her Aunt Eunice his whole life, and now he's trying to call her Mother. So if you and Leo call her Gramma, that might make it easier for him."

"Will that make Gramma Eunice nicer?"

"If we're nice, then it'll be easier for Gramma Eunice to be nice in return. So let's give it a try, shall we?" The approaching duo interrupted their conversation. "Here come your daddy and Leo. Our little secret, all right?"

The kids started fidgeting again. Leo picked at a scab on his elbow. Rita slapped his arm. He rotated to block her stings with his back, then resumed his self-surgery. Under the dual pressure of a turbulent stomach and the anticipation of their arrival, Marie returned to staring out the passenger-side window, which gave Rita an opening.

"Rita, *stop it!*"

Marie turned with a start. Rita had parried her Raggedy Ann's red-haired mop top into her brother's ear. Marie felt like she was about to throw up. The car slowed, made a sharp swerve, then took an abrupt dip into and out of a pothole, before coming to a stop.

"We're here!" Henry announced in a rising tenor, which seemed to Marie to be forced. She twisted forward and looked through the windshield. There, parked for all to see, was the yellow Pontiac convertible with its black ragtop, Lete's pride and joy. Jostled by Henry's parking and sickened by the sight of the Bonneville, Marie opened her door, leaned outside, and vomited.

The Eriksons lived in a modest single-family house in a working-class neighborhood built in a wooded area away from the city proper—more rural than urban. A narrow side driveway fed a single-car garage, in front of which JP's faded green Studebaker was parked. A postage stamp–size lawn fronted the property. Beside the garage, a south-facing garden, sprouting the nascent stems of Eunice's vegetables, sought the rare Rochester sunshine. Two apple trees in full bloom marked the backyard border between the Eriksons and neighbors who were likely content to leave them be.

Bang!

The wood-on-wood crash signaled that the cousins must have burst through the back-porch screen door. The twins shuddered in unison. Marie braced herself.

Gunnar and Lars—eleven and nine years old—appeared in full

view, cutting across the front yard on a gangling, dead run for the station wagon. In the weeks since Ma's funeral, the Erikson boys seemed to have grown like weeds on a creek bank. Lete's sons were almost as tall as Henry, who stood a full head below his half brother.

"Is this for Gramma?" Gunnar shouted, as he yanked the flower basket from the back of the Nomad. "She won't like flowers, ya know. Our daddy says flowers are a waste of money. We got Gramma a cheese wedge. She likes cheese."

Try as she might, Marie shrank from these children. With the taste of vomit's residue in her mouth, she felt her nausea resurging. Placing a hand on Gunnar's shoulder, she wrested the flower basket from his hands. With strained civility, she said, "It's Mother's Day, Gunnar. We want Gramma Eunice to have some nice flowers."

Marie looked into the pair of bug eyes gawking back, and her chest sank. From her other side, Lars ripped the basket away from her. He punched his brother in the stomach, then ran up the front-porch stairs. Eunice stood on the threshold, holding open the outward-swinging storm door. Winter's glass panes were gone, replaced with wire-mesh screens, which allowed the flow of fresh air and at the same time fended off squadrons of persistent mosquitoes.

"They brought ya flowers, Gramma. Pretty stupid, huh? Don't let them have any of yar cheese. Ya can't eat no flowers, can ya?"

"Hello, Mother," Henry croaked, as he rounded the station wagon.

Eunice's erect posture suggested the force of her will. "We expected you an hour ago."

"We left early, Aunt Eu—uh, Mother. A jackknifed tractor trailer slowed us down. The truck driver missed the exit and blocked the ramp. No one could move. I'm sorry, I . . . ," Henry stammered, seeming unable to end his rambling explanation.

Eunice cut him off. "Well, we need to eat. Food's been ready for some time. So get those two washed up and to the table straightaway."

"Nice to see you, Eunice," Marie said, as she stepped past. "Happy Mother's Day."

Marie's nausea was impossible to assuage during the meal. The Erikson boys made disturbing gorging sounds as they shoveled their food. Leo seemed mesmerized by Lars, seated across the table from him. At one point, while staring at his cousin, Leo stalled his forkful in midair, then missed his mouth and poked himself in the cheek. Rita's eyes remained locked on Gunnar, who was head down, wolfing his food like his father and grandfather. As she chewed behind tight lips, she glared at him. Finished with his meal, he stopped short of licking his empty plate, then ran from the table. In apparent payback for the punch to the gut, he smacked the back of Lars's head as he left the dining room in a sprint.

Lete's wife, Fran—a stout, frumpy woman with mousy brown, flyaway hair and gnarled, discolored teeth—stood with her plate and reached for her husband's.

"Don't touch it! Ain't done, goddammit," Lete scolded. His forearms and fists slammed onto the table in a protective corral that surrounded his plate.

"Help me with the dishes, Marie?" Fran asked, blushing.

"My pleasure," Marie said, with sincere gratitude for the ticket out of the dining room. She smiled at Eunice and held her hand out. "May I take yours?"

"Much appreciated," Eunice said, with a strained smile.

Once in the kitchen, Fran said, "Marie, is it okay if I wash and you dry?" Her breath carried a stench of halitosis so intense that Marie swooned as she faced her at the sink.

"Either way, Fran," Marie said, grabbing a dish towel and twisting into a shoulder-to-shoulder stance over the running water. She took a sideways breath through her mouth, and said, "I hope the kids can get along outside. They don't know each other very well."

"Those boys of mine probably won't let that happen. I'm sorry, Marie. Can't seem to control them one bit."

"They have to control themselves, right? Everybody eventually learns how to work things out," she said.

"You sound like Eunice."

"Fran, I'm trying to get used to the idea of Eunice as my mother-in-law. Frankly, I don't know how you do it. You're so patient with everything."

"No choice. It's my life, I guess."

"How do you talk to her? I don't think she's said five words to me, ever." Marie's annual Mother's Day encounters with Eunice had yielded little connection over the years. Each of their conversations had been succinct, utilitarian. Since the revelations at Ma's funeral, little had changed.

"She's not so bad, I guess. Had a hard life. Can't expect her to be like you, Marie."

"I'm sorry?"

"Oh dear, I went and did it again. Stuck my foot in my big mouth." Fran scrubbed the single plate in her hand as if the grime of her offense had been baked into the porcelain at the kiln. "I just meant that you seem so happy, that's all. I feel trapped. Both Eunice and I had to get married." Fran's hands stalled in the soapy water. "I'm sorry, Marie—I should just shut up."

She pitied Fran, and yet Marie hoped the woman, as the only ally she'd found among her in-laws, could help her navigate the Erikson family. "Fran, I know I'm very lucky. I don't know what else to say but thank you for being so open. It takes a lot of courage to tell someone such things."

Fran heaved as she washed the dish in her grip. After rinsing it, she handed the dripping plate to Marie and smiled. "Thanks, Marie. You're so nice. It's easy to talk to you."

The running water drowned out the kids' voices in the backyard. Marched to the door by their grandmother, Rita and Leo had been expelled toward their prowling cousins. Marie suspected that her children were being taunted, regardless of the guise of any game being played. A trusting boy by nature, Leo could be coaxed into treacherous situations. Given prior experiences with his cousins, she hoped his guard was up.

Marie looked through the window to catch a glimpse of the activity. When she tapped the glass, Rita cast back a look of reassurance.

A clean, slippery bowl was passed to her for drying. "Marie, can I talk to you about something?"

"Of course, Fran. What's on your mind?"

"It's makes me crazy every time I come over here." Fran dropped the dishrag into the soapy water, braced herself against the wall of the sink, and, fighting for composure, mewled, "I see Eunice, and it's like looking into a mirror."

"Fran, how can you say that? You're as sweet a woman as I know," Marie countered, thinking how the physical attributes, not just the demeanors, of the two women couldn't be further apart.

"I don't think Eunice is that bad. And we do have a lot in common, I'm sad to say."

"My word, Fran. Something must be very wrong for you to say that. I don't know either of you very well, but from what I can see, you're worlds apart."

"Eunice eats and drinks without gaining an ounce. I get fat just *smelling* food. I've never seen her cry in all these years, and I bawl whenever I pass a puppy. I'm not talking about our personalities; I'm talking about our lives, Marie. I look at her life and see my own future."

"You're not going to turn into a hard person like she is."

"Who knows how she was before she married JP?"

"From the stories I've heard, I know her life was always pretty tough." Marie caught herself. She wondered how she herself would have come through all that Eunice had endured.

"Marie, I had four sisters, and we seldom quarreled. Our parents were teetotalers who read the Bible to us every night. Simple people, kind and loving."

"So, then how can you see your future in Eunice?"

"We both got pregnant and had to get married. God forgive me for this, but look at my sons. They're the spitting image of Lete, ears and all." She retrieved the dishrag and swooshed her hand in the cloudy water to find something to scrub. Empty. She pulled the plug from the drain, wrung out the dishrag, and slumped again. "Oh, I'm a terrible person. I married the man, and then I had another child with him. At least Eunice had Henry. He might be a bastard, but he's one helluva better man than Lete." Fran turned and shot a frightened look at Marie. "Oh my God! I'm so sorry, Marie. I didn't mean to call Henry that. I'm so embarrassed."

"Fran, it's okay. Thank you for apologizing. Henry has dealt with his murky history for a long time. After Ma died, he became more confused. When he looks into a mirror, he still sees an illegitimate son. Different mother, same sad outcome for my Henry."

"He must hate Eunice for deceiving him for so many years. Why does he even come to see her on Mother's Day?"

"Tradition, for one thing. Every Mother's Day since he can remember, Eunice has visited the farm. They told him she was there to see Ma. She was always nice to him, he remembers. As nice as he ever saw her with anyone, even Lete."

"Did Henry ever talk about how Lete treated him when they were kids?"

"Henry said that Lete would torment him. Older cousin showing off. Eunice never laid a hand on Henry, but she'd give Lete what Pa called a whoopin' when he didn't let up, which was most years. That would usually end the Mother's Day visit, and the two of them would drive away."

Bracing her hands against the sink, Fran sobbed. "Marie, I'm losing my mind, I swear. Lete's a terrible father and a lousy husband. I don't want to end up like Eunice. She's given up. I just can't imagine staying with Lete for the rest of my life."

"Does he hit you?"

Fran gripped the sink harder and dropped her head. She tried to speak, but could only nod as she stared into the water and whimpered.

Through the woman's sniffles, Marie asked, "Do you believe in divorce?"

"My parents tell me to be a loving wife. That God'll soften Lete's heart. 'Trust the Lord' is what they say." She bowed her head and shook it from side to side. "Oh, I'm such a bad mother. On Mother's Day! Forgive me, Marie. Please forgive me."

"Fran, there's nothing to forgive. You're in a very difficult situation."

"I'm going to run away," she announced. "I don't know when,

but just telling you makes me feel like it's possible. I can't leave those boys alone with Lete, so I have to think about this. Not sure I can wait until they're old enough to join up, like Henry did. Marines, right?"

"Yup. Sixteen years old. Pa wouldn't sign the papers to let him enlist early. Wanted him to work the farm—free labor, I guess. Henry ran away and forged his enlistment documents." Marie looked through the window. There was no one in sight. "Fran, do you hear the kids?"

Fran leaned toward the screen that covered the open bottom half of the window. "Not anymore. Maybe they're out front."

"Wait, I think I heard Leo."

Sounds of youngsters at forced play passed through the screen—the less-than-enthused voices of her own kids and the barking of their cousins.

"Lars, let go of me!" Leo screamed. "Ouch! Stop it, Gunnar!"

Pint-size feet stomped up the back stairs. Thrown open, the screen door collided into the wall of the back porch. Rita smacked the hardwood interior door and ran crying into the kitchen. At full speed, she toppled into her mother's dress as Marie stood with wet hands suspended over the sink. "Mommy, Gunnar and Lars pulled down Leo's pants and are trying to shove a stick in his bottom."

JP shouted from the dining room, "Shut that kid up, god-dammit! Get 'er back outside!"

Eunice burst into the kitchen with a fixed intensity on her face that Marie had never before witnessed. The back door flew open before Marie could get there. Eunice cleared the porch stairs and, clenching one of the cousins in each of her hands, tore the bullies from Leo. Gunnar and Lars went flying in opposite directions, sliding across the soaked lawn. On all fours, the grass-stained, muddied boys looked up at their grandmother. They scrambled to their feet and started to run.

"Stop! You boys'll stop right there if you know what's good for you."

Breathing hard as they pulled up, once again they slipped and fell onto their already filthy hands and knees. Eunice's fierce stare held the two perpetrators as they stumbled to regain their balance. Lars lost his tentative stance, and his feet flew out from under him. He crashed onto his shoulder, close to his nape. Marie thought he might have broken his neck if the muck had proved less forgiving. Gunnar laughed at him.

Eunice commanded them to walk ahead of her. Caked with slabs of mud, they marched toward the outside spigot extending from the side of the house. Their darting eyes betrayed that each wanted to run, while gauging the staying power of the other.

Marie pulled up Leo's pants and, glancing over his shoulder, watched Eunice do what Fran couldn't and Lete wouldn't. Leo was calming down inside his mother's hug. As Marie rubbed his back, she guessed that Gunnar and Lars must have heard that tone from their grandmother before and knew she wasn't bluffing. If they disobeyed, it would be harder on them.

Marie watched Eunice unfurl a garden hose, then, by feel, as she bore her ice-blue eyes into her grandsons, turn the spigot. The boys clung to each other as she stung them with the cold spray. She shouted for them to clasp their hands behind their heads, elbows out, so she could clear the last bit of territory that they held in their own embrace. When all the mud was gone, she kept them shivering in the stream of cold water for a few more seconds in what seemed to Marie a preemptive act to flush away further shenanigans.

The two boys huddled, trembling. Eunice lowered the hose.

As they wiped their eyes, she spoke. "You don't have any dry clothes here, and anyway, it's hot out, so you two go play in the woods by yourselves. Stay outta this yard until I whistle for you." She blew a shrill whistle through the reed formed by her fingers. The boys cupped their wet hands over their ears. "When you hear that, start running back here, 'cause you'll be heading home."

As the boys hightailed it toward the woods, Eunice rewound the hose. Marie escorted Leo into the house. Her mother-in-law stomped up the porch stairs and entered the kitchen. When the screen door clapped back behind her, she nodded at Marie, then stepped to the sink to wash her hands. Eunice turned with a dish towel and looked at Henry and the kids. Marie tried to conjure what Eunice might be thinking. Her son's family. Three of her own blood. Marie wanted to know if this woman saw a red stain, too.

Marie knew that Leo's melancholy was meant to milk the comfort of her embrace. How many more years would he encourage, much less tolerate, such public affection? She pulled him close and looked over at Rita, who had found her father's chair and rested against Henry's hip, her skinny legs angled out, heels dug into the floor, holding his arm as he squeezed her waist.

Rita didn't blink or look away from Eunice. Behind the safety of her father's embrace, she stared at her grandmother. Marie was pleased to see Eunice gift her only granddaughter a slight smile.

"Play outside," Eunice said to both kids, though her gaze never left Rita. "They'll stay in the woods, so you don't have to worry." Rita blinked once and swallowed but didn't take her eyes off her grandmother. Marie knew she had a spunky little girl, but she had never seen Rita so bold with an adult. Marie didn't think Rita was scared of Eunice one bit, and that gave her a Mother's Day chill that accompanied the proud warmth radiating through her body.

"We're thirsty, Gramma," Rita proclaimed.

Eunice's smile widened; then she looked over at Marie. After a slight hunch of her shoulders, she turned back to her two grandchildren and said, "All right, then. I've got some ginger ale in the basement. Do you like ginger ale?"

"I like it!" Leo said.

Rita looked at Marie, who guessed what her daughter would have asked her if they'd been alone. *Do I like ginger ale, Mommy?* Marie nodded at her.

Eunice must have seen the silent exchange, because she said, "The two of you can go down into the basement and get yourselves a ginger ale. While you're at it, bring up four cans for the adults, please."

The tollbooth agent dipped her head to look inside the car and make eye contact with Marie, who was sitting on the passenger side. As Henry took the ticket, the agent spoke past him and said, "Happy Mother's Day!"

"Thank you," Marie replied.

"They're giving you a nice gift," the agent said, as she nodded toward the twins—fast asleep, splayed flat across the cargo space. Marie inspected the woman's midriff inching into view above the gate of the tollbooth—seven months pregnant, she guessed. The operator touched her stomach. "Next year, they promised, I can have off. First-time mother and all."

The Nomad pulled onto I-90. Marie lowered her head on an angle and stared through the windshield at the polka-dotted sky. "Looks like our car, doesn't it? All that blue, with those puffy white clouds. Such a pretty day."

Henry smiled as he raised his gaze to the heavens. "At first look, it's like elephants flying; then they turn into ships, or barns.

Used to lie in the grass and stare up at 'em when I was a kid. Loved it when a big, fat shadow would pass over me."

Henry grew silent. *Let him be*, she thought, as he settled into the slow lane. Marie looked back at the kids. Side to side, Rita's head rolled with every slight swerve of the station wagon. The road curved to circumvent a hill, and the sun burst through the passenger-side windows. Under the heat of the rays, Leo mumbled. Around the hill, the road returned to its eastern line. Marie turned to face the dashboard and slid closer to Henry. She stretched both arms atop the seat back, yawned, and raised her left hand to stroke her husband's head. His ear shone crimson from the sun he'd gotten while playing outside with the kids at Eunice's. She traced the contour of his ruddy ear with her finger, then tugged on his lobe. Short, black hair formed a perfect horizontal sideburn—a clean line delineating his smooth-shaven cheek. Held in a curl, her two longest fingers felt the edge of it.

"Hmm, I've only ever seen you in a brush cut, Henry. Bet you'd look like Elvis if you grew out your hair."

"Imagine me with a ducktail! That'd go over big with my mother, wouldn't it?"

Marie doubted Eunice would care enough to comment.

"Henry, what did Eunice say to you when you were sitting together on the porch?" JP and Lete had been drinking in the dining room when Fran waddled down to the woods to check on her two troublesome pups. From the top step, Marie had sat watching Henry and their kids in the front yard. Eunice marched out to the porch and plunked down next to Marie. The two women were silent as they watched Fran retreat and Henry play with loving ease, as natural as any man could be, with his children. Then, in an unspoken transfer, the couple swapped places and Henry sat next to his mother.

"Do you want to talk about it?" she asked.

"Check on them again, please. Are they out?"

"Appears so. I'll keep an eye on them."

Once again, Henry checked every mirror and studied the speedometer. Marie waited; then he cleared his throat. "Mother was her usual self—didn't offer much and waited for me to talk. I didn't know what to say, so I just stared out at you and the kids for what seemed the longest time. Finally, I asked her: Why?"

"Why she sent you away—as her sister's baby?"

"No, I sort of get that, I guess." Henry's voice croaked. He coughed and said, "Give me a minute." He rolled down his window, propped his elbow on the sill, and held his forehead with his left hand while his right wrist capped the steering wheel and he stared ahead.

Marie shook her head and glowered through the windshield at the road zinging at them. Painted white stripes zipped past in a steady beat; sunlight hitting the black asphalt caused the road to sparkle with false gems. *No woman could justify what Eunice did to him*, she thought. *Not as a child, not as a man.* She wanted to scream but kept quiet. Then Henry broke their silence.

"Marie, I've got a brother. A brother!" he blurted.

"Lete's only a half-brother. You're nothing like him, darling."

"No, not Lete. A full brother."

"What? I thought she had a single indiscretion," she said, avoiding the use of "one-night stand," a phrase certain to deepen his trauma.

"Evidently, twins run on *my* side of the family."

"You had a twin brother?" Tears started to well as Marie absorbed the news. Her left hand caressing his neck, she cried, thinking his twin had died so young. A brother who could have changed everything in his childhood. Every lonely night, every friendless day.

"Not 'had,' *have*. I have an identical twin brother."

With uncharacteristic bluntness, he told the story, channeling Eunice's matter-of-fact delivery. Marie stared at the greenery of the rural New York spring and caught glimpses of the now ice-less ditches as he told of the kidnapping. She spun in disbelief.

Her gaze returned to the windshield. The road came at her in a blur as she processed the truth. The thump of the tires lulled her. Minutes passed in shared silence until the twisted carcass of a slain deer broke the monotonous shoulder of gravel. Gone in a flash, the dead animal was behind them, and then she said, "Why didn't Eunice try to find the father so she could hand you over, too? That would have solved all her problems." Gasping at her own words, she patted her eyes. "I'm sorry, Henry. You know what I meant, right?"

A tear welled in his eye. "I know what you meant."

Against her hand, the muscles in his neck jerked taut like steel cables. She massaged him until her hand cramped; then she rested her head on his shoulder. Eyes closed, she listened as he recounted Eunice's explanation, which included the counsel of her confidant, a woman named Gussie, the only trusted friend his mother had ever earned. A Negro woman, as strong as any man, a powerful, protective ally. Gussie had advised her to get the twins someplace safe, had said not to give JP the chance he'd boasted he'd take.

"Safe? Eunice thought that shipping you off to Pa was safe? Didn't he use to tell you that he would have drowned you if he could've gotten away with it?"

"Yes, he did. When I came back from the Marines, he said that when I was a baby, he should've. Told me that nobody would've looked for a half-breed infant buried in the woods."

"Sounds like something Pa would say."

Henry released an uneasy laugh. "Yeah, he said it would've been easy to do back when he was born."

Maybe Pa's own parents should've, she mused, then chastised herself for sinking to the man's level. "If the Negro woman told her not to keep the babies, why'd she ship you off to Pa's with Aunt Rita? Why didn't she leave you at an orphanage?"

"I asked her that question."

"And? Did she answer you?"

"Yeah. When Fran and the kids were walking back from the woods. Remember when they stopped and Fran made those boys apologize to Leo?"

"I do. It wasn't the most sincere remorse I've witnessed, but I appreciated poor Fran's attempt to make them somewhat civilized. She's got her hands full."

"Well, Mother would agree, I suppose."

"Why do you say that?"

"She looked at all of you standing out there. Turned to me with those ice-blue eyes, then glanced back over her shoulder toward the screen door. Back where we could hear JP and Lete laughing like drunken goons. Then she mumbled that what JP put in her was his doing. What the Indian put in her was her doing."

"That's an interesting way of saying things."

"I guess it's her way of taking responsibility. She told me that every year on Mother's Day, she faces her three biggest mistakes: Uli, JP, and the Indian."

"Oh, Henry. That's terrible!"

"And then she said that she had thought about trying to find the Indian but didn't see how it would have changed anything. Said she liked to think that my twin brother was safe and happy. And that every year on Mother's Day, at least she could see."

"What does that mean?"

"That's all she said. Each year she could see."

"That one of her twins was still alive?" Marie speculated. "Or see what Pa wanted her to see—what she'd brought on the family?"

"No. I think just the difference."

"Difference?"

"Yeah. Between what she did and what JP did *to* her. The difference between Lete and me. That's what she saw every year."

A barrage of vermillion volleys from the sunset at their backs shot high over the Nomad and splashed into the cumulus clouds that floated before them, as if painted zeppelins had been raised to signal the end of the day for mothers. Marie thought about telling him, *That was Eunice's clumsy way of letting you know that she loves you.* Thought about telling him, *Eunice didn't want to lose you like she lost your twin.* Instead, she slipped her left arm behind Henry's lower back, then brought her right arm across the front of his waist. She squeezed him, closed her eyes, and nestled her head into his rib cage. At low frequency, the steering wheel vibrated inside his right palm. He crossed his left hand underneath and stroked her hair as they drove in silence toward Schenectady.

CHAPTER FOURTEEN

———•—

T he prior year, on their first visit to Eunice's house, Marie had
been nauseous from the child not to be, another in her string
of miscarriages since the twins were born, a string interrupted
only by the stillbirth more than two years ago. In the morning on
the next Mother's Day, when the couple was alone in the kitchen,
Henry suggested to Marie that today's trip might be their last as a
family to Rochester, or to the farm, for that matter. An odd tradition, he said, one that he should no longer foist upon his wife and
children. He told her that next year he could drive up late on Saturday night and stay at the nearby Howard Johnson motel, save
the whole family the hassle—a euphemism, she assumed, for repeating last year's traumatic visit to Gramma's. He said he could
visit Eunice before Lete got there and be back in Schenectady by
lunchtime to spend the bulk of the day with Marie and the kids.
Then he grew quiet as he fumbled to refill his empty coffee cup.
Let's see how this year goes, she told him, although her hopes
were modest at best.

A convenience store waited for the kids just beyond the gas
pumps. Henry agreed with Marie that he should put up the backseat so the twins could remain primped and proper for their ar-

rival at Gramma Eunice's house. Both children had been instructed to use the restroom. Leo ran with thanks, while Rita capitulated after given her choice of obstinance or treats.

The twins emerged from the store, Marie's hands clasping their shoulders, carrying brown paper bags of candy. Henry paid the teenage attendant, who had topped off the gas tank and washed the bug-splattered windshield. Eyes cast down into his palm, the lad stared at the fifty-cent piece before thanking Henry for the generous tip. Then he turned to Marie and said, "Happy Mother's Day, ma'am."

Marie straightened Rita's dress and tightened her ponytail, then tucked in Leo's shirt. Out of habit, she rubbed her hand backward from the top of her son's forehead, enjoying the soft fleece of his close-cropped brush cut. *Like father, like son*, she thought.

Quiet settled inside the car once the doors closed; then Henry pulled the Nomad out of the gas station for the last leg of their journey. The drizzle started. "Good thing he cleaned the windshield," Henry said, as he turned on the wipers.

Marie's gaze drifted into the mist as she took in the signs of rural life—farmhouses, barns, silos, and fence-lined pastures—all being cleansed by the early-morning rinse. Lulled by the gray day and its sprinkles, she felt sanguine about the visit. Despite having to suffer JP and Lete, Marie was less anxious than she had been last year. Henry was on high alert about those two, and she had complete confidence in the ex-Marine when it came to protecting his family. She wasn't suffering morning sickness, and there were no adolescent hyenas awaiting their arrival—Gunnar and Lars wouldn't be there this year.

The storm intensified, and a hard rain came upon them fast, as was common in upstate New York. Lines of trucks and cars slowed. Only the most confident or foolish—often in dangerous combination—passed them on the left. Bombarded by fat raindrops the size of gumballs, the Nomad cruised west. The driving rain rumbled like a drum corps advancing across the hood, climbing up the windshield, then marching double-time atop the roof of the station wagon.

"Listen to that. Whoa—look at it pour, kids!" Marie twisted her torso and stretched her left arm over the top of the bench seat. "Let's leave that ball in the car, Leo. I promise we'll get out on the way home at a rest stop if the rain lets up."

"Mommy, if it's not raining when we get to Gramma Eunice's, can we still bounce it outside in the driveway, like you said?"

"Sure, Leo, if it's okay with Gramma." Back home in Schenectady, after a short bout of negotiation, Marie had agreed to let Leo bring his ten-inch red-rubber ball, but she worried it might set off Eunice, JP, or both, so no promises.

"Maybe it'll only be drizzling at Gramma's. Can we play if it's only drizzling?"

"Let's wait and see, honey."

Right before they'd left, she'd picked up a call from Fran. Lete might stop by for his traditional Mother's Day drink with Eunice, but Fran and the boys wouldn't be coming this year. Then tears. Then Fran's croaked admission of a black eye. Then a click to end the sobbing on the other end of the line.

"Yes, Leo, I do think it's only drizzling now," Marie responded, as she sat on Eunice's porch with her two children. "Let's give it a couple more minutes. See how the sky's starting to clear?"

"Can I go get my ball from the car?"

"*May* I, Leo," Rita corrected.

"May I, Mom?" he asked, without acknowledging his sister.

"Yes, dear. But please bring it right back here." She gripped his forearm, and he gazed up at her with a perplexed look. "Run fast!" Marie instructed, as she released her hold.

"Race you," Rita shouted, as she rushed down the porch stairs ahead of him.

"Not fair! It's not a race, Rita, if you cheat. Don't touch my ball, either," Leo snapped, chasing his sister.

Marie watched them bolt toward the Nomad and wondered when Leo would have *his* growth spurt. Last week, he'd cringed at the dinner table when Rita had told him he wasn't short, he was "fun-size." In private, Marie secured Rita's cooperation to keep Leo from feeling sad about her extra two inches. When his mother had later tried to soothe him, he'd appeared hopeful but unconvinced as she had explained that girls mature sooner than boys. "Look at the children in your class, and then look at the older kids in school," she had suggested. "It's certain to change. The boys grow later, and when they do, they shoot right past their sisters. You'll be taller than Rita someday," she promised. She'd been relieved when Leo said okay. But then, in the next breath, he'd asked, "She's already smarter—why does she have to be taller, too?"

A dark cloud roamed overhead, its looming shadow surprising Marie, who had anticipated sunshine, not another deluge. The children, laughing as the drizzle became a pounding rain, closed themselves inside the car. They waved to their mother on the porch, who, with a smile and an open hand in the air, instructed them to sit in there until the thick cloud had passed.

Through the downpour, she watched the twins inside the station wagon turned playhouse and marveled at how, for such different kids, they got along so well. Leo was his father's son:

likable and disarming, deflecting antagonists everywhere, from playground to classroom. The consummate agreeable child, Leo still enjoyed being doted upon by his sister. When other children might have bristled at the mothering attempts of a sibling, Leo accepted Rita's care as he might an offered treat.

Even as a toddler, Rita had been a powerful force and prone to bouts of righteous indignation—a crusader. The mother of a classmate of the twins had commented that Rita was a red-dress, not a pink-dress, little girl. Marie often wished that she herself had a bit more of Rita's red-dress-ness. With a sigh, she concluded that her daughter had inherited her spunk, at least in part, from Eunice.

The rogue rain cloud passed, and Marie beckoned the kids forward from the Nomad with a wave of her hand. Leo sprinted back to the porch with the ball tucked under his arm like a running back with a football. In unspoken collusion with her mother, Rita trudged up the porch steps behind her brother and said, "I had a head start, and he almost beat me to the car, Mommy. Leo's really fast!"

"You're both fast, but I think you're right, Rita. Leo's *really* fast!"

Leo beamed and then said, "Mommy, we didn't get even a little wet. Can we bounce the ball, like you promised?"

JP's Studebaker was parked in the garage, leaving an open court for her son's passion. "All right, honey. But just bounce it back and forth on the cement with Rita. No wall ball, okay?"

An early-May breeze rustled the slick green leaves, still shiny from their recent sprouting. Moisture dripped from the branches and the wind gusted into a whistle while the whir of distant cars accompanied the distinct *plop* of the bouncing ball. The sound must have drawn Eunice to the porch. She sat down next to

Marie, who worried that her mother-in-law would stop the fun. Instead, Eunice smiled as she observed the kids at play.

Leo slammed the ball downward onto the concrete surface with a two-handed pass that sent it sailing over Rita's head. Down the narrow driveway the ball bounded, hopping toward the street in strides reminiscent of a white-tailed deer in frantic escape. Leo passed Rita in a sprint. To Marie, it all happened in slow motion, even while her abject fear was instantaneous. She was rising as Eunice shouted, "*Stop!* Don't you two move an inch."

Leo pulled up, and Rita stopped short of colliding with her brother's back. Both children stared toward the porch. Leo stood gripped by apparent guilt and terror, while his accomplice, brave Rita, seemed to have abandoned her usual resolve.

"Let the ball go. Don't run into the street," Eunice commanded. Cemented, neither twin moved their feet. Turned at the waist, they stood at contorted attention, watching the red rubber ball cross the street. It bounced without damage into a chain-link fence, then commenced its return trip, which ended when the ball dribbled to a stop at the curb in front of Eunice's house.

A car horn blasted, and Lete shouted, "Happy Mother's Day, Mother!" as his banana-colored vehicle rounded the street corner. The morning rain had cleansed the air. Not as hot as last year, it was a typical warm Sunday in early May. Rolling gray clouds threatened to repeat the rinse cycle with a gully washer. Most would have considered it a risky day to roll down the ragtop of a convertible in order to make an entrance.

He waved a pint bottle above his head as he steered the unwieldy Bonneville toward the curb with one hand. The car lunged. The right-side front tire squeezed the red rubber ball into the curb, squishing it. Rubber on rubber, the ball exploded like a gunshot through the quiet neighborhood.

"Whoa, did ya hear that?" Lete laughed and tripped as he exited the driver's-side door, which he slammed shut with a curse. In clumsy theater, he displayed his pint bottle in the air for his audience, then deposited the whiskey atop the Pontiac's hood. Like a circus clown, he spun with fake confusion. Pretending to search for the source of the popping sound, he held a hand cupped around one of his wing-nut ears and twisted in a downward spiral near to the ground. One hip leaned against the car, preventing his fall. His bug eyes widened as he feigned amazement while reaching down under the tire to grab Leo's deflated ball, which was wedged and did not release at Lete's tug. He yanked and grew angry, ending his awkward comedy. In a curse-filled sweat, he forced it out from under the tire. Then, victorious, he straightened himself and held it out on display, like a dead rabbit days after being caught in a trap.

Lete wiped his wet brow on his sleeve and retrieved his bottle from atop the hood. Holding out the shredded ball, he walked to the twin balustrades planted in the driveway and dropped the scraps into Leo's cupped hands. "Looks like its bouncing days are over."

Leo stared down at the mangled ball and remained silent. Lete laughed at the stunned boy, but his giggling halted as he confronted Rita. The startled drunk reeled at her scowl, which Marie assumed might have been the same look Eunice had used throughout Lete's life to keep her son under some semblance of control.

After repeated blinks, Lete refocused, then sneered at Rita. He exhaled a demeaning snort in her direction, then raised the bottle back to his lips without looking away, as if he were worried that she might grab him by the balls. Marie's red-dress fantasies took a nasty turn as she squeezed her hands into angry fists.

"Don't take it so hard, kid. Yar brother'll get over it."

Lete took another swig, then brought the bottle down and stepped past Rita, giving her a wide berth. Up the front-porch stairs he stumbled, catching himself on the top step with the outstretched hand that held his bottle. He passed Eunice, who had averted her eyes. Lete hiccupped as he crossed the threshold.

Gramma's raised, open palm stopped Leo's progress at the bottom of the stairs. As she descended, Eunice instructed him to hold out the filthy remains for her. She pinched the rubber between her thumb and index finger.

"Sorry about that. Better the ball than you, Leo. You two go get washed up, now. Lunch is ready."

After helping Eunice with the dishes, Marie found her usual perch at the top of the porch stairs. The children were playing in the yard again. The creak of the front door caused her to shudder, but the sound of Henry's voice brought relief and a smile to her face.

"It's getting a bit sloppy in there," he said, looking down at her as he rested against the porch railing, half standing, half leaning. "Thought I'd come out for a little fresh air."

Marie watched her husband descend the stairs, then chase the kids. He laughed and they giggled as their impromptu cat-and-mouse game unfolded. Rita escaped a feeble, two-armed swipe and cackled as she ran in a loop away from Henry's half-hearted pursuit. Leo snuck up behind his daddy's back and flirted with capture when he tickled Henry's ribs.

Once more, the door announced a refugee from the two drunks inside the house. "Could just grab them if he wanted to, huh?" Eunice observed, as she placed her feet on the first step and sat down next to Marie. "Who's teasing who? If they get a little bit closer, he's gonna nab them, I bet."

"That's how it often happens. The kids'll giggle while he pretends they're just out of reach. Watch—Leo's usually the one who tests his father's wingspan. Henry'll grab him; then Rita'll come to the rescue. Both'll be laughing in his embrace in about a minute."

Leo yelled, "No!" as Henry gathered him up in both arms and then pretended to chew on his neck with loud, guttural, toothless chomps. The savior cued, Rita swooped in. Henry swept her into a one-arm hug, then leaned back, raising both of his captives off the ground. They kicked the air and giggled, demanding to be released, in hopes of repeating the contest.

"They ain't scared of their father, are they?"

"Not in the least."

"They scared of their mother?"

"Well, Eunice, let's just say that I tend to be the disciplinarian. Henry likes being the fun daddy."

"What happens if you're not around? Do they run roughshod on him?"

"They seem to test me more than they do him. Something about the man just makes them want to please him, I suppose."

A comfortable silence settled on the porch as the two women watched the carefree game in the yard. Marie glanced over at her mother-in-law, wondering what Eunice thought of her son as playful father.

"Eunice, may I ask you about Henry?"

Eunice smiled and nodded, without taking her eyes off the laughing scrum on her lawn. "Do you want him to visit you like this?"

Eunice raised her glass and took a sip from the drink she had nursed through the several JP and Lete had downed. "Been seeing each other every Mother's Day since he was born. I'd miss it."

"The kids aren't very keen to visit. It's not you, but it's difficult for them."

"They scared of JP?"

"Yes. And also of Lete and his two boys."

"You scared, too?"

"Not scared, but definitely uncomfortable."

With his thumb bent backward by tiny fingers, Henry released his grip, and Rita escaped in a spin. Hands on her hips, she stood a few feet away, glaring at her father in mock challenge, daring him to chase her, while he held Leo pinned to his hip, the boy's feet still off the ground.

"She reminds me of you, Eunice. Henry says so, too."

"I can see it. Strong kid. Doesn't take nothing from nobody, does she?"

"She's got a sense of right and wrong, which makes her persistent at times. Especially whenever she thinks Leo's suffering some injustice."

"I've seen her take up for her brother. Tough little girl. I was tough like that, too, back then. Sometimes that's what a girl needs to get by. Nothing wrong with that."

The sky had cleared since they'd arrived. Past the street, the distant blue was pocked with white puffs. No ominous gray clouds hovered in view, yet Marie could feel a storm in the air. Then, from behind the house, sneaking over the roof, the rain came falling down without warning. The kids ran to the porch, giggling, as Henry jumped into the station wagon to ready the car for the trip home. From the backseat window, he waved at Marie, then motioned that he'd get the seat folded down while waiting out the cloudburst. The pounding on the porch roof sounded like gravel being dropped into a wheelbarrow. Careening off the eaves, water formed a curtain to the ground.

Lete staggered out through the front door, shoved Leo out of the way, and hurried down the steps. After two unsteady paces along the cement walkway, he attempted to sprint across the slippery lawn toward his prized Bonnie. Its top was down, and rain was pummeling the black upholstery. The grass was as slick as a sheet of sprayed plastic, and Lete never secured solid footing. His arms waved, his legs split, and his feet rose toward the overhead rain cloud, and then he crashed flat on his back. Splayed in the grass, he wriggled to raise himself as the kids tried to stifle their laughter. Bug eyes wild, he spun in the mud to glower at them. When Marie met his gaze, he snarled, "What the fuck are *you* looking at?"

Marie's eyes shot to the Nomad, where Henry was still head down as the rain nailed the roof above him. She was relieved he hadn't heard his half-brother swearing at her or their children. Without turning her head, she sensed Eunice locking eyes with her oldest son.

Lete's knees sank into the lawn and slowly split apart. He shifted for traction, then struggled to his feet. Before arriving at his convertible, he slipped twice more, each time cursing as he rose. Drenched by the time he reached the car, he pulled open the driver's-side door with such force that it rebounded and the frame clipped his side.

"Shit! That hurt, goddammit!" he shouted, rubbing where the door had grazed his hip bone.

The violent rain started to subside as he slouched into position behind the steering wheel. The black roof unfolded to the whiny sounds of the car's auxiliary motors. Blinking upward into the rain, he watched the ragtop cover his head.

"Gramma, may we please go get a ginger ale?" Leo asked.

"That's fine. Bring up a couple of cans for your mother and me, too, please."

Once the front door slammed behind her kids, Marie turned back toward the street, her gaze oscillating between the Nomad and the Bonneville. Henry was now observing his half-brother wrestling with the ragtop's ceiling hooks inside the convertible. Lete wiped mud across his chest in an effort to improve his grip. By the time the top was locked in place, the rain had reduced to a drizzle. With odd synchronicity, two driver's-side doors opened and the half-brothers stepped from their respective vehicles.

Almost as dry as their audience on the porch, Henry gave way to a sopping Lete when they both arrived at the sidewalk. Lete swayed in place as he stood at the foot of the stairs to address Eunice. Although drunk, he was drenched and knew better than to attempt entry through the front door.

"Mother, I'll go through the cellar door to grab those overalls in the basement. I need a towel to wipe down the inside of the Bonnie."

"Overalls are fine, but no towels. Take a few rags from the bin next to my canned vegetables. And take those boots off at the top of the cement steps. Come back out that way. I don't want you tromping through the house."

Lete's thin blond hair had matted to his forehead. He wiped away the wet strands that poked at his eyes, then disappeared around the side of the house. On the porch, under a quiet roof, an awkward lull among the three adults replaced the din of rain. Drops fell from the eaves and dripped onto the flower beds. Long after Lete vanished, Eunice monitored the corner of the building he'd rounded. When Marie heard the exterior iron door to the cellar fall open with a crash, Eunice turned back to stare at the lawn. Her eyes traced the gouges her eldest son had made in his scramble to reach his exposed convertible.

She stood, tugged her dress into shape, and said, "I better go make sure JP doesn't bother those kids. They should have come up from the basement with those ginger ales by now."

"Right behind you, Eunice. I need to powder my nose," Marie said. Henry motioned toward the Nomad, smiled at his wife, then headed back down the stairs. He must have forgotten something, she thought.

Eunice stepped toward the kitchen in search of the twins while Marie walked upstairs to the only bathroom in the house, but before she closed the door behind her, she heard Leo yelling for her. She ran downstairs and found her son standing alone in the open doorway to the basement. He stammered, "Uncle Lete won't let Rita come upstairs."

In her fury, Marie slipped on the first wooden step and grabbed the handrail. Eunice was ahead of her and had commandeered a cast-iron skillet from the kitchen. Brandishing it in the air, she screamed, "Get out of her way, Lete!"

"What ya got that for, Mother? Can't do no cooking down here, can ya?" He continued to block his niece's path, waiting for his mother to respond.

"You heard me. Get out of her way—now!" He smirked as he shuffled to the side. "Come here, Rita," Eunice said. Rita started past Lete, who reached for her as if he was going to pinch her. Eunice pulled the girl to her and lifted the skillet. "Knock it off, Lete!"

"Now, Mother. Just havin' some fun with the lil' bastard's lil' bitch."

Eunice raised the skillet higher and shook it at him. "Don't test me, boy!"

"Ya gonna smash me in the head like ya did ole Uncle Uli?"

"What happened to Uli was an accident. You'll get what's coming to you."

Lete wobbled in place. He seemed to bring the skillet into focus as he laughed; then his gaze met his mother's icy stare. "Aw, Mother, ya ain't gotta be so damn sen-see-tif. Ya just protecting her 'cause she a girl. Ya got two real grandchildren. She ain't shit! Just that lil' bastard's lil' bitch is all she is."

Eunice squeezed the child's shoulder with her free hand and once more brandished the skillet. "I've got four grandchildren. Rita here is the best of the lot, and you ain't going to get your hands on her."

He grabbed his loose belt and belched. "Sen-see-tif. That's the truth, Mother. Just too damn sen-see-tif."

Leo was sulking a bit, sitting in the Nomad by himself, reading his comic books until it was time to drive home. Out of character, Rita had refused his invitation to play. She wouldn't leave Marie's side while they waited for Henry to gather them for the ride home. After hearing about the basement incident and convincing Marie that he had calmed down, he was indoors having "a word" with his half-brother.

On the front porch, Marie and Rita sat with Eunice on the top step. Marie listened for an argument to stream through the screen door. Henry and Lete must still be in the basement, she thought, and then cringed at JP, whom she heard snoring inside. She jerked when the metal cellar door crashed down. Lete stumbled out from around the side of the house in his father's co-opted overalls. He didn't glance up at the female troika on the porch or mutter a word as he staggered across the lawn on the way to his

Bonnie. He slammed the driver's door to make a point and peeled out so fast that he caused the tires to hike gravel.

"Bet you're glad to see him leave, huh?" Eunice said to Rita.

With a shoulder bump, Marie nudged Rita, who sat in between the two women. She caught her daughter's eye and nodded encouragement to speak her mind. It seldom took more than a nudge.

"He's drunk every time we come here, Gramma. Is he like that all the time?"

"Pretty much every time I see him these days."

"Was he always so mean?"

"Pretty much. You can see it in your cousins, too, I bet."

Marie felt Rita react. She wondered if her daughter's body had jerked at the repetitious "pretty much" or at the mere mention of the gangling Erikson boys.

"Yeah. Aunt Fran's nice, though. Are they always mean to her?"

"Pretty much. Your aunt Fran's got it tough. She tries, but it ain't easy with her crew."

Rita leaned her shoulder into Marie to signal her unspoken observation on Eunice's diction, then said, "Uncle Lete's not nice, her kids are mean, and her breath stinks. I feel sorry for Aunt Fran."

All three held their vision toward the street. Marie wondered how Eunice would handle her red-dress granddaughter. As Marie inhaled a calming breath, she remembered Henry's saying that Eunice had always been nice to him when she came to the farm on Mother's Day, as nice as he'd seen her be with anyone.

Eunice said, "I gave Fran some mints, but they didn't help much. Don't last long, I guess."

"She needs braces, Gramma."

"She doesn't have polio, Rita. She's got bad breath."

"Not braces for her legs, Gramma, for her teeth. I have a friend whose mommy had crooked teeth like Aunt Fran's. Her breath was even worse! Remember, Mommy? I couldn't play over there sometimes, it stunk so bad."

"Yes, darling. Those braces gave her a nice smile."

"And her breath doesn't stink anymore. Aunt Fran should get braces for her teeth." Marie watched Eunice absorb her introduction to orthodontia. *Out of the minty-fresh mouths of babes*, she thought. She knew the classmate's mother, whose parents had died and left her a nice little inheritance by Schenectady standards. First she'd gotten a divorce; then she'd fixed her teeth.

"Good to know, Rita. You sure are a smart kid, aren't you?"

"Pretty much, Gramma." Marie gaped at her daughter and laughed. Two peas in a pod.

"Would you be mad at Aunt Fran if she got a divorce?" Rita asked, plowing ahead. Marie wondered which conversations her curious daughter had overheard.

"Wouldn't blame her, Rita. But I heard that it takes a lot of money for a woman to get a divorce if the man doesn't want one. Fran doesn't have any money, far as I know. Don't think Lete would stand for it."

Eunice continued to stare out toward the street. Through the screen door, Marie heard JP snort; then his snoring settled back into its usual cadence.

CHAPTER FIFTEEN

The previous weekend had been dark and stormy and had kept the twins indoors until they walked to school in the drizzle Monday morning. Today, the Friday before Mother's Day, was a bright day. Chubby cumulus clouds flew over Schenectady, cloaked neighborhoods with their passing shadows, then plodded away like a herd of skyborne pachyderms. When the kids got home, Marie let them play outdoors after they agreed to finish their homework before dinner. Tomorrow, they'd watch cartoons in the morning and then want to play outside on what promised to be the first conducive Saturday of spring.

Late in the afternoon, Marie was prepping for dinner when a familiar rumble filled the narrow driveway. She looked outside through the window screen above the kitchen sink. Their blue-and-white station wagon stopped in front of the closed garage. Henry was home from work.

When he raised the door to the single-car garage, Marie heard its hinges squeal for the grease gun. The screech drew her onto her tiptoes, and she angled her gaze as he disappeared inside the garage. She heard the wheels first, then watched as Henry pushed the lawn mower outside and parked it on the grass. During breakfast that morning, he'd said that if the weather held, he'd mow the lawn after work. He wanted to get it done tonight so he could enjoy the family tomorrow without interruption before he drove to Howard Johnson's. He planned to head over Saturday night so he could see Eunice first thing on Mother's Day morning, then hustle home to spend the bulk of the day with Marie and the kids.

Henry stepped into the kitchen and embraced his wife, as was his habit at the end of each day. "Wow, what a beautiful spring evening! Can you believe how nice it was today?"

As Marie savored their hello hug, she said, "The kids are getting antsy about summer vacation, and it's still five weeks away. Spring's in the air, and they're ready to bolt."

"Where's my fan club?"

"They're doing their homework. The weather was so nice, I let them play outside after school. I just checked on them. Rita's finished and helping Leo with his math."

"Perfect. I'll be quick with the lawn," he promised. He turned at the doorway and asked with a smile, "What's for dinner?"

"Meat loaf." She paused. "Henry, your mother called."

"What?"

"Meat loaf."

"I heard that part. What did Eunice say?"

"Said she wanted to make sure the kids and I felt 'welcomed' this Sunday."

"Welcomed? Really?"

"She wanted to know if they might like some other kind of soda pop. She said that on her way home today she'd be stopping to cash her check and pick up some things."

"Did you tell her that you and the kids aren't coming this year?"

"Henry," she said, scolding him with an incredulous frown.

"Marie, you don't have to. You know that, right?"

"The kids and I talked about it. Leo negotiated for ice cream cones. I think Rita wants to see Gramma."

"Are you sure? Do you want to sleep on it?"

"I told Eunice that we're coming. All four of us. Now, please, go mow the lawn."

"Marie."

"Cut the grass, then collect the kids for dinner. And be happy, Daddy."

Friday had been Eunice's payday since they'd moved upstate to Rochester. Erect in her ever-strict posture, she strode down the sidewalk of the lower-middle-class neighborhood on her way to the corner store. Delight in her achievements was complemented by the pleasant weather, which had refused the entire month of April. Today was a day she'd imagined over decades of grueling work in the laundry and dry-cleaning industry. Victorious over endless piles of dirty-dirties, she had persevered where others, even those desperate for work of any kind, had not lasted one full day. She thought about David Welles, estimating his current advanced age as she stepped over the cracks in the cement. Old Man Welles would be impressed by the size of the paycheck snug in her handbag. She wondered if he'd be more impressed by the folded papers that rested alongside her wages.

The owners' teenage son, Kevin, was outside with a hand crank to let down the awning that blocked the late-afternoon sunshine from penetrating the wide storefront window. Each Friday on her way home, she cashed her check at the corner store and picked up last-minute necessities for the weekend. She watched the lad struggling and wondered why he hadn't yet mastered such a simple daily task in the family business.

"Kevin."

Her salutation surprised the boy. The unwieldy crank tilted behind him, tapping the glass, before he pulled the rod in with both hands. "Hi, Mrs. Erikson. Good afternoon."

"I'd like to cash my check. Is your mother around?"

"In the back room. Please, after you, ma'am," Kevin said, as he stepped out of the way of the entrance. The handle of the crank knocked an apple from the top of the sloped display. It rolled downhill toward Eunice, who caught it in one hand before it fell to the pavement. In her other hand, she gripped the handle of her purse, the body of which dangled knee-high.

"Good catch, Mrs. Erikson!"

She grinned and said, "Add it to my total, Kevin."

Kevin's mother had not yet emerged from the stockroom, and he looked at the draped curtain as if his wordless appeal might beckon her to the front.

"Do you want a case of ginger ale, Mrs. Erikson?"

Eunice, chewing with her mouth closed, nodded confirmation of her standing order. Kevin selected one of the two-wheeled grocery caddies that his parents kept for the regulars and rolled it up to the stack.

"Anything else that's heavy before I get my mom, Mrs. Erikson?" Kevin asked, as he offered her a trash bin to dispose of the core.

"What kind of soda pop do kids like?"

Kevin's shoulders straightened. "Well, I used to like grape soda when I was little, before I switched to orange. This one here," he said, as he reached for a bottle of Nesbitt's Orange in the cooler. "My pals and I, we all drink root beer now."

She wondered if those boys liked the taste or just the idea of drinking something named "beer."

"Kevin, let's get another case. Two sixers of root beer, and one each of grape and orange."

"Anything else, Mrs. Erikson?"

"What do you and your pals like to eat when you drink root beer?"

"Potato chips and pretzels. Anything with salt. Salt goes real good with root beer."

"All right, then. I'll get some of those, too."

"One big bag of chips and one of pretzels?"

"Sounds about right. One each."

"Here you go, Mrs. Erikson. I'll fetch my mom to cash your check."

"Thank you, Kevin," she said, as she retrieved the check and a worn leather billfold from the belly of her purse.

Once she left the corner store, Eunice rehearsed out loud what the divorce lawyer had suggested: Tell JP that he'd get more money if he didn't contest her petition. He'd get half of the house. Nothing much left in her savings at the bank, and she had no idea if he even had an account, but he'd get half of hers, and vice versa. She'd paid the attorney a thief's ransom in advance for both divorces: hers and Fran's. And the fancy dentist had taken a pile that made her shake her head, but little Rita was right: Nothing short of braces was going to cut it. Breath mints hadn't done the trick—that was for sure.

She hadn't told the attorney that since she'd moved upstate, on every Mother's Day trip to the farm, she'd hidden in a glass canning jar the extra cash that she'd been able to save throughout the year. When she was a young woman, the librarian in New York had told her she'd have to buy her freedom. She'd told Eunice to save every cent she could and had given her advice not to leave it in a bank, where the court could seize it. JP hadn't contributed anywhere near half to their expenses, and she wouldn't risk exposing her stash until their divorce was official; that was the word the lawyer used. "When it's done, it's done," he'd said.

Soon after Eunice left the store, one of the two wheels on the caddy started to wobble. All the way home, it got caught on cracks in the cement that weren't high enough to trip even the clumsiest pedestrian. By the time she turned the corner of her street, she was so frustrated that she wanted to pick up the cart and carry it the rest of the way. No matter how troublesome, the errant wheel could not stymie her resolve to confront JP. Tomorrow, she'd make sure he was gone when Henry came with his family. Lete could take him to a bar, for all she cared.

Eunice dragged the cart along the broken sidewalk next to their overgrown lawn, which was pocked with fresh dandelions and spring crabgrass. JP had few assigned chores and had to be badgered to get anything done. Last week, every day before the rains started, she'd asked him to mow the lawn. Today, the skies had been partly cloudy and still he'd left the yard fallow. Fuming at the grass gone to seed, she planned to hand the ne'er-do-well the divorce papers, then march outside and mow the damn lawn herself. For the first time in memory, she hoped JP was home.

Bypassing the concrete path to the front porch, she bullied the cart to the end of the driveway, where she stopped to stare. The garage door was up, exposing an empty bay where JP's helmet-green Studebaker should have been sheltered. Instead, the faded old vehicle sat in the driveway, as if it were awaiting permission to park itself inside. The driver's-side door was flung open. Reflected in the chipped chrome bumper, an intermittent glow from the right-hand turn signal blinked at her. JP must have had another lapse. Of late, his memory seemed to visit less often than his own son.

Any other day, JP's oversight would have been raw meat slapping against the head of an irritable tigress. Today, she shrugged and then reached inside to turn off the blinker. JP's keys dangled from the ignition. The stale odor of the man lingered in the cab. She extracted the key and palmed the bundle. After returning the blinker to its neutral position on the steering column, she closed the door without slamming it.

She left the cases out back by the slanted cellar door and grabbed the chips and pretzels. After changing her shoes to mow, she'd take the soda pop to the basement via the shortest route. Then she would park the caddy inside the garage and return it to the store in the morning.

On the back porch, she tugged open the screen door. She touched the knob of the heavy interior door, which swung into the kitchen with ease—JP hadn't pushed it back into position when he'd entered the house. Eunice looked through the kitchen, past the dining room table. The glow of the television bathed the front room and sprayed a dull gray light up the length of the entry door.

Per his custom when alone in the house, the volume of the television was turned up high. Every night, he arrived home before Eunice and turned on the TV set. It was always blaring when she entered. She'd seen him address the television many times over the years with an irritating ritual. After powering up the appliance, he'd squeeze the aluminum foil that he had crumpled years ago onto the extended tips of the rabbit-ear antennae—an enhancement that he claimed guaranteed better reception. He would select one of three available channels, then plunk down into the molded cup of his easy chair. Settled, with a triple pour of whiskey in hand, he would drift into the static of a black-and-white escape.

When she walked inside each night, Eunice would drop her purse on the dining room table, step in front of the television set, blocking his view, and crank the volume down all the way. Then she'd retreat to the kitchen without comment. He'd grumble, demand that she return to adjust the volume; then, in response to the clanks of pots and pans from the kitchen, he'd stagger to his feet. He'd set the volume at the edge of her irritation, replant himself in his easy chair, and then—completing their cycle—mutter some insult in Swedish that she never cared to understand.

"Forget something?" she asked, dropping the keys into his lap.

The overloaded ring of cut metal bounced off the trampoline formed by the crotch of his pants, which were stretched taut between his outward-pointed knees. JP didn't move, look up, or in any way acknowledge her presence. He stared straight ahead in the direction of the game show that preceded the evening news report by the most trusted man in America: Walter Cronkite.

Decades ago, when they had occasionally spoken to each other in full sentences, Eunice had prophesied to JP that one day she'd get a divorce and leave him to his bottle. He'd laughed at her back then. Now, she pulled the petition from her purse and held the envelope in the air within view. He didn't move his head or alter his blank stare. Not one of his muscles twitched. She shook her head in disgust. This, of all days.

"You know what this is?"

Silence. JP didn't budge. She stepped in front of the television to capture his attention. Twisting at the waist, she lowered the volume with an angry turn. Then, scowling at him, she waved the envelope in his face.

"JP, listen to me! These are legal divorce papers." He stared straight ahead at her waistline. No emotion, not the subtlest of reactions—he gave her nothing.

The glow from the television hit her in the back and forked around her body into a split stream that flowed toward JP's easy chair. His breathing was slow. He didn't shift in his seat or even raise his head as she stood over him. She assumed he was drunk, though she could not locate a glass, much less the bottle he was accustomed to keeping within reach. The side table was bare. His hands were empty; his right one curled like a monkey's paw. No telltale accident had found the floor; no broken glass; no puddle of amber. Once more, drawing closer, Eunice waved the divorce papers in front of his face, then snapped her fingers within inches of his unblinking, bulging eyes.

The half-hour news show had neared its end. As on any other evening in their cramped house, they sat in separate chairs facing the TV set. Memories of the years—like winged snippets—flew about her mind, circled, and made repeated passes. JP hadn't said a word—like most nights. But unlike on those previous evenings of suffering his grunts and grumbles, she sat there knowing that he wasn't going to speak, not tonight or ever again.

JP farted. The unwelcome sound merged with Cronkite's voice. Then she heard a wet-sounding rumble from his chair and knew he'd crapped himself. Eunice closed her eyes and held them tight as the expected odor followed. The putrid smell brought her back to the sorting room and Welles's proposition: "Lift the patient, then pull the sheet out, diaper and all. We'll return every article clean, pressed, and folded." Now, with an unwanted patient sitting by her side, Eunice realized that up until tonight, she had endured the less trying turns of a cycle that had paid her way since she was ten years old.

JP's angry words were gone forever. The shells from years of his drunken outbursts were scattered on the floor at his feet like shucked peanuts as he sat melted into the formed depression of his easy chair. Cronkite finished his report of the nightly news, ending the thirty minutes during which his voice had roamed the room with details undetected by either person facing his flickering image. The most trusted man in America looked through the camera, stared into their living room, and called her to action. Added to the fresh stench, Cronkite's signature sign-off broke her spell and cued her that it was time to get to work.

"And that's the way it is."

Saturday morning, on the eve of their next trip to Rochester, Henry received a brief, matter-of-fact phone call from Eunice. After hearing his report, Marie understood that their family had until their arrival to digest JP's condition. Other than a few cuss words in Swedish, he couldn't talk and was paralyzed down his entire right side.

The Mother's Day visit didn't last long. Marie cleaned house a bit while Henry and Eunice cleared the dining room and carried the table to the garage. He then helped her set up the hospital bed that she'd rented. The twins sat on the porch, each with a book in their lap. They were unwilling to go back into the front room to watch TV alone with the patient, who sat in his chair, as Eunice had found him on her payday.

After they got the hospital bed set up where the dining table had been, Eunice asked Henry and Marie to assist her in moving the patient.

"He's heavy," she stated, before they tried to budge the chair.

"If we can get the rug out from under it, we can slide him over to the bed. Do you have some old towels or dishrags we can put under the feet?" Henry asked.

"Can you get the corners up high enough to yank the carpet out and for me to slip the rags underneath?"

"I think so, Mother." Henry crouched down in a tuck, got his hands under the frame of the chair, straightened his legs in a lift like a veteran teamster, and brought one corner off the floor. Eunice inched the edge of the carpet away, and Henry set the chair's foot down on the bare hardwood.

Eunice smiled. "You're strong as an ox, boy." She turned toward the kitchen. "I'll be right back with some rags. Good idea, Henry."

Marie almost cried when she saw how Eunice's approval affected her husband. The sounds—moans, shrieks, and angry grunts—that emanated from JP during his transfer to the dining room penetrated the walls and drove the kids to stare through the porch window. Marie saw their foreheads pressed against the glass and their faces cupped in their hands so they could watch the clumsy scrum that had been wrestling with the big Swede.

They'd gotten to work as soon as they'd arrived, around noon. After spending a couple of hours helping out, they hadn't eaten lunch yet. The kids remained polite, but Marie knew they were hungry. Eunice seemed to have no idea. Everyone was showing stress, and, after offering another round of her soda pops to the family, Eunice thanked them for all the help, then insisted they leave to drive back to Schenectady. She told them JP would fall asleep soon. She'd get Lete and Fran to help move him back into his chair in the morning before she went to work. When Marie asked who would stay with him during the day, Eunice offered a puzzled look.

Monday evening, Marie called her sister-in-law and learned that, throughout the day, Fran sat in the front room, attending to the man who had heaped insults on her since the day she'd wed his son. Three adults were required to lift JP from his chair and get him into the bed, then reverse the process in the morning. Without Fran and Lete, Marie knew that Eunice would be stranded.

Saturday, Marie telephoned Fran, wondering how she was holding up. Amid her subsequent daily visits, Fran said that she felt she had earned something akin to respect from their mother-in-law, who Marie knew had pitied the poor woman from the time she had gotten pregnant in high school.

At the beginning of the week, Fran said that each morning after breakfast, she and Lete had each driven their respective cars over to Eunice's. After he knocked off work, Lete stopped by to help get his father into bed. By Thursday, that track record had been broken. He helped with the transfer to the chair that morning but didn't show up as promised at night, leaving his mother and wife to change his father's diaper and attempt to clean JP with an awkward sponge bath while he remained molded into his chair. There he sat throughout the night.

Friday morning, Lete didn't follow Fran on her drive over to watch JP, saying it was a waste of time, since his father was already in the chair. He said he'd help move JP to the bed after work, but he never showed up. Eunice decided JP wasn't going anywhere, so she followed Fran home in the Studebaker. She wanted to have it out with Lete. They arrived to an empty house—the boys were nowhere to be seen, and they assumed Lete was at a bar. When Eunice called for Lete in the morning, Fran handed him the phone and then listened to him shout at his mother to get off his back. He told Eunice that Fran had to take care of her own chores this weekend, screamed that he'd help with the transfer Monday night, then slammed the phone down.

After ending the phone call with her sister-in-law, Marie told Henry that she thought Eunice and Fran might have to forgo the chair altogether in favor of the bed. They'd have to move JP once more, and that wouldn't happen until Henry visited or Lete had a change of heart. Marie asked him if there was anything he could do to help the two women.

When they finished dinner, Henry spent some time alone in the garage. About an hour later, he emerged and suggested to Marie an idea that she embraced and encouraged him to share with Eunice. He thought he could jury-rig a lift that two people could manage, thereby avoiding accidental injury to either patient or caregivers.

On the phone, Eunice thanked him and said she wanted to give it a try—she didn't know what else to do. During his lunch break on Monday, Henry went to a scrap yard and then stopped by the shop of a welder friend. With the backseat flattened and the cargo space loaded, he drove the station wagon to Rochester the following weekend, bringing the welded metal frame, along with a canvas harness and a converted block and tackle. He hoped the casters in the bottom of the frame would enable them to transport the patient between the bed and the chair in the front room.

After some jiggering in the dining room, the contraption seemed up to the job. Before he headed back to Schenectady, Henry helped Eunice get JP into bed, where he'd stay until Fran came over Monday morning.

Midday on Monday, Eunice called Marie to tell her how relieved she was. She and Fran had been able to negotiate the transfer by themselves. Eunice asked her to please tell Henry how grateful she was for everything. Then she made comments that halted Marie's breath: "Lete's worthless. Fran does the best she can, but I'd be up shit's creek without you and Henry."

CHAPTER SIXTEEN

E ven during the snowbound depths of winter, Henry had driven to Rochester at least twice each month over the course of the past year, which gave Eunice and Fran a much-needed helping hand and some welcome breaks. Although it had been a tough year for the two Rochester women, he told Marie that life there seemed to have settled into predictable patterns.

Marie always called her sister-in-law on the heels of each of Henry's visits, so she knew that Gunnar and Lars rode their bikes to school when the weather permitted; otherwise, they'd trudge on foot to avoid truancy, which was their natural bent. After school let out, they'd ride or walk to Gramma's house and create chaos until Eunice came home from work. On weekends, Eunice would take over full-time, save getting Fran's help transferring JP a couple of times each day. As for her job at the laundry, Eunice had no problem getting Saturdays off but felt the financial hit of a six-day workweek being reduced to five. Whenever there was a school vacation or shutdown day, Fran brought the boys with her. Gunnar and Lars would often not even go inside. Where they went, she didn't wish to imagine; their actions were hidden from parental view, as might be expected from pubescent boys who were granted any latitude. Marie told Henry that she thought it was a recipe for disaster, given the ingredients.

It had been a year since she and the twins had last visited Rochester. Given that Mother's Day was Sunday, Marie had called Fran a few days earlier to get the latest. She didn't want to surprise the kids—or herself—if things had taken a turn for the worse. Fran reported that everything remained the same and that Eunice was looking forward to their visit on Sunday. She had mandated that Fran take a well-deserved break after they got JP into bed on Friday evening. He could rest there through Saturday night. She could take better care of him when he was lying down and would move him to the chair soon after Henry arrived with his family on Sunday. Eunice had invited Fran to come for Mother's Day lunch but insisted that in the meantime she try to get some rest. Don't worry about JP, she said.

Before their call ended, Marie asked, "Fran, since you're not going to be there Saturday, should we volunteer to drive up a day earlier to help out?"

"That's kind of you, Marie. Frankly, I think Eunice might want a little time alone before seeing everyone on Mother's Day. It's been a strenuous year."

"You must be exhausted," Marie said. "How's Eunice holding up?"

"She hasn't been herself lately."

"I can only imagine how tired she must be, too."

"Not so much tired," Fran responded. "She seems . . . weak."

Burp.

The steering wheel jerked under Henry's grip, the station wagon swerved, and Marie bumped against the passenger-side door.

"Leo! What do you say?" she demanded, as she pushed herself off the window crank that had been jammed into her fore-arm.

The boy sighed. "Excuse me."

"He's laughing, Mom."

"It's gas from the root beer And, I was only smiling, not laughing. The gas made me smile, that's all."

"There's no excuse for a belch that loud, young man. It al-most caused your father to drive off the road. Use your head, Leo."

"Sorry. Do you think Gramma Eunice will have any root beer?"

"She bought some last year, remember? Anyway, I thought you liked the grape soda she had."

"Yeah, but now I like root beer a lot better. She'll have orange for Rita, I bet. Can we stop and get some more root beer? Please?"

Henry glanced into the rearview mirror. "We're almost there, Leo. If Gramma doesn't have any root beer, you and Rita can walk down to the corner store and get some. Okay?"

"I guess." Leo turned to confirm his accomplice. "Rita, you'll go, right?"

"Maybe. But you better stop burping in here if you want me to do anything. Your breath smells worse than your stinky sneak-ers."

The fact that the store in question would be closed on Sun-day was lost on her children. Henry knew better, but he wasn't himself today. Wanting the drive to end, Marie waved it off. Everyone was anxious, and she needed to get the twins settled down before they got to the house.

"Okay, kids, we're getting close. Read your books and leave each other alone for the rest of the drive."

"Comic books don't count, do they, Mom?"

"He's fine, Rita. Let's just calm down and have a little quiet before we get there." She calibrated the remaining drive time against the approaching scenery. "How long, Henry?"

"Not even fifteen minutes," he responded.

"Hear that, kids? Let's button our lips for fifteen minutes. Got it?"

"Got it" came the forlorn chorus, as the twins lowered eyes toward their respective reads.

As the car slowed to the curb, Leo gripped the handle next to his elbow. He flung open the door, jumped from the station wagon, sprinted toward the house, and ran up the stairs onto the front porch. The other three exited the Nomad. Henry stretched. Rita straightened her dress and followed her mother's eyes toward the porch. "He's going to pee his pants, Mom."

"Rita, don't you say a word. Let him get inside, please."

"So, I can't call him a root beer float again?"

"No. He did drink way too much root beer, but don't make him laugh or yell. The last thing any of us needs right now is an accident."

Leo shouted, "Mom, no one's answering!" He writhed as he tapped a wild dance atop what the twins had once called the "not welcome" mat. He rapped his knuckles on the wooden door in obvious desperation while, with the thumb of his other hand, he pressed the doorbell's button over and over.

"Leo, stop! Gramma's heard you by now. She'll only be a minute." If not as mean as her kids had once thought, the Gramma Eunice whom Marie expected would be stern with her grandson if he was unruly. She had had plenty of practice with Gunnar and Lars.

"Mom, I can't hold it!"

Book in hand, Rita outran her mother to Leo's side. Marie arrived just in time to grab the girl's elbow before Rita could drive her wiggling fingers into her brother's armpit. Marie knew a single tickle could trigger a flood. "Rita! I'm not kidding. Knock it off!"

"He just went at the gas station."

"Rita, please! Go sit on the new porch swing and read. Behave. It's Mother's Day, for goodness' sake." Marie caught herself before she said, *Do it for Gramma Eunice.* Her mother-in-law had had a horrific year. With each of their brief phone calls, Marie's heart had softened toward Eunice. The day Henry had surprised her and set up the porch swing as a gift, she had hugged her thanks, bringing him to tears. Soon after he arrived home in Schenectady that evening, he admitted that he had pulled over to blow his nose and wipe his eyes before he took the ticket at the thruway tollbooth.

Every morning, Fran came over to the house and they "got to work" before Eunice went to the laundry. The extended conversations between Marie and Fran filled in the details of the strain that had blunted their mother-in-law's characteristic intensity. Fran said that by the time Eunice came home at night, she looked like a wisp of her former self, and that she seemed crushed by a life that had grown too heavy. In truth, Eunice had been acting as if her body had been broken. Yet those crystalline blue eyes persisted, Fran said. Whenever she looked into Eunice's eyes, she saw defiance—a refusal to submit to any dilemma, despite overwhelming challenges.

Eyes watering, Leo tapped his knees together, like an organ grinder's monkey clashing tiny cymbals. As if he were breaking news to his father, who approached with a vase of cut flowers, Leo yelled down at the front lawn, "Dad, I really gotta pee!"

Henry deposited the vase on the bottom tread. "Run, Leo!

Follow me." As the boy leaped down the porch steps, Henry shouted over his shoulder, "Marie, wait here with Rita! We're going around to the back door."

Rita folded her book over her index finger, then, rising from the swing, stepped to the window and gawked inside. "Mom, look! Gramma's lying on the floor!"

Marie stepped next to her daughter and peered through the sheer lace curtain. The TV stand was turned toward JP's bed in the dining room. Eunice was splayed out on the floor in front of the television, which was on, but there was no picture, just a mash of black-and-white sparkles. She didn't move; her body appeared stiff, like a statue that teenage vandals had tipped over in a local park.

Henry opened the front door from the inside. He held his hand up to stop them from charging into the house. Marie knew before he whispered into her ear. Blocking Rita, she stood at the open door and kept her eyes on the staircase. She fought not to spy into the front room.

When Leo descended, Marie could see that he seemed confused by his quiet father, waiting at the bottom of the staircase. Other than the muted slaps of his sneaker's rubber soles on each step, the TV's static was the only sound in the house. The putrid odors that had gagged Marie upon entry rose up the stairwell to meet him. With a quick index finger, Leo pulled out his collar and dipped his nose inside his T-shirt. He found his mother's eyes, and she beckoned him to her while hoping she could hold his gaze.

One hand on the banister, the other pressing his handkerchief to his own nostrils, Henry stood looking up at Leo. He waved the boy down to floor level as he shifted his own body to block Leo's view. "Let's go back outside, son," Henry instructed, cupping his hand around the back of the boy's neck and spinning him away from the grisly scene.

"Mom, why're you still on the porch?" Leo asked, releasing his breath. She shook her head and cried. Leo inhaled. The odors of an unattended JP and a decomposing grandmother overpowered the boy, who then vomited in the foyer.

The pleasant scent of the fresh grave wafted past the four children standing on the green grass at its edge. Marie heard Henry take a slow, deep breath. She wondered what he smelled. While they'd been dating, Henry had waxed on about the scents unleashed when they plowed the fields in the spring and the earth opened to receive the seeds that promised bounty at harvest. The dates on nearby markers indicated that the soil here had hibernated without interruption for well over a century. After the trees had been cleared and the field consecrated as holy ground, no blade or root had pierced the spot. Whatever had fallen here had long ago decomposed and fed the humus that now infiltrated the nostrils of the living who came today to bury their dead.

Gunnar went first, after he ripped the shovel from his brother's grip. He poured dirt down onto the casket, then drove the sharp tip of the spade at Lars's shoe. Lars jumped back to save his toes, before grabbing the handle and poking the blade at his laughing sibling. Fran stood close by and moved in to control her sons. When Lars won the tug-of-war with Gunnar, she received the butt of the handle in the stomach. Lete smacked Lars in the back of the head, then staggered back to his perch and planted his buttocks against the headstone of an adjoining plot. He stared down at the far wall of his mother's grave, her casket lowered out of view. He held a pint bottle in one hand and with the other wiped the thigh of his pant leg.

Lars scooped up and deposited into the grave a minimal amount of dirt, then dropped the tool on the ground. Rita picked up the shovel at her feet, cupped a small ceremonial load onto its tip, and poured the dirt down on top of the casket.

Distracted by strangers visiting a far-off grave, Leo jerked when the handle touched his arm. "Leo, take it! It's your turn," Rita scolded in a whisper as she passed the shovel.

Marie cleared her throat to pull the boy's attention back to their own deceased. As Leo recovered and scooped up his shovelful, she gazed over to where he'd been looking. In an older section of the cemetery, two somber figures stood over a weathered white marker. Shoulder to shoulder, they faced the mourners standing around Eunice's open grave, as if drawn by primal curiosity to a stranger's farewell. The faces of the two men were up, angled away from the gravestone of their own loved one. Unlike the oily black crows cawing in the oak trees scattered throughout the graveyard, they were respectful observers.

Two men of equal size, they looked familiar. But that was impossible, she thought. She knew no one else in Rochester—only these people gathered here at her mother-in-law's gravesite. Why did the strangers seem captivated? Was it simply the magnetism of a life having just ended? Perhaps they hadn't attended the burial of their own loved one and were making a vicarious grasp at the event they'd missed. *It doesn't matter*, she thought. Whatever had brought them here, they now stood gazing across the field of markers at Eunice's service, their fallen arms as limp as worn ropes.

Out of place, these two men seemed. Maybe it was the old pickup truck parked near where they stood. The block letters and numbers on its white license plate—not New York's orange—were illegible from such a distance, but they weren't locals, she surmised from the scant information.

The dirt from Leo's deposit crashed onto the coffin. He looked around, holding the shovel. No one moved to take it from him. A breeze passed through the gathered as the insistent caws of the crows accompanied the sound of one person crying.

Marie turned to follow the low sobs back to Fran. The boys would be in high school soon. She wondered how long her sister-in-law would stay with Lete. In a few years, she concluded, Fran would be gone. Marie asked herself who then would care enough to stand over Eunice's grave. Someone to clean things up a bit, offer a flower or a prayer? Would there be any regular callers, or even such rare visitors as those two far-off men? She wondered if they had paused to take note of the sky today, closed their eyes to feel the weather, licked their lips to taste the air, or registered any of the various notes of life played out here during their visit, other than the distant spectacle of Eunice's burial. Would there be anyone like those men to commune with her deceased mother-in-law? Would someone speak down toward the grass to tell deaf, decayed ears about the day's weather, if only to have such thoughts fade between visiting Eunice's grave and their own?

"Mom?" Leo pleaded, holding out the shovel for her like a burden he couldn't bear.

"Oh, thank you, dear," she said. She took it, then drove the blade into the soft pile of soil. Muffled by the dirt already accumulated on top of the casket, her small load landed, then slid down along the side of the wooden box onto the grave's cool pan. *Who's next?* she wondered, as she turned toward the group. Fran nodded and reached out. Neither Lete nor Henry seemed to notice. The half-brothers Eunice had borne stared into the hole. One mourning son sipped from his pint bottle and mumbled toward his mother's grave. The other, Marie knew, mourned not only a mother lost but the death of her long-hidden love for him and its brief reveal.

Henry paid the preacher, told the mortician he'd speak to his brother about the balance due, and asked him if he should tip the diggers. After handing a few bucks to the men standing by the backhoe, Henry turned to walk in the direction of the two remaining vehicles. Marie heard him call out to Lete.

Several steps ahead of Fran and the boys, Lete teetered toward his Pontiac, ignoring his half-brother's voice. He discarded his empty pint bottle on the grass of the nearest grave, then reached inside the Bonnie. Braced against the door frame, he once again snubbed Henry's plea. The seal on Lete's second bottle of whiskey proved a difficult puzzle and dominated his attention. Problem solved, he dropped the wrapper on the ground, pulled out the bottle's stopper, and took a swig. After replacing the cork, he belched, slid beneath the steering wheel, slammed the door, and started his engine.

Drawn by the draft of the departing hearse, Eunice's sons drove their respective families to the cemetery's entrance. Behind the yellow Bonneville, the blue-and-white station wagon was the last in the scant procession to pull away from the gravesite. Lete stopped in between the two brick pillars that formed the gateway. Marie was thankful, thinking he'd paused to check oncoming traffic. Then his door swung open. It bounced back on its hinges, and he blocked its recoil with an angry slap as he rose to exit.

Lete sprayed a saliva-laced rant into the Nomad. As he spat incomprehensible words at Henry through the rolled-down win-

dow, Marie kept her gaze locked on the windshield. She squeezed
her husband's arm as she looked back at the twins, whose eyes
were also averted. In a slow, quiet voice, Henry responded to his
brother's vitriol with a request to meet at the house to talk to the
nurse about JP.

Lete stumbled backward, then, leaning forward again,
lobbed preemptive curses through the open window. Marie felt
Henry's arm muscles tense as Lete swung around and crashed his
rear end against his brother's door. Henry grabbed the door handle, but Lete shoved off, then stumbled the few feet back to the
Bonneville.

"Daddy, why's he always so angry?" Rita asked.

Henry held his eyes shut for a long pause, then opened them
and swiveled his head to look both ways. He pulled out behind
the Bonneville without answering his daughter. Marie slid closer,
rubbed his shoulder, then turned to address the kids. "Honey,
Uncle Lete just buried his mother. I think he's had a little too
much to drink, too."

"Why are we going over to Gramma's house, anyway? Can't
we just go back to Howard Johnson's?"

"Yeah, Daddy. You said we could go swimming in the pool,"
Leo said.

"We have to eat lunch first, kids," Marie said, in as matter-of-
fact a voice as she could muster. With widened eyes and slight
head shakes, she implored the twins not to aggravate their father.
Then, switching back to her feigned calm demeanor, she said,
"After Daddy talks to the nurse, we can all go swimming."

At the next intersection, Lete turned in the direction opposite his parents' house. Rubber burned as he floored the Pontiac.
He then extended his left arm through the open driver's-side
window with his hand clenched in a one-finger farewell.

The Studebaker was parked in the driveway in front of the closed garage door. The nurse waved as the Nomad pulled in and stopped behind JP's car. She was sitting on the porch swing with a cardboard shoebox in her lap. Henry didn't notice, but Marie knew. Fran had pulled her aside at the cemetery. Before the funeral, Lete had been rifling through the house and found the shoebox on the top shelf of Eunice's bedroom closet. Among its inventory was an envelope she had left for Henry. Fran reported that Lete had torn it open, then tossed it into the trash bin once he determined that it contained nothing of value to him. She'd retrieved the envelope, stuffed it back into the shoebox, and asked the nurse to give the container to Henry when he stopped by.

"Mom, do we have to go inside?" Rita asked.

"No, you kids can sit on the porch swing."

The nurse handed the shoebox to Henry and told him what Fran had requested. He said that he'd be a few minutes and then would help her with JP.

He took the box to the top step and sat on the edge of the porch. He motioned for Marie to join him.

"Do you want some privacy?"

"No, darling. Please, sit."

The contents were sparse. An old savings account passbook sat atop a yellowed wedding certificate. Digging deeper, he found a stack of weathered black-and-white photographs bundled together with a rubber band. It snapped off at first touch, indicating that Lete—no slave to nostalgia—had not stopped to ponder images of the family's history. At the bottom of the box sat a manila envelope with "For Henry" printed across the front in his mother's bold hand.

As Fran had warned, it had been ripped open. Henry felt the lumpy envelope, then spread apart its torn mouth. Inside was a wrinkled photograph of his stiff-backed mother as a stern-looking young woman, two birth certificates for unnamed twin boys, and a musty red bandanna.

After he and the nurse had attended JP, Henry drove the family back to the motel. Marie called Fran to ask when she would be back to relieve the nurse; they'd come over to say goodbye and discuss the schedule for the upcoming week. She then went poolside to relax in a chaise lounge and watch the kids frolic in the shallow end with Henry. When their play had been exhausted, they toweled off; then the whole family got ice cream cones.

"Mom, can we stop for another ice cream later?" Leo asked.

"Please," Rita added, poking her brother with her elbow.

"We'll see, kids," Marie said. "We've got to swing by the house again before we get on the thruway. Maybe we can get burgers and fries on the way home. You can have a cone if you eat your meal."

"Yay!" Leo shouted.

"Why do we have to go back to the house?" Rita challenged.

"The nurse has to go home, and Daddy wants to make sure Aunt Fran's there before we leave. It won't take long." *If Fran's there,* she thought. Now that Eunice was in the ground, Fran's fears seemed to be manifest: Eunice's past had become Fran's present.

The Nomad pulled past a pickup truck that sat at the curb where Marie had hoped to see Fran's car parked. White license plates. The same truck she'd seen at the cemetery. Its cabin was vacant. The street was almost devoid of cars, and there were plenty of parking spots, yet it sat right in front of Eunice's house.

Henry drove into the driveway and rolled up behind JP's green Studebaker. As he rose from the driver's seat, he glanced toward the street, drawn by the presence of the weathered pickup.

No one was on the porch swing and Marie doubted anyone who could avoid it would have entered the house. She glanced about to see if someone was approaching on foot; the sidewalks were deserted. It might take longer than she had intimated to the twins.

"Hey, that's the truck that was at the cemetery," Leo proclaimed. Marie's eyes went again to the white plates on the battered bumper: Idaho. Sprinting across the lawn, Leo ran to the pickup as they all approached to take a closer look. Toolboxes and a couple of duffel bags huddled in the open bay. Cut grass and other rural debris had been baked into its flatbed. Marie recalled the story of the kidnapping and wondered, *Wasn't the reservation in Idaho?*

Henry gave Marie a knowing look, then slipped his arm into the crook of her elbow and escorted her away from the vehicle. They turned in silence and walked, slump-shouldered, toward the house. As they ascended the wooden steps with leaden feet, the nurse opened the front door with a serious expression on her face.

"You have visitors, Mr. Ritter."

Marie steeled herself and asked the kids to wait on the porch swing. When she and Henry stepped inside, JP was sitting in the easy chair with his eyes protruding in a blank stare. Illuminating the grotesque, the glow from the TV bathed the old man's droopy face. The volume was off.

Two men of equal height and similar build faced Henry. They were used to the outdoors, and the sun had turned the skin of both a deep, ruddy color. The two visitors stared at her husband through dark brown eyes set in round faces above high, prominent cheekbones. The younger man was Henry's identical twin—identical except for his long black hair. Undeniable—the three men were father and sons, their faces separated only by years. The older man's straight white hair, striped with gray strands, fell beyond shoulder length. He held a faded red bandanna in one hand, fingering the material like worry beads.

CHAPTER SEVENTEEN

—·—

D ressed for the storm in foul-weather gear, Sheriff George Mc-
Cheyne stood in pouring rain as the first tow truck pulled
the convertible back from the point of collision so that both of
the two-man ambulance crews could get to the victims in the
other vehicle. His deputy had been first on the scene and radioed
that the couple in the blue station wagon had been killed upon
impact—a conclusion the sheriff had just reached, too, while trying to keep his stomach under control. The woman on the passenger side had been pregnant when Lete Erikson's Bonneville
plowed their car into one of the brick pillars marking the cemetery entrance. Brown, shoulder-length, blood-splattered hair
wrapped her smashed skull. Her round belly appeared to have
been unaffected by the turmoil. The fatal accident had occurred
less than an hour ago. McCheyne wondered how long the tiny
heart had continued to beat.

The sheriff's deputy had already retrieved their driver's licenses from the wreck, but McCheyne was waiting to hear back
from Dispatch about cross-checking the address on the vehicle's
temporary registration. They said it might have to wait until tomorrow, when the DMV offices were open. The Chevrolet Impala
station wagon was brand new, with less than one thousand miles
on the odometer. The original window sticker was folded up and

stored in the glove box. It noted the color as Marina Blue. New car for a growing family, McCheyne assumed.

Their licenses indicated that they weren't Rochester residents, so he might need to call Albany to get a New York state trooper to chase down next of kin. The sheriff worried that the unborn baby would not have been the couple's first and only child. He said a private prayer that no children had been orphaned by the crash. "Mother's Day, for chrissakes," he mumbled aloud, then cringed at how he had closed his heartfelt petition.

The rotating beams of the light bar signaled that his deputy's car was returning. Hit-and-run had been their mutual assumption. "No sign of him up that way, Sheriff," the deputy said, speaking into the rain through the half-rolled-down window of the patrol car. His windshield wipers were spitting at the sheriff, who leaned closer to hear above the whir.

"All right. Take a lap in the other direction. He's not going far on foot. He hitched a ride or is hiding out someplace. Did you see where he landed?"

When the deputy had radioed Dispatch, he had reported his suspicion that Lete had been catapulted from the convertible. McCheyne concurred when he first got on-site and peered inside the Bonneville: Its cockpit was compressed, the steering wheel less than the width of a fist from the driver's seat. Lete hadn't stepped away from the collision—he had flown over it.

"Yeah. Got tossed about twenty yards into the grass over there. Found a shoe and this," the deputy said, as he poked a waterlogged leather wallet through the window.

The winch snapped its cable tight. Metallic screeches cut through the din of the storm. Rain smacked Lete's crumpled Pontiac; yellow paint had chipped off at the creases, exposing silver streaks of bare metal. The haunting sounds invaded Mc-

Cheyne's ears, and memories of all the bad wrecks he'd seen
rushed back.

It would take the salvage crew some time to clear access to
the gravel driveway. The sheriff decided he'd better walk inside,
beyond the wreckage, to take a look around. The sheets of rain
were unrelenting as he slogged down the driveway to its mid-
point, where he stopped. The roar made it sound as if he stood
inside the eye of a circular waterfall. As he gazed about, everything in view appeared blurred. He thought he was alone in the
cemetery and decided to trudge back to his patrol car. Then he
spotted a lone figure resting his backside against a marker deep
inside the grid of gravesites.

After an involuntary airborne escape from the violent crash,
Erikson had managed to locate his mother's grave. He wore a
soaked white T-shirt pasted onto his pale torso. One of his shoes
was missing; his exposed sock was wet and no longer white,
thanks to grass stains and muck.

No quick movements toward Erikson, the sheriff told himself,
recalling firsthand experience with the man's temper and history
with the bottle. The dripping peace officer stared at Lete's injury:
a compound fracture—the radius bone of Lete's left arm stuck
out; clumps of bloody flesh hung off jagged shards. McCheyne
grabbed the walkie-talkie strapped onto his chest, hoping his
deputy was in range so he could radio for another ambulance.
The deputy picked up and told him the ambulance would be
there in no time. *Thank God,* McCheyne thought. They'd know
better how to dodge an angry poke from the infamous drunk.

An empty pint bottle rested on top of Lete's mother's marker.
A vase of fresh-cut flowers sat in the grass next to the marble. The
sheriff read the carved dates; the Erikson woman had died a year
ago, almost to the day. He turned to look at Lete.

"That arm looks pretty bad," the sheriff said from under the runoff spilling over his plastic-covered, broad-brimmed hat. No response; Lete just gawked down at the grass that led to his mother's gravestone. Mixing with the booze, shock must have worked its way through his brain, McCheyne concluded. "Lete, you hear me? I said that arm looks bad."

Lete lifted his head in slow motion and squinted into the rainfall. "Sheriff, glad to see ya. I fucked up my arm pretty bad."

"Yeah, I can see that," the sheriff said, determining that the broken arm was Erikson's only apparent injury, though internal bleeding could well be in play. No external sign of head trauma, but he assumed Lete had suffered a concussion, too, given the brutality of the crash and how far he had been catapulted. *Let the doctors figure all that out*, the sheriff said to himself. McCheyne had seen his share of gruesome collisions over the course of his career, but never before had he seen someone survive, much less walk away from, anything this bad.

"Lete, I gotta arrest you for drunk driving and the crash."

"Huh?"

"You wrecked your car, Lete."

"Just got my Bonnie paid off."

"Lete, the two people in that station wagon you ran into are dead."

"Station wagon?" Erikson's voice trailed off. When he shifted his position on the gravestone, his arm moved. He shrieked and winced in pain.

"Why'd you have your top down?"

"Those punk kids asked me the same damn thing."

"What kids?"

"In the pickup. Back there at the red light. Laughing at me about my convertible. What's the point of having a ragtop if you can't lower it when the weather gets nice? Been a shit-cold winter, Sheriff."

"Was it raining when you put the roof down?"

"Hell no. Only drizzlin'. Nice day. Put down the top to go visit my mother. Just like I did every Mother's Day since I got my Bonnie. Gonna keep right on doing it, too. A little drizzle ain't no rain, Sheriff."

"Well, you got tossed out of your car, Lete, when you plowed into the station wagon."

"Station wagon?" Lete repeated.

The sheriff took out Lete's mushy wallet and extracted his driver's license. He brought it underneath his hat and out of the rain. McCheyne wiped a thumb across the license to squeegee away the beads. He brought it close to his eyes, then pressed ahead. "This still your address?"

"Naw. My old lady kicked me out. Living at my father's house."

Down the country road, the unnecessary sirens faded as the two ambulances carried the dead couple away. The departing ambulances must have driven past their colleagues heading this way. The rising wail of a siren announced that Lete's emergency medical team was fast approaching. The sheriff replaced the driver's license and handed the waterlogged wallet to Lete, who grimaced as he struggled to insert it into the seat pocket of his wet pants. The siren's volume peaked, then trailed off as the crew parked the ambulance on the shoulder near the crash site.

"Does your father live nearby? You want me to swing by and tell him?"

Lete laughed and then said, "You can tell him anything you want, Sheriff, but he won't get it. Like talking to a tree stump. Bad stroke."

"How about contacting your wife? You still married?"

"Been served. Don't say nothing to that fat bitch. Both my boys are in juvie because she's such a shitty mother. Not like my dear mother there," Lete said. With his other hand, he wiped wet hair out of his eyes, then nodded at the grave.

Water peeled off McCheyne when he stepped out of the way as the two-man ambulance crew scrambled to Lete's side. *Let them do their jobs*, he mused.

"Mister, let us take a look at that arm," one of the men said.

"Sure thing, Doc. I fucked it up pretty bad, huh?"

"Yeah, you sure did, but we're gonna take good care of you, Mister. Breathe out slowly. This'll prick a little."

"Shit, I don't like needles, Doc."

"Well, you won't like us messing with your arm if we don't give you this first." The man administered the shot of morphine before he had finished his sentence. Practiced hands then immobilized Lete's arm inside a splint.

The man held the broken limb parallel to the ground as he and his colleague guided Lete off his perch and onto his feet. Rain-rippled puddles undulated throughout the cemetery's gravel driveway. Together, they all started a slow, weaving walk in the direction of the ambulance parked outside the cemetery's entrance. "So, you came out here to visit your mother's grave on Mother's Day?" the sheriff asked, as he walked alongside Lete and his two handlers.

The morphine had started to kick in, lifting the patient into good spirits. "Sheriff, let me tell ya something. Long as I remember, I always had a drink with my dear mother every Mother's Day. Just 'cause she's dead 'n gone don't mean I can't share a Mother's Day toast with her. Get what I mean?"

"Yeah, Lete, I get what you mean," McCheyne said, squeezing the ambulance door hard.

The wind had died down, its whistle replaced by the water's droning. In the right moment, McCheyne thought, in the right setting, nothing seemed more serene than nature's steady thrum —background music apropos for a graveyard. The rain should continue for several hours. He hoped it would cleanse the scene. Washed anew, the dead could return to their sleep and be left once more to rest in peace.

"I'd prefer it, but I don't think you should cuff his free wrist to the gurney, Sheriff," the driver said.

Procedure warranted at least one handcuff, but such an injury overrode that protocol. McCheyne could see that the man wasn't happy about driving the patient—a drunk who had yet to realize he'd been arrested for manslaughter—secured only by gurney straps. "We've got two patrol cars. I'll send my deputy behind you. Just pull over if he starts acting up. I'm gonna stay here till the site's cleared."

"Okay, Sheriff," he said, then sent the back door swinging fast toward Lete's feet. The driver hunched over and circled the ambulance in a light-footed prance. McCheyne smiled as he watched the man act as if he could avoid getting wetter. The sheriff shook his head as the driver hopped into the cab and pulled the door shut. The engine turned over, and the wipers engaged. The flashers came on, then the siren.

As his deputy followed, the ambulance pulled out past the crumpled Bonneville as it was being chained to the bed of the tow truck. "*Only drizzlin',*" McCheyne recalled from Lete's rambling explanation. *Until the booze and the drugs wear off, there's no need to rush over to the hospital to conduct a full interrogation,* McCheyne thought. Lete's driving with the ragtop down had saved his life.

"Sheriff, are we good to go?" the salvage driver asked.

"Yeah, go ahead and pull out. I'll see you down at the salvage yard in a few minutes."

McCheyne exhaled a solemn sigh as he inspected the point of collision. The eight-foot-high-by-two-foot-wide brick column at the far side of the entrance had been toppled. He kicked broken bricks out of the way. Glass crinkled under his boots as he stepped across the wreck's litter.

"Can we get in there, Sheriff?"

"Oh, sorry." McCheyne hopped to the side to let the second tow truck maneuver into position. The wreckers worked their craft, unfazed by the pouring rain. Unlike the last ambulance crew, they seemed to understand that they couldn't get more soaked. He knew from experience that as long as the grips were solid, it wouldn't matter where they placed the hooks for the winch. With a broken axle and three flat tires, the second wrecked vehicle wasn't going to roll anywhere.

The winch stopped. As the salvage crew made adjustments to their rigging, the sounds of the storm swamped the sheriff's eardrums.

McCheyne cringed when the hoist reengaged. The cable grew taut and, with an invasive metallic strum, cut a discord through the timeless chorus of waterfall. Loose bricks cascaded with the rain shower as the winch pulled back the crushed, blood-splattered wreckage. A rogue gust of wind fought the downpour and swept a descending wave across the crumpled blue station wagon scraping up onto the flatbed of the tow truck.

CHAPTER EIGHTEEN

M other's Day—it had been a year since Uncle Lete was arrested
for manslaughter. A year when Grampa Joseph had visited
them twice in Schenectady. Today he was driving home after staying two full weeks. Rita and Leo had both wanted to drive with him
to Rochester on the family trip to visit Gramma's grave. Daddy and
Mom followed in the station wagon, the blue-and-white '55 Chevy
Nomad—the only family car the children had ever known. They'd
get off the thruway at the same exit, but their parents would drive
over to pick up Aunt Fran, before meeting them at the cemetery.
Leo knew that Uncle Lete was in the maximum-security prison in
Auburn and had lobbied Grampa to see it. They had plenty of time
for the side trip. The thought gave Rita the creeps, but she went
along with the plan for her brother's sake.

The gentle bounce of Rita's head against the window reminded her of her mother. For as long as she could remember,
whenever they'd driven anywhere as a family, that had always
been Mom's seat: in the front, on the passenger side, where she
would rest until she sensed Daddy wanted her near or she wanted
to be near him. She'd slide over and set her head on his shoulder.
Rita imagined her mother's pleasant purr, the happy moan she
always made when she settled next to him on those trips. The girl
closed her eyes, saw her mother and father as if she were in the

backseat of the Nomad; then a second soft murmur left her lips, like a kiss blown into the glass.

Without raising her head, Rita opened her eyes and let the window continue to lift her off its surface, then catch her, tossing her up and down in benign, rapid beats. There was no backseat, no place for her and Leo to sit other than on the pickup's bench seat. Its tired springs creaked and poked up from beneath the cushion's cracked upholstery like poles supporting a sagging tent.

The twins sat next to their grandfather as he drove westward in the direction of Idaho. In four days' drive, maybe five, he expected to be home. His home, not theirs—a home their father had never visited. Next summer, the whole family would drive out— that was what Daddy said. Drive cross-country, stop at Yellowstone to see Old Faithful leap into the air on schedule, then visit Grampa Joseph in the village he loved. They had met Uncle Jackson two years ago but had seen him only that once, the day Gramma was buried. Grampa said their uncle might be able to get time off work and drive up from Boise for a whole week during their vacation. Rita knew that was what Daddy hoped for. Jackson was the first attorney from their village, one of three from the entire reservation. Rita wanted to meet his wife and their only child, a girl born two years before her and Leo, an older cousin she expected to be far afield of Gunnar and Lars.

"You were asleep. Or were you just resting?" Grampa asked.

She cringed from the cramps in her stomach but smiled for her grandfather as she turned toward the steering wheel. Last month, her first period had arrived. It hadn't been as bad as she feared. Mom's cramps had always seemed a lot worse. Rita stretched and looked about. "I think I did fall asleep. Where are we, Grampa?"

Leo piped up, "Almost to the jail. Grampa said it's the next exit."

The bent knuckles of her index fingers curled into the sockets of Rita's drowsy eyes. After a prolonged yawn, she scanned the cab's interior, noting telltale signs of time spent on the reservation: the aged wooden handle on Grampa's cold metal hammer that showed the dents and dings from jobs completed; dust and bits from many a season's harvest—dried leaves and broken stalks; and a single burlap scrap torn from a sack caught long ago, seized by one of the truck's exposed barbs, the way the sliver of a wooden window frame had once snagged a bandanna. That was her favorite tale about Grampa Joseph.

She looked up and to her left. The sunlight caused her brother's lip to reveal the downy fuzz that he would one day shave in hopes of stampeding the hairs of a burgeoning mustache. He'd finally grown this year, as Mom had promised—an inch taller than Rita and eating as much as two grown men, swallowing his food past a voice box that, with every spoken word of late, croaked his imminent change into manhood.

The driver offered Rita an interesting study. He sat next to his grandson, whose facial muscles were relaxed, portraying a sense of safety. The teenage boy focused his eyes through the windshield on the landscape racing toward them. Leo seemed calmed by the man whose cotton work clothes were as thin as veils, faded from repeated cycles of sweat to soap suds. Grampa's white ponytail flapped in and out of the window as the wind whipped it from side to side. The steering wheel vibrated in his callused hands. She wondered if Mom would agree that they looked alike. Maybe not as much as Daddy and Grampa, but, from the side, Leo displayed the same chiseled bones.

It wasn't an unpleasant potpourri that had crinkled her nose as she inhaled the trace scents in an old man's pickup, smells hinting at his habits of life and labor. The dust must have caused her to sneeze. From the other side of the window, the freshness of the sunny spring day teased her. The crank rolled in her hand; the glass slid down; then her arm, bent at the elbow, pressed on the sill as the wind swept up inside the sleeve of the last red dress her mother had bought her. Rita, too, had grown over the year since Uncle Lete had been arrested; she had newer clothes, but this was a dress she loved. It had become too tight, and she wouldn't be able to wear it to school in the fall. At the thought of it, a sad groan passed over her elbow into the breeze.

Once more, Rita closed her eyes and ignored her flailing hair. She winced and rubbed her stomach with her left hand. The wind's rush soothed her as she listened to the breeze accompanying the unfolding conversation inside the cab.

"Grampa?"

"Yes, Leo?"

"The story your grandfather told you—he said that *everybody* has two wolves, right?"

"Yup. That's what he told us."

"So, even Uncle Lete has two wolves?"

"Far as I know. There's a good wolf and a bad wolf within everyone, and they're constantly fighting each other for control of the person."

Curious, Rita rotated her head a few degrees and opened her left eye a slit. Her brother was looking into the windshield and had stretched his toes under the dashboard. The slit closed when she heard Leo's voice.

"Which one wins?"

With her eyes shut, Rita smiled and nodded when her grandfather said, "Whichever is fed the most." That was her second-favorite Grampa Joseph story.

"Does that mean some people end up with only one wolf?"

"Good question, Leo. That's exactly what my cousin Jackson asked our grandfather."

"What'd he say?"

"He said he didn't think so. He told us one wolf could grow so strong as to cower the other. But it's still in there, inside the person, waiting for a chance to take control."

Leo looked down at his hands.

"What's got your tongue, Leo?"

"Uncle Lete's bad wolf must've killed his good wolf. I don't see how it could still be alive."

"I've known some men that made me wonder, too. My older cousin Ellis, for many years, seemed as if his bad wolf roamed alone inside him. Then he changed. Stopped drinking. That one thing gave his good wolf a chance. Maybe it can happen to your uncle. You think?"

"Nope. I don't. Not after what he's done."

"Well, you're probably right, but I do like to think it's possible. Makes it a little easier to get along. You know, give a person a chance to change."

The cab grew quiet, except for the sounds of the tires and the air rushing past the open windows. Rita was happy that Leo had Grampa on their drive. They both did, but it was different, she thought; Leo was a boy. Rita wondered what it would be like if either of her grandmothers were alive. Another cramp—the strongest yet—grabbed her, and she thought more about Mom, about wanting to be near her as the pain surged.

"Still want me to drive by the prison? We've got plenty of time."

"I do, Grampa, but I don't think Rita does."

"I'm okay. It's not like we're going to visit him." The words slipped into the cab from the left side of her mouth as she held her chin on her folded arm and her gaze on the passing stripes of a planted field—raised rows of rich, dark soil with green sprouts lined up like birthday candles pointing toward the sky.

Grampa steered the pickup into the right lane, accompanied by the faint ticks of the turn signal. Rita read the exit sign's declaration of Weedsport and the nearby city that housed the convicts: Auburn.

As Grampa brought the pickup around the street corner, Leo gawked up at the gun tower. Like the slanted banks of a pharaoh's pyramid, gray cement walls tilted toward the prisoners on the other side. "Do you think he'll get out of there someday?" asked Leo.

Rita grumbled at the concrete fortress, "I hope not."

Twenty years. If he served the full sentence, when released he'd be older than Gramma had been when she died. Mom had told them that the soonest Uncle Lete could get out would be eight years, which meant he had more than another seven to go. After Rita had heard Mom's explanation of "good behavior," she had asked if the warden could make him stay longer if he continued his "bad behavior." The walls looked impenetrable. As they cruised by, she grew calmer, convinced he'd be in there for at least twenty.

The old truck rattled into the final turn, which would complete their lap around the prison. Grampa pulled away from the penitentiary and drove back toward the tollbooth. From prior trips along the New York State Thruway, Rita anticipated the upcoming exits—family markers—that would soon meet them. First Waterloo, then Geneva, where their father had grown up on Pa's brother's farm. They'd drive past towns where they had sometimes stopped for gas but never dawdled. She suspected that, just like on the Mother's Day trips with her parents, they'd reach their destination on the outskirts of Rochester in silence.

The difference between the pillars hadn't been evident as they approached the cemetery, where the two eight-foot-high stacks denoted the entrance. An overhead cloud passed its shadow, as dark as the blackened breath of a smokestack, across the bricks. The gloom masked both the old masonry and the new. By the time they'd driven off the road onto the gravel driveway, the cloud had moved on. Rita glanced out her window at the faded column on her right, then cast her gaze past Leo's frozen-straight-ahead stare and over the steering arms of their grandfather. The far pillar was made of unblemished bricks with mortar that appeared to be in motion. The cement looked fresh and soft, as if it were seeping from the crevices between the stacked vermillion blocks. She felt nauseous, then turned to match her brother's angle on the graveyard. He was searching for the marker where they'd soon set the vase of cut flowers wedged between luggage and tools in the back of the pickup. They'd leave the vase and half a dozen individual red roses—one for each of them in the cab, one for each of her parents, and one for Aunt Fran, whom Rita hadn't seen since Gramma's funeral almost two full years ago.

Grampa Joseph stopped on the gravel driveway as close to Gramma's gravesite as he could park. He turned to them and smiled, untied his ponytail, and shook his head. The breeze flew through the window and whipped his white hair around in a swirl, sending loose strands over his shoulders. He crooked his neck to relieve muscles strained from driving, then opened his door and stepped out.

As the trio walked up to the marble headstone, a murder of crows cawed from the trees lining the far end of the cemetery. Finger-length grass had grown up like frilly trim along the edges of Gramma Eunice's memorial where the mower hadn't reached. Rita studied the nearby graves. Most of the tombstones were surrounded by the same border of skinny green blades. A few gravestones, those adorned by fresh flowers, seemed to have had the errant grass trimmed away by loving hands. Leo knelt. Without a word, she followed her brother's descent and, kneeling side by side, they cleared the base of their grandmother's marker.

Leo returned from his jaunt reading tombstones. "Just like you said, Grampa. All those little flags were just for one guy. He got killed in Vietnam last month."

How long will we have to stand here? Rita wondered. She stared back at the road through the gap between the brick pillars, wishing her parents would soon arrive with her aunt. Then she saw her family's blue-and-white station wagon. It slowed as her father negotiated the entrance, and Mom waved. Her head rested against Daddy's shoulder, and Rita felt relief that soon she could tell her mother about her cramps.

"Here they come," Rita announced. "Don't say anything about Gunnar and Lars, okay, Leo?"

"Why?" Leo asked. "I thought they're supposed to get out before Christmas. Isn't that what Aunt Fran told Mom?"

"Yeah, but they got caught burglarizing their own school. I think she must be pretty embarrassed. Right, Grampa?"

Grampa Joseph nodded his head while keeping his lips sealed. He glanced at Leo and waited for the boy's response.

"I'm not going to say anything," Leo said, as the Nomad slowed its roll over the gravel. The tires made popping sounds until the vehicle came to a stop in the driveway behind Grampa's pickup truck. Aunt Fran waved from the backseat; her fleshy arm jiggled next to a broad grin of once-crooked teeth that sparkled with metal braces as she aimed her perfect smile at the twins. The front doors swung open. Daddy hopped out, opened Aunt Fran's back door, and extended a hand inside to help her rise from the seat.

The two exchanged words that Rita couldn't hear. Her aunt—pale and far larger than she remembered—struggled to exit the car. With a look of intense concentration on his face, Daddy set himself to the formidable task of helping her maintain her tenuous balance. Aunt Fran clutched his hand as if he offered a bulwark against a gathering tempest. A loud grunt escaped as she strained to rise up. Rita watched her take several rapid, shallow breaths.

Aunt Fran shuffled her feet as she twisted to find Mom. With one hand still in Daddy's grip, Aunt Fran placed the other on the car's frame and continued her shallow breathing, as if the mere act of leaving the backseat had exhausted her strength. She rotated with tentative, labored steps and set her shoulders forward in the direction of Rita, who was frantic to talk to her mother.

Daddy left Aunt Fran and rushed to the front passenger door to offer his hand to Mom, who had told Rita that the new twins would arrive before the end of summer. When the doctor had reported that he heard two strong heartbeats, Mom had announced that night at dinner that she knew the babies would be fine. As she rounded the Nomad with one arm in Daddy's and her free hand on her protruding tummy, Mom sent Rita a knowing look that calmed her. The cramps—far more intense than a month ago—were twisting her insides. Mom had promised her that they wouldn't be here long. Today's visit was important to Daddy, and also to Aunt Fran. Over the past year since Uncle Lete had been arrested, Rita had asked her mother the kinds of questions that girls who are soon to be women ask. Many times, they'd talked about Gramma Eunice and her hard life. How afraid Aunt Fran had been that she was doomed to repeat Gramma's ordeal.

Daddy once more held out his hand to Aunt Fran. She let go of the car's frame, accepting his support the way a falling woman on a staircase makes a desperate grab for the banister. Mom extended her bent arm for her sister-in-law. Daddy took the hand squeezing his own, then slid it into the crook of his elbow, which he had raised at an angle to match Mom's. With a quick glance to her left, then to her right, Aunt Fran nodded that she was ready. Then the couple guided her toward Rita on the remaining journey to Gramma's grave.

ACKNOWLEDGMENTS

Kathleen Wood, my sister the writer, for her early guidance and steady encouragement along the way.

My ninety-four-year-old father, Frank Rose, an avid nonfiction reader, who, after reading an early draft of *The Sorting Room*, commented that he had known people whose characters and lives were reminiscent of those imagined.

Pattie Lawton, who, after reading every word in every major draft, offered her love and encouragement without fail—my, my, my!

Hilde Wesselink, who helped me navigate living in a strange land, and whose voluntary editing of my early words made clear that my journey to craft was neither sprint nor marathon, both of which would have suggested too near a destination.

Jessica Lipnack and John Kersic—two writers and friends who knew the travails ahead for an aged novice, yet never pulled their punches.

Joritt Van Der Togt for his encouraging friendship and stimulating conversations near the waters of the North Sea and the Pacific Ocean.

For the following friends and family who were kind enough to slog through my earliest attempts and provide their thoughts and encouragement: Bill Gregorak, Bob Sadler, Marcus Harwood, Laura Rockwell, Craig Vent, Gerard Penning, Jim Arena, Mary K. Sharp, Marjorie Derr, Frank Vafier, and Theresa Beaumont.

Roland Merullo, a patient writing teacher and frank critic whose gifts to me are uncountable.

And, finally, my tenth grade high school English teacher, Ron Ventura, who wrangled unruly Catholic school boys and led at least one of us to a life of reading.

ABOUT THE AUTHOR

MICHAEL ROSE was raised on a small family dairy farm in Upstate New York. He retired after serving in executive positions for several global multinational enterprises. He has been a non-executive director for three public companies headquartered in the US. *The Sorting Room* is his debut novel. He lives and writes in San Francisco.

SELECTED TITLES FROM SPARKPRESS

SparkPress is an independent boutique publisher delivering high-quality, entertaining, and engaging content that enhances readers' lives, with a special focus on female-driven work. www.gosparkpress.com

Attachments: A Novel, Jeff Arch, $16.95, 9781684630813. What happens when the mistakes we make in the past don't stay in the past? When no amount of running from the things we've done can keep them from catching up to us? When everything depends on what we do next?

When We Were All Still Alive: A Novel, Keith McWalter, $16.95, 9781684630776. The last great question of every long marriage—*Who will die first?*—has been answered for Conrad Burrell. After losing his wife to a violent accident, he discovers that he has one more lesson to learn about love from the women of his past, and the one woman he's certain he can't live without.

Absolution: A Novel, Regina Buttner, $16.95, 978-1-68463-061-5. A guilt-ridden young wife and mother struggles to keep a long-ago sexual assault and pregnancy a secret from her ambitious husband whose career aspirations depend upon her silence and unswerving loyalty to him.

The Takeaway Men: A Novel, Meryl Ain, $16.95, 978-1-68463-047-9. Twin sisters Bronka and JoJo Lubinski are brought to America from Germany by their Polish refugee parents after World War II—but in "idyllic" America, political, cultural, and family turmoil awaits them. As the girls grow older, they eventually begin to ask questions of and demand the truth from their parents.

Enemy Queen: A Novel, Robert Steven Goldstein, $16.95, 978-1-68463-026-4. A woman initiates passionate sexual encounters with two articulate but bumbling and crass middle-aged men, but what she demands in return soon becomes untenable. A short time later she goes missing, prompting the county sheriff to open a murder investigation.

About SparkPress

SparkPress is an independent, hybrid imprint focused on merging the best of the traditional publishing model with new and innovative strategies. We deliver high-quality, entertaining, and engaging content that enhances readers' lives. We are proud to bring to market a list of *New York Times* best-selling, award-winning, and debut authors who represent a wide array of genres, as well as our established, industry-wide reputation for creative, results-driven success in working with authors. SparkPress, a BookSparks imprint, is a division of SparkPoint Studio LLC.

Learn more at GoSparkPress.com